Texas Strong

Book Four

The Lone Star Series

by

Bobby Akart

Copyright Information

Other Works by Bestselling Author Bobby Akart

The Lone Star Series

Axis of Evil

Beyond Borders

Lines in the Sand

Texas Strong

Fifth Column

Suicide Six

The Pandemic Series

Beginnings

The Innocents

Level 6

Quietus

The Blackout Series

36 Hours

Zero Hour

Turning Point

Shiloh Ranch

Hornet's Nest

Devil's Homecoming

The Boston Brahmin Series

The Loyal Nine

Cyber Attack

Martial Law

False Flag

The Mechanics

Choose Freedom

Patriot's Farewell

Seeds of Liberty (Companion Guide)

The Prepping for Tomorrow Series

Cyber Warfare

EMP: Electromagnetic Pulse

Economic Collapse

Dedications

Every day, I wake up to a beautiful world filled with the undying love of my wife and the loyalty of our pups. Without them, none of my books would be possible. I wish every family could have what we have.

The Lone Star Series is dedicated to the love and support of my family. I will always protect you from anything that would disrupt our happiness.

ACKNOWLEDGEMENTS

Writing a book that is both informative and entertaining requires a tremendous team effort. Writing is the easy part. For their efforts in making *Beyond Borders*, book two in the Lone Star series, a reality, I would like to thank Hristo Argirov Kovatliev for his incredible cover art, Pauline Nolet for her editorial prowess, Stef Mcdaid for making this manuscript decipherable in so many formats, Sean Runnette and the folks at Audible Studios for producing the incredible narration, and the Team—Shirley, Denise, Joe, and Jim, whose advice, friendship and attention to detail is priceless.

A special thank-you to Kevin Baron and the team at *Defense One* for providing invaluable insight into the North Korean threat and how we'd defend against it. Also, thank you to Michaela Dodge, senior policy analyst at the Heritage Foundation, Center for National Defense, for her extensive background material on missile defense, nuclear weapons modernization and arms control.

Thank you all!
Choose Freedom!

About the Author

Bobby Akart

Bestselling author Bobby Akart has been ranked by Amazon as the #3 Bestselling Religion & Spirituality Author, the #5 Bestselling Science Fiction Author, the #7 Bestselling Historical Author and the #10 Bestselling Horror Author. He has written twenty international bestsellers, in forty different fiction and nonfiction genres, including the critically acclaimed Boston Brahmin series, the bestselling Blackout series, the frighteningly realistic Pandemic Series, his highly cited nonfiction Prepping for Tomorrow series and his latest project—the Lone Star series, which has already produced four #1 bestsellers.

Bobby has provided his readers a diverse range of topics that are both informative and entertaining. His attention to detail and impeccable research have allowed him to capture the imaginations of his readers through his fictional works and bring them valuable knowledge through his nonfiction books.

SIGN UP to Bobby Akart's mailing list to receive special offers, bonus content, and you'll be the first to receive news about new releases in the Lone Star series, updates on his other series, special offers, and bonus content. You can contact Bobby directly by email (BobbyAkart@gmail.com) or through his website:

BobbyAkart.com

FOREWORD

by Dr. Peter Vincent Pry
Chief of Staff,
Congressional EMP Commission

Executive Director, Task Force
on National and Homeland Security

The recent escalating war of words and actions with rogue nations like North Korea and Iran has given rise to a new sense of urgency about threats we face—especially the existential threat that is a nuclear electromagnetic pulse (EMP) attack. I am pleased to write this foreword for author Bobby Akart as he continues to inform his readers, through his works of fiction, about the EMP threat, both man-made and naturally occurring.

With the Lone Star series, you will learn about the potential of nuclear-armed satellites flying over America daily in low Earth orbit, positioned to collapse our power grid, destroy our way of life, and possibly kill up to ninety percent of Americans.

The Congressional EMP Commission warns North Korea may already pose a worldwide threat, not only by ICBM, but by satellites, two of which presently orbit over the United States and every country on Earth.

A single satellite, if nuclear-armed, detonated at high-altitude would generate an EMP capable of blacking out power grids and life-sustaining critical infrastructure.

Yet, after massive intelligence failures grossly underestimating North Korea's nuclear capabilities, their biggest threat to the U.S. and the world remains unacknowledged—nuclear EMP attack.

The EMP threat continues to be low priority and largely ignored, even though on September 2, 2017, North Korea confirmed the EMP Commission's assessment by testing an H-Bomb that could make a devastating EMP attack.

Two days after their H-Bomb test, on September 4, Pyongyang also released a technical report "The EMP Might of Nuclear Weapons" accurately describing a "super-EMP" weapon generating 100,000 volts/meter.

North Korea's development of a super-EMP weapon that generates 100,000 volts/meter is a technological watershed more threatening than the development of an H-Bomb and ICBM because even the U.S. nuclear deterrent, the best-protected U.S. military forces, are EMP hardened to survive only 50,000 volts/meter.

My colleague EMP Commission Chairman William Robert Graham warned Congress in 2008 that Russia had developed super-EMP weapons and most likely transferred that technology to North Korea allegedly *by accident*, according to Russian generals.

The result of this newly discovered relationship between Russia and North Korea is that the DPRK now has the technology to win a nuclear war. At the very least, a North Korean EMP attack could paralyze the U.S. nuclear deterrent and prevent U.S. retaliation, perhaps even by U.S. submarines at sea that cannot launch missiles without receiving an Emergency Action Message from the president.

However, the warning signs have gone largely ignored. Although North Korea, Russia, and China have all made nuclear threats against the United States recently, in the case of North Korea and Russia repeatedly, most analysts dismiss the war of words as *mere bluster* and *nuclear sabre rattling*, not to be taken seriously.

In the West, generations of leaders and citizens have been educated that use of nuclear weapons is unthinkable and the ultimate horror. Not so in Russia, China, and North Korea, where their nuclear capabilities are publicly paraded—missile launches and exercises are televised as a show of strength, an important part of national pride.

Then there is the issue of an EMP attack. An electromagnetic pulse attack would be perfect for implementing Russia's strategy of "de-escalation," where a conflict with the U.S. and its allies would be won by limited nuclear use. It's their version of "shock and awe" to cow the U.S. into submission. The same kind of attack is viewed as an acceptable option by China and North Korea as well.

An EMP attack would be the most militarily effective use of one or a few nuclear weapons, while also being the most acceptable nuclear option in world opinion, the option most likely to be construed in the U.S. and internationally as "restrained" and a "warning shot" without direct loss of life.

Because an electromagnetic pulse destroys electronics instead of blasting cities, even some analysts in Germany and Japan, among the most antinuclear nations, regard EMP attacks as an acceptable use of nuclear weapons. A high-altitude EMP ("HEMP") attack entails detonating a nuclear weapon at 30–400 kilometers altitude—above the atmosphere, in outer space, so high that no nuclear effects, not even the sound of the explosion, would be experienced on the ground, except the resulting EMP.

An EMP attack will kill far more people than nuclear blasting a city through indirect effects—by blacking out electric grids and destroying life-sustaining critical infrastructures like communications, transportation, food and water—in the long run. But the millions of fatalities likely to eventually result from EMP will take months to develop, as slow as starvation.

Thus, a nation hit with an EMP attack will have powerful incentives to cease hostilities, focus on repairing their critical infrastructures while there is still time and opportunity to recover, and avert national extinction.

Indeed, an EMP attack or demonstration made to "de-escalate" a crisis or conflict is very likely to raise a chorus of voices in the West against nuclear escalation and send Western leaders in a panicked search for the first "off ramp."

Axis of Evil and the entire Lone Star series are books of fiction that are based upon historical fact. The geopolitical factors in this series leading up to a potentially catastrophic collapse of America's power grid are based upon real-world scenarios.

Author Bobby Akart has written several fiction and nonfiction books with the intent to raise awareness about the threats we face from an EMP, whether via a massive solar storm or delivered by a nuclear warhead. While many books have been written about the results of nuclear war and EMPs, few have tackled the subject of using satellites as a means of delivering the fatal blow, until now.

The Lone Star series is written to be thought-provoking. It will be a reminder to us all that, as Bobby says, you never know when the day before is the day before. Prepare for tomorrow.

Dr. Peter Vincent Pry
Chief of Staff
Congressional EMP Commission
Executive Director
Task Force on National and Homeland Security

About Dr. Peter Vincent Pry

Dr. Peter Vincent Pry served as chief of staff of Congressional Electromagnetic Pulse (EMP) Commission (2001-2017), and is currently the executive director of the Task Force on National and Homeland Security, a Congressional Advisory Board dedicated to achieving protection of the United States from electromagnetic pulse (EMP), cyber warfare, mass-destruction terrorism and other threats to civilian critical infrastructures, on an accelerated basis. Dr. Pry also is director of the United States Nuclear Strategy Forum, an advisory board to Congress on policies to counter weapons of mass destruction. Foreign governments, including the United Kingdom, Israel, Canada, and Kazakhstan consult with Dr. Pry on EMP, cyber, and other strategic threats.

Dr. Pry served on the staffs of the Congressional Commission on the Strategic Posture of the United States (2008–2009); the Commission on the New Strategic Posture of the United States (2006–2008); and the Commission to Assess the Threat to the United States from Electromagnetic Pulse (EMP) Attack (2001–2008).

Dr. Pry served as professional staff on the House Armed Services Committee (HASC) of the U.S. Congress, with portfolios in nuclear strategy, WMD, Russia, China, NATO, the Middle East, Intelligence, and Terrorism (1995–2001). While serving on the HASC, Dr. Pry was chief advisor to the vice chairman of the House Armed Services Committee and the vice chairman of the House Homeland Security Committee, and to the chairman of the Terrorism Panel. Dr. Pry played a key role: running hearings in Congress that warned terrorists and rogue states could pose EMP and cyber threats, establishing the Congressional EMP Commission, helping the commission develop plans to protect the United States from EMP and cyber warfare, and working closely with senior scientists and the nation's top experts on critical infrastructures, EMP and cyber warfare.

Dr. Pry was an intelligence officer with the Central Intelligence Agency, responsible for analyzing Soviet and Russian nuclear strategy, operational plans, military doctrine, threat perceptions, and developing U.S. paradigms for strategic warning (1985–1995). He also served as a verification analyst at the U.S. Arms Control and Disarmament Agency responsible for assessing Soviet arms control treaty compliance (1984–1985).

Dr. Pry has written numerous books on national security issues, including *Blackout Wars*; *Apocalypse Unknown: The Struggle To Protect America From An Electromagnetic Pulse Catastrophe*; *Electric Armageddon: Civil-Military Preparedness For An Electromagnetic Pulse Catastrophe*; *War Scare: Russia and America on the Nuclear Brink*; *Nuclear Wars: Exchanges and Outcomes*; *The Strategic Nuclear Balance: And Why It Matters*; and *Israel's Nuclear Arsenal.* You may view his canon of work by visiting his Amazon Author page.

Dr. Pry often appears on TV and radio as an expert on national security issues. The BBC made his book *War Scare* into a two-hour TV documentary *Soviet War Scare 1983*, and his book *Electric Armageddon* was the basis for another TV documentary *Electronic Armageddon* made by National Geographic.

EPIGRAPH

"Texas is the obsession, the proper study, and the passionate possession of all Texans."
~ John Steinbeck

*****

"Texas can make it without the United States but the United States cannot make it without Texas."
~ Sam Houston

*****

Texas is a state of mind.
~ Anonymous

*****

Clear eyes, full hearts, can't lose.
~ Coach Eric Taylor, *Friday Night Lights*

*****

The backbone of surprise is fusing speed with secrecy.
~ Carl von Clausewitz

*****

A nation can survive its fools, and even the ambitious, but it cannot survive treason from within. An enemy at the gates is less formidable for he is known and he carries his banners openly.
~ Marcus Tullius Cicero, Roman Philosopher

Part One

CHAPTER 1

Christmas Day 2022
The Armstrong Ranch
Borden County, Texas

"Daddy," whispered Palmer, the youngest of the Armstrong children and the only daughter. If there ever was an apple of a father's eye, Palmer fit the bill. In Major's eyes, she was the spittin' image of his darling Lucy. As Palmer grew out of her pigtails and found herself as a young woman, Major talked to and treated her with utmost respect. He set expectations of how a man should treat a lady and hoped she'd never settle for anything less. Above all, he loved her and took pride in her accomplishments as she grew up. A bond existed between them as a result, one that was somewhat different from the bond between Major and his sons.

"Yes, honey," he replied as the conversation between the boys and Preacher continued.

"I've never seen Momma like this. Anytime we try to get together and talk about what we've been through, and especially what might happen next, she breaks up the conversation. Is she okay?"

Major furrowed his brows before answering. He'd asked himself the same question. Lucy had remained strong throughout this ordeal. She acted very much like a general on a battlefield. She was organized, authoritative, and unflappable most of the time. Naturally, she worried about her children's safety but not to the point of emotional breakdown.

But as those fears were set aside on Christmas Eve with the reunification of their family, she'd become focused in a way that was out of the norm. Lucy was the consummate multitasker. All mothers are. She took care of their home, helped run the ranch, and watched over everything related to their preparedness activities.

Major replied as he tried to make sense of it all, "Since you guys returned yesterday, it's been all about Christmas. Last night's service in the barn was spiritually moving until, of course, the military jets flew past us."

"Yeah, that kinda brought us back to the present, didn't it?" asked Palmer.

Major thought for a moment. "You know, honey, maybe that's it. Since Black Friday when the EMP hit, we've been on edge here at the ranch. God only knows what it was like for you all on the road. Now our family is together again just in time for Christmas. Maybe your mother—"

Before Major could continue, Miss Lucy walked out of the kitchen and into the family room of their ranch house. She was wearing a classic bib apron embroidered with a western design including holly, a horseshoe, a cowboy boot, and a felt hat. Her hair was pulled back into a ponytail and tied with a red ribbon.

Major hadn't seen her dress like this for Christmas dinner since their children were in grade school. He wasn't sure what to make of it. Lucy had gone all out for this Christmas and refused to let the family be distracted by the outside world while they celebrated.

"Okay, okay, enough shop talk, or whatever y'all are mumbling about," Lucy announced as she wiped her hands on a towel and shoved it into the front pocket of her apron. "It's time for Christmas dinner. Would y'all please grab a serving dish from the kitchen? I see that everyone else has arrived."

Riley, who was the first to respond, had remained closest to Lucy since their return. "You got it, Momma. Are there any samples you'd like me to taste? You know, to make sure it's really good?"

Lucy retrieved the kitchen towel from her apron, took both ends and began to twist it into a weapon. She snapped it towards Riley's backside. "One unauthorized nibble, young man, and you'll get a whoopin'!" she threatened, to the group's delight.

Major smiled as he admired his family. His adorable wife wasn't troubled and hadn't changed. She was just intent on making this Christmas special.

The group made its way to the barn to greet the ranch hands and their families, who'd brought dishes of their own for this potluck-style Christmas feast.

Picnic tables were retrieved from all around the ranch and set up in rows in the main barn. They were covered with white sheets adorned with each family's unique Christmas décor, candles, and many different types of foods.

The Texas love of barbecue was evident, as roasted chicken, smoked turkeys, and pulled pork were abundant. The Mexican women prepared tamales, menudo, and cinnamon buñuelos, a dish made with deep-fried tortilla wedges covered in a sugary cinnamon mix.

Lucy had discussed the meal planning with Major yesterday afternoon. They both were keenly aware that food supplies in Texas were dwindling and they'd have to rely completely upon their food storage moving forward. However, this was also the most significant Christmas in their lives, and they intended to make it the most memorable, which included a fabulous meal.

Throughout dinner, people talked, laughed, and allowed an occasional muted belch as their compliment to the chef. Miss Lucy was thanked repeatedly for creating this wonderful opportunity to come together as a family, share Christmas joy, and exchange their hope for the future.

Sook was especially appreciative, as she'd never experienced a Christmas dinner. She explained to everyone the risks that she and her family had taken as Christians in North Korea. In a country teeming with fear and mistrust, they'd practiced their faith within the confines of the familial home without revealing their belief in God to anyone.

After the group had finished eating, Major stood from their table located at the center of the barn. The soft chatter stopped, and he was given everyone's full attention.

"I'm looking around this barn, thinking of the day Christ was born. His birth was a tremendous gift to this world, just like all of you are a gift to me. Better than any presents wrapped up under a tree, when I see all of you holding hands and loving one another, it warms my heart."

Major dropped his chin to his chest and wiped a tear from his face. He gathered himself, reached for Lucy's hand to gain strength, and then continued. "Dallas is not here with us today, God rest his soul. Like Jesus died on the cross for our sins, something he believed was his destiny, Dallas died for the country he loved, protecting all of us from the evil beyond our borders.

"At night, I look into the heavens and search for answers as to why he was taken from us. The answer I receive is that God has a plan, and the stars of freedom shine brightly to remind me of how lucky those of us on this planet really are."

Major then paused and reached to take Sook's hand, who immediately welled up in tears.

"But then God finds a way to surprise us all. Our oldest son might have suffered the same fate as Dallas if not for this angel, this beautiful young woman from a faraway place. In her country, it's forbidden to be a Christian, yet here she is. In her country, her family could've been sent to prison camps or executed for saving my son's life, yet there she sits.

"I will thank God every day for you, Sook. Miss Lucy and I lost one child to the ugliness of war, but we gained another loving member of our very large family when you came into our lives."

Again Major paused and then looked skyward for guidance to find the right words. He furrowed his brow as he continued. Lucy's warm hand squeezed his, and their eyes met. In that moment, he understood her demeanor of the last twenty-four hours. He nodded, and she returned his look with a smile of encouragement.

"We face troubling times that will be dangerous. The world as we know it has been devastated by death and destruction. The evil in men continues to exist, so I have no illusions of what our future brings.

"As the children of God, our fate rests in His hands. We're all knockin' on Heaven's door as we persevere in this new life. Together, as a family, we will enjoy life's greatest blessing—our love for one another, and it is our love that will help us endure what comes our way."

CHAPTER 2

Christmas Day
The Armstrong Ranch
Borden County, Texas

"Major, that was beautiful," said Lucy as she stood up from the table. Major gave her a hug and a lingering kiss. A tear came from her eye, and he quickly kissed her wet cheek. His puzzled look caused her to smile. "Honey, I'm fine. Don't worry."

Everyone congregated for several minutes before Preacher reminded them that banditos didn't take Christmas off and they were most likely enjoying fried chicken in their barnyard right about now. This drew a laugh from the ranch hands, who promptly retrieved their rifles and headed for their horses. The wives and children assisted Miss Lucy in clearing the tables after everyone voiced their appreciation for the wonderful dinner.

Preacher began to walk toward his horse when Lucy called after him, "Preach, before you go, would you mind comin' inside for a few minutes? I'd like the family to get together for a moment and that, naturally, includes you."

"Of course, Miss Lucy," he replied. "Let me load up some of these dishes. Heck, I'll help ya wash them."

She smiled and touched his arm. "No, that's not necessary, but thank you. It's time to get the kids back in the swing of doin' chores. That's part of what I want to talk about, among other things."

After several trips to the barn and back, the farmhouse-style sink was overflowing with dishes and serving pieces. Lucy would get her crew together to tackle the mess later. For now, she wanted to address several things while she had their attention. Somehow, after this meal, the concept of family gatherings would change from cheerful dinners to strategic planning sessions about security and food levels.

Duncan stoked the fire, and the flames danced inside the massive stone fireplace. Lucy and Major shared the settee while the boys scattered about the floor and on the fireplace hearth. Preacher took up a spot on the sofa, where Palmer joined him. The room was quiet in anticipation of what the matriarch of the Armstrong family had to say.

"Everyone, I'd like to apologize if I've been a little more ornery than usual," Lucy began as she dropped her eyes to the floor and exhaled. She nervously fiddled with a kitchen towel as she spoke. One by one, she made eye contact with her kids. "I'm not going to get emotional again. But thank God you're home."

Palmer was the first to rush to her side and sit on the roll-top arm of the settee. The two hugged as the tears flowed. There wasn't a dry eye in the room as the emotions poured out of them. Somehow, since the kids had arrived home, the Armstrongs had managed to keep their emotions in check in order to enjoy Christmas, but now they were allowed to let it out.

The room burst into a combination of tears, laughter, and conversation as everyone began telling their stories.

Finally, Lucy stood and waved her kitchen towel over her head. "Now do you see why I wanted y'all to wait until after Christmas? There is so much to talk about. I wanna know about Coop's ride. Riley has been dyin' to talk about this Red Rover truck. Duncan has one heckuva whopper to tell us about his exploits in North Korea. And I wanna get to know this angel who brought him back to us."

Major took Lucy by the hand and gave it a loving squeeze. After the emotional moment, the rodeo kids took the sofa relinquished by Preacher, who readily took a seat on the *king's throne*, as Major called his leather La-Z-Boy recliner near the fireplace. Duncan and Sook, who were inseparable, holding hands everywhere they went, remained on the hearth.

Duncan squeezed Sook's hand, and she kissed him on the cheek to give him strength to tell his story. "I guess I'd better start because, without exaggeration, I believe this whole thing is my fault."

"Son, whadya mean?" asked Major.

"Dad, you know I'm not supposed to discuss my job, but the world has turned upside down, and I couldn't tell you at this point if I work for the United States government or if I'm a citizen of Texas or what."

"You're a Texan," Riley chimed in.

"I guess so," said Duncan with hesitation. "I really don't know where I stand with Washington, the CIA, or my handlers. All I do know is they left me to die."

Lucy sat up on the edge of her seat. "What? Son, why don't you tell us what you can, you know, without giving up state secrets or whatever."

"Listen, Momma. I don't work for them anymore. I quit the day they left me and my partner, Min Park, behind in North Korea."

"Fair enough, son," interrupted Major. "Why don't you tell us what happened and why you think everything from the EMP forward is your fault."

Duncan gulped and looked around the room at his family. They were all listening intently to his next words.

"Yes, Duncan," Sook encouraged.

He nodded and began. "I was sent to assassinate Kim Jong-un."

His words exploded into the room, but nary a sound could be heard. Everyone looked at one another in disbelief and then back to Duncan for further explanation.

"Park and I were assigned to a patrol vessel in the Persian Gulf region when we suddenly received orders to report to a military facility in Japan. We were tasked to take out Kim Jong-un as he oversaw a missile test in the western part of North Korea. Y'all, there are so many details, this story might take hours to tell."

"I reckon you missed, huh?" said Riley with a chuckle.

"No, actually, I hit the target, but it must have been a body double," replied Duncan. "Park and I left the sniper hide thinking *mission accomplished*, at least the shooting part of it. After the shot, we had to get out of the country without getting caught or killed."

"It sounds like a suicide mission to this old man," grumbled Preacher.

"In a way it was, Preacher," said Duncan, who immediately looked to his mother, whose eyes began to well up in tears. "Momma, there was a viable plan of extraction. Otherwise I wouldn't have gone in. Again, without going into long details, I sensed something was off when the place was crawling with North Korean soldiers within minutes of the shot.

"They had us surrounded, but Park and I fought our way through to the extraction point at Sinmi-do, a tiny island on the Yellow Sea. We managed to hit the beach ahead of schedule where the pickup was to take place. But they never came. He and I decided to find our way back to South Korea by taking a boat from the village where Sook lived.

"That's when we ran headfirst into a North Korean patrol. Park got hit, and I tried to carry him to safety. They shot at us moving through the woods. Park was hit four times in the back, killing him. The impact of the rounds knocked me down, and I fell thirty feet off a cliff into a river."

Duncan shook his head and took a deep breath. He gave his mother, who had Major's hand in a death grip, a reassuring smile.

"I should've died that night, but Park shielded me from the bullets, and then Sook, together with her father, pulled me out of the water. They kept me safe and nursed me back to health."

"Sounds like a Rambo movie," quipped Riley.

"How'd you get out of the country?" asked Cooper.

"Sook's father led us out to sea with a fishing boat, which we then drove toward South Korea. After a brief skirmish with a North Korean patrol, we made our way to the south. The rest is a long story too."

Major leaned back on the settee and put his arms around Lucy. She quizzed Duncan. "Why would they leave you behind?"

"That's how these things go sometimes," Duncan replied. "You know the drill—deny, deny, deny, and then if that doesn't work—

disavow. They probably had some type of dirty dossier on me that linked me to a radical group in South Korea that was acting independently of the Seoul government and certainly without any U.S. government authority. Dad, you can imagine, right?"

Major raised his eyebrows and nodded.

"But, honey, this never made the news," continued Lucy. "If you killed a man who was supposed to be that dictator, why didn't he throw it in our faces that we shot the wrong guy?"

Sook spoke up for the first time. "May I answer that question?"

"Yes, honey, please," said Lucy with a smile and a nod of approval.

"The Kim dynasty has ruled our people with fear and intimidation for many years. Any attempt on his life would be seen as a sign of weakness. He attended his parades and public appearances as if nothing had happened."

"And although Park and I had deep cover stories, it wouldn't take long for his team of hackers to determine that my partner was an American of Korean descent," Duncan added.

Major shook his head and grimaced. "Kim Jong-un responded, but not publicly. He orchestrated the EMP attacks and sent us back to the nineteenth century, except for Texas, of course."

"Here's what I don't understand," said Cooper. "If Kim wanted to settle the score with us by using the EMPs, then why did everybody start firin' off the nukes?"

"We may never know, Coop," said Duncan. "I will, however, find out who left me there to die. Somebody made that call, and I wanna find out who it is."

CHAPTER 3

Christmas Day
The Armstrong Ranch
Borden County, Texas

The rodeo kids took their turn at describing their month-long journey home. It started with Riley's dramatic play-by-play of Cooper's ride atop One Night Stand. Riley jumped up and down, spun around on the floor and then jumped into the air with his arms raised in victory as if he'd ridden the beast himself. The hilarity lightened the mood, so they could begin to relay what they'd seen during their journey from Calgary to the ranch.

To an extent, Cooper, Riley, and Palmer kept their promise to shield their mother from the ugliest aspects of the trip, especially the kills made by Riley and Cooper. As agreed, Coop, the oldest of the three, was allowed to discuss it with their father. It would be left up to him whether their mother found out.

Preacher thanked Lucy for a wonderful meal, and he left to check on security. Duncan and Cooper walked outside to get some fresh air. It was the first time the two had been alone together since their return.

"Coop, I wanted—" started Duncan before stopping.

"Can we talk for a minute?" said Cooper simultaneously.

"You first," they said together nervously. The two brothers began to laugh.

Cooper put his hand up and smiled. "No, please. Age before beauty."

"Yeah, yeah," said Duncan with a laugh. "I've heard the buckle-bunnies throw themselves at you bull riders. Is it true?"

"Yeah, sorta," replied Cooper. "I'm real focused on the road, so I don't pay them any mind. There was one girl in Calgary. I got her number but lost it, I think. It was before the lights went out."

"Well, brother, congratulations on your ride. It sucks that the Vegas thing was cancelled. Heck, everything's been cancelled."

"No doubt," said Cooper. "Duncan, um, I had a lot of time to think while we were on the road home. It's amazing how you see things differently when there aren't distractions to clutter your brain."

Duncan laughed. "You mean insignificant distractions like the apocalypse?"

"Right, the apocalypse ain't nothin'," Cooper answered with a laugh. "Nah, I'm talkin' about what a jerk I've been to you over the last few years. Duncan, I've missed my big brother, and I realized it when we were on the road. I was afraid I'd never see ya again."

"No such luck, Coop. Y'all can't get rid of me that easy. It's like I've got nine lives."

Duncan got suddenly quiet and began to kick at the gravel in front of the house. They needed to address the elephant in the room.

"Coop, I have a lot of regrets in my life, and taking the shot to kill Kim Jong-un isn't one of them. I wish I could take one of those nine lives I just mentioned and give it to Dallas. I'd give anything to bring him back."

Cooper started to get emotional and kicked at the same rocks Duncan had swatted with his boot earlier. "I know, Duncan. I've always known that you took his death as hard as I did. But it wasn't your fault, just as shooting the phony dictator didn't trigger this war. People with more power than we have are responsible for both."

"Thanks, Coop, but the fact is I could've discouraged Dallas from entering the service. I knew what war was like. One of the reasons I became a special ops guy was the promise that I could fight the enemy without the gloves on. If you're gonna fight a war, you do it balls to the wall. Dallas was over there doin' police duty. He never had a chance against roadside bombs or fools wearing suicide vests."

Cooper moved to hug his brother. He comforted Duncan as he realized the wall between them over the death of Dallas had just been torn down, never to return. The guys hugged it out, then, to show they were still macho men, pounded each other on the chest.

"So we're good?" asked Duncan.

"Yup," replied Cooper with a nod. "But I need help on something."

"You name it."

"Duncan, I killed two guys over in Patricia when our truck ran out of gas. They were attacking—"

"I know all about it, Coop. Sook and I came upon them on the road back to the ranch. Y'all tied one of 'em to the sign, right?"

"Yeah," Cooper answered. "Duncan, I wanted to kill him too."

"I don't blame you," said Duncan. "After the idiot told me the whole story, it was all I could do to get on that horse and not beat him to death myself. Listen, you were protecting Riley."

Cooper returned to kicking rocks. "Defending Riley was actually easy. After a while, I thought back on what happened. It was all so fast. Amazingly, I hit those guys exactly where I aimed."

"That's good," said Duncan with a laugh. "Especially with Riley and Palmer nearby. I need to talk with you about the concept of friendly fire."

"But listen. It really messed me up, you know? I wanted to shoot the third guy. Just kill him in cold blood."

"Yeah, but you showed restraint and didn't," interjected Duncan.

"I threw up instead."

"Coop, we're in the midst of a war, believe it or not," started Duncan. "There may not be tanks rolling through the countryside or bombs falling from jets over our heads. There are, however, desperate people out there, and I'm not just talking about outside the Texas borders. People are in trouble here too, and we're gonna have to deal with them."

"Daddy and Preacher already have," added Cooper.

Duncan continued. "There are mental breakdowns that soldiers experience as a result of getting shot at and killing others. Post-traumatic stress disorder is very real. Some guys get PTSD really bad. Others don't. Truthfully, I can kill without doubt or remorse. It's a curse, not a gift, trust me."

"Riley's the same way," said Cooper. "He killed while we were on the road, and it didn't even faze him. I kill two guys and I blow chow all over the highway."

Duncan put his arm around Cooper's shoulder. "We're not wired to kill each other. You ever heard the word *posturing* before?"

"Yeah, like a couple of cowboys about to fight over a girl," Cooper began to reply. "They get all bowed up, sticking their chests out, lean forward, and ball up their fists."

"Exactly, Coop. Animals do the same thing. Heck, even rattlesnakes, which will kill a human without hesitation, avoid killing another rattlesnake if possible. People think PTSD comes from a fear of dying, but really, it comes from the memories of killing another human being."

"How do you do it?"

"Coop, it's my job. Plain and simple. Now, it helps that the person in the line of fire is the enemy, or at least perceived to be the enemy. The day a human being decides to kill for fun or sport, then they lose their soul and become a murderer."

Major approached them from the house, and Cooper decided to cut the conversation off. "Can we talk some more about this later?"

"Absolutely, just between us," replied Duncan.

"Hey, fellas, am I breaking something up here?" asked Major.

"No, Dad," replied Duncan. "As a matter of fact, there's something I want to discuss with you and Coop in private."

CHAPTER 4

Christmas Day
The Armstrong Ranch
Borden County, Texas

"Are you boys all right?" asked Major. He'd tried unsuccessfully for years to get Cooper to let go of his animosity toward his brother. Dallas's death had been an emotional blow to the family, but it was exacerbated by Cooper's resentment. As he approached his two oldest sons, his reading of their body language indicated a thaw in the chilly relationship they'd endured for a while.

"Yeah, Daddy, we're good," started Cooper with a smile. "Right, Duncan?"

"Yessir," Duncan said as he grabbed his brother's shoulder and gave it a squeeze. He turned his attention back to Major. "Daddy, I'm glad the three of us are alone."

"Is there somethin' else, Duncan?" asked Major.

"I believe so, but I didn't want to mention it earlier. We had two encounters on the road. One was near Winslow, Arizona, which involved me killing a couple of thugs. The other was in New Mexico as we looked for a safe way across the Pecos River."

Major looked back toward the house and pointed toward the barn, indicating the boys should follow him. All the hands had cleared out and were on the ranch tending to the cattle or performing security functions.

"Were they related somehow? There's a lot of geography between those two points."

They settled in the barn and sat on top of the picnic tables, which had been cleared of their Christmas decorations. As Miss Lucy had predicted, after Christmas dinner, it was immediately back to living life in a post-apocalyptic world.

"When I relayed what happened in Winslow earlier, I failed to mention that the men who attacked the convoy were Koreans. I'm no expert on the demographics of Northern Arizona, but I doubt there are many Koreans."

"Agreed, go on," interjected Major.

"When Sook's horse died on the highway, a convoy of trucks was heading south from Roswell. I wasn't sure they'd be friendlies, so I hoisted Sook on my horse, and we found a place to hide. The convoy stopped to check on her dead horse and began shouting instructions to one another."

Duncan hesitated, so Cooper urged him on. "What is it, Duncan?"

"Coop, they were Koreans, too. North Koreans, to be exact."

Cooper asked, "Did you get a close look at 'em? How would you know that?"

"Sook immediately recognized their Pyongyang dialect, as she called it. Koreans are able to differentiate North from South by the different Korean dialects."

Major took a deep breath and let out a noticeable exhale. "Is there any chance it was part of the same group? I mean, that would be a heckuva coincidence."

"I don't know, 'cause I never really got a good look at them during either encounter. I know this, however, there aren't a lot of Koreans in America anyway. Running across the same group twice would be highly improbable. If it's two different groups, then don't you think it's pretty bold for Koreans to be running around attacking and commandeering convoys?"

Major nodded in agreement. "Something's wrong with this picture, and we need to send it up the chain of command, so to speak. I reckon we oughta make a trip to Austin, sooner rather than later."

"I'm in, too," started Cooper.

Major patted Cooper on the shoulder and shook his head. "No, Coop, I'm gonna need you to stay here at the ranch."

"Why?"

"Son, we're gonna begin making some changes around here," replied Major as he addressed both of his sons. "Boys, I believe we've been very fortunate that Texas maintained a separate power grid. Just because we have power doesn't mean we're sleeping on a bed of roses. We've had incidents here at the ranch, and I imagine you two have seen things outside our borders you haven't fully disclosed to me yet. Until things settle down, which may take years, I need to delegate some of my responsibilities so I can attend to the whole operation."

"Whadya mean, Daddy?" asked Cooper.

"Coop, I'm gonna start grooming you to take over for me and run the ranch," replied Major, who then turned to Duncan. "Duncan, I'm putting you in charge of security. We have a good thing going here, whether the power stays on or not. I'm entrusting Cooper to maintain the status quo, and then make it better using the energy that he has and I don't anymore."

Duncan stretched his hand out to his father. They shook, and then Cooper said, "Daddy, I won't let you down."

"I know you won't, Coop," started Major as he gestured in a circle with his arm. "Duncan, don't feel slighted by my decision because your job is equally important. No matter what we've managed to achieve here, if we can't defend it, it isn't ours. There's no man better to defend the Armstrong Ranch than you."

CHAPTER 5

December 26
Office of the President
The Mansion
Austin, Texas

Every politician dreams of becoming President of the United States. When Harold Fauntleroy was elected county selectman in Bug Tussle, Texas, he mused with his wife that he could be president one day—*one never knew*. When Marion Burnett first ran for statewide office in Texas, she not only knew she'd win, but she felt in her bones that she'd be the governor of Texas someday, and maybe, just maybe, she'd make her way to Washington for the *big job*. Well, Marion Burnett was president now, but of the Republic of Texas rather than the United States. The *big job* might have eluded her, but the task ahead of her was ginormous nonetheless.

"Madam President, good morning," greeted her running mate and the new vice president of Texas, Montgomery Gregg. Gregg had worn many hats during his illustrious career in the United States military and then in civilian life as the Secretary of Defense. Like President Burnett, he had high aspirations, but the title that he had earned in the recent election was never on his political radar.

"Hi, Monty," said President Burnett cheerfully. She'd welcomed a day away from the trials and tribulations of establishing a new government, not to mention the indicators of collapse that were surfacing around Texas. "Did you enjoy Christmas with your missus?"

"I did, although most of the time she complained of the constant security detail surrounding our place. She's not adjusting too well, to put it mildly."

"Is there anything I can do to make things better for her? Other than pull the detail, of course. She does understand that we receive death threats daily, right?"

Gregg unbuttoned his jacket and took a seat across the desk from the president. With a sigh, he responded, "I try not to throw that in her face. In Washington, we had military personnel stationed outside our home, but the level of security was much less. In a way, it might be good if she were able to see what's going on around America and even in our state. She might appreciate how lucky we are."

President Burnett chuckled. "Ah, the media. Both a blessing and a curse, depending upon which side you're on."

"True. The press is called the fourth estate for a reason. The media's power is overwhelming, but their misuse of that power to advance a political ideology is criminal."

President Burnett left her desk to refill her coffee. "Would you like some?"

"No, thanks."

As she returned to her desk, she slid a report across the top for Gregg to see. "I just received this from the adjutant general's office," started the president. "On the surface, it looks glum. I'll bottom line it for you."

"Okay."

"Texas will be running out of food soon."

"Have we already exhausted the strategic reserves we gained access to?" he asked as he thumbed through the graphs, spreadsheets, and projections.

"No, but based upon rationing and other means of allocating the reserves, by February, roughly ninety days after the EMPs hit the U.S., the total food storage within grocery-store-chain warehouses, emergency supplies, and people's homes will be exhausted."

Gregg furrowed his brow as he placed the report back on her desk. "While there was no good time for the catastrophe inflicted upon us by Iran and North Korea, entering our winter months was by far the worst timing. The growing season was over. Most livestock had been sold and sent to slaughterhouses around America."

President Burnett took another sip of coffee and then swallowed hard as she began to speak. "Now food imports have slowed to a crawl because U.S. ports can't process the container ships, and we can't allow them into Houston because the dredging operation is still under way."

Texas was employing a variety of dredging techniques to open the Port of Galveston and the Houston Ship Channel after the nuclear explosion off Galveston Island displaced a million square feet of sea bottom. These ungainly workhorses sucked mud and sand from the murky floor, working twenty-four hours a day in a frantic attempt to open ship traffic.

The dredges had to maintain the channel at a depth of forty-five feet or more for the deep-draft ships delivering cargo to the Houston docks. The dredging operations had been a part of the Galveston District of the Army Corps of Engineers for over a hundred years. Mother Nature worked against the corps due to hurricanes from offshore and heavy flooding in the Houston area. The muck dredged one month could quickly be replaced the next by a category three hurricane or larger.

"And the natives are growing restless," started Gregg. "Preparing Texas for this calamity was one thing, but getting the citizenry prepared was another. Despite the major hurricanes and tornadoes that Texans endured in recent years, families still did not heed the warnings. They didn't stockpile food, water, and medical supplies, as the public service announcements suggested."

"I have to admit something that stays within these four walls," began the president. "Texas was so proud to exercise its independent streak and maintain a power grid under ERCOT, which survived this attack. But we overlooked the day-to-day preparedness measures that should've been addressed. Honestly, Monty, we totally overlooked the fact that if the U.S. grid failed, our source of food, supplies, and medications dried up too."

Gregg gathered his thoughts as he rubbed his temple. Fighting wars was much easier for him than tedious government administration. "We need to establish international trading partners. Our deal with Washington doesn't do us that much good today, only down the road when America gets on her feet."

"That could take years," interrupted the president.

"Most likely, yes. The alternative is to establish international trade partners and start getting shipments into Houston. What is the time frame on the dredging operation?"

President Burnett rustled through some paperwork on her desk until she found the report from the port authority of the Houston Ship Channel. "Assuming decent weather, which is likely for this time of year, they'll need another four to six weeks," started Burnett as she threw the report back on her desk. She sat back in her chair and sighed. "Got any ideas?"

Gregg stroked his chin and nodded his head. "I do, actually. I need to make a call to Hong Kong and a company called Transward."

"What do they do?"

"It's a process called midstream operation," replied Gregg. "Basically, Transward loads and unloads cargo containers at the ship while it's still at sea. The containers are placed on flat-bottom barges, which don't have much draw, and are then guided into port using tugs. It's very effective in Hong Kong."

President Burnett sat up in her chair. "That could work, but why Hong Kong? Isn't there a company closer to home?"

"No, and here's why. Midstream operations have been abandoned most everywhere in the world except for Hong Kong, where the ports are insufficient to handle heavy traffic and the fees are high. In addition, environmentalists stopped the practice in most countries, including the U.S., because of the danger of spillage and container ships colliding."

"We could bring container ships into the Gulf of Mexico, right off Galveston Island, and ferry the freight into Houston on barges," summarized the president, nodding her head with approval. "What's not to love about that plan?"

Gregg leaned back in his seat and smiled, gloating slightly at his innovative idea.

CHAPTER 6

December 26
Route 115
Patricia, Texas

Preacher drove the Dodge Ram four-door flatbed work truck, which towed an open trailer behind it. Duncan and Riley rode in the backseat while Chris Slaughter of the Lazy S Ranch accompanied Preacher in the front. They'd made another trip to the Slaughters' ranch to retrieve additional milking equipment, and their next stop was to retrieve Red Rover, the 1982 Land Rover Defender given to the Rodeo Kids in Montana for the trip back to Texas. After it ran out of diesel fuel, Riley had reluctantly agreed to leave it behind as long as they could return quickly to bring it to the ranch.

"Yessir!" exclaimed Riley from the backseat as he leaned forward between Slaughter and Preacher. "There's my Landy!"

The rest of the group didn't share the same enthusiasm as Riley. Duncan handed Slaughter the binoculars as Preacher slowed his approach.

"Looks clear except for the four dead bodies," he observed.

"Wait, let me see," said Riley, reaching for the binoculars. "There should only be—dang, there is a fourth body. And I think it's moving!"

"Stop the truck, Preacher," instructed Duncan from the backseat. "We need to be very careful here. Riley, grab your rifle and open your door. After you get outside, leave the door open for cover. I'll do the same. Chris, you monitor every move with the binoculars. If anything looks out of place, let us know. Preacher, drive forward slowly so the doors don't slam shut on us. We'll use the doors as cover and be prepared for anything, right, Riley?"

"Dang straight. They'd better not have messed with my truck!"

Duncan and Riley exited the flatbed and took up their positions behind the doors. Preacher began to roll forward, allowing the idle speed of the Ram truck to determine the speed. As they got closer, Slaughter described what he saw.

"I've got one guy tied to a road sign, body is limp and head rolled to the side. If he's alive, I'd be surprised. Jeez, looks like the crows pecked at his face. Two guys lying on the ground. Dried blood near their bodies. Fourth body appears to be a boy. Not a child, but not a teen either. I'm gonna guess seven to ten years old, maybe?"

Duncan looked ahead and assessed the situation. There were no other opportunities for an attacker to hide themselves besides the truck itself. The land was completely flat, and there was nothing but scrub brush around.

"Chris, can you see under the truck or even inside?" asked Duncan.

"Not really, we need to get closer. Hey, it is a young boy. He just raised his arm and tried to wave."

"Step it up, Preacher," instructed Duncan. "C'mon, Riley, break cover. Keep your rifle's sights on the kid. I've got everything else."

Duncan slammed his door shut and began running the final hundred yards to Red Rover. Riley was clomping down the highway in his boots, so Duncan made a mental note to discuss footwear with his siblings. You couldn't sneak up on anybody wearing cowboy boots.

As the guys drew closer, Duncan lowered himself and scanned his rifle's scope under the truck, looking for any unwelcome surprise. He could see to the front now, and there were no legs or bodies in view.

"Stay frosty, Riley! Keep your rifle on the kid!"

"Got it," he responded as he closed the gap.

Duncan reached the Landy first and looked inside the windows. The supplies and clothing left behind when he'd discovered Red Rover on Christmas Eve were all gone. The entire truck had been cleaned out.

Riley shouldered his rifle and knelt down next to the young Hispanic boy. “Hey, little man. What’s your name?”

The boy barely turned his head to reveal a black eye and a bloodied nose, which had crusted over. He moved his mouth, but nothing but dry air came out.

Riley turned to Slaughter, who had just arrived in the truck. “Bring me a bottle of water. Hurry!”

“We’re clear,” announced Duncan as Preacher joined the group. Preacher was carrying his rifle and began to walk slowly around the perimeter.

Slaughter tossed the water to Riley, who spun off the cap.

“Go slowly,” warned Duncan. “Just enough to wet the inside of his mouth at first. Then a little more to moisten and cool his throat. There’s no need to talk yet.”

Duncan removed his camouflage shemagh, the scarf he was given in the Middle East, and handed it to Riley. Riley moistened it and began to wipe the dried blood off the young boy’s face, who winced at the slightest pressure.

Riley moistened the scarf again and wiped off the boy’s lips. A slight smile came across his battered face as he looked up to his rescuer. There was a sparkle in the youngster’s eyes as he blinked and managed a smile.

Riley tried to assess his injuries. “Don’t talk, okay? Can you nod or blink?”

The young man smiled and nodded. He tried to speak, and a coughing fit overcame him. He reached for the water bottle, and Riley allowed him to have a little until he was satisfied.

“Better?”

The boy nodded and then winced again.

Duncan and Slaughter positioned themselves to block the sun from the boy’s eyes. It was fairly cool, so heat was not an issue. But the combination of the dry air and the unobstructed sun had caused the youngster to dehydrate.

“Are you hurt anywhere else?”

“No, just my face,” the boy replied, surprising everyone with his quick recovery.

Riley set the water aside and placed his hand behind the boy's back, encouraging him to sit upright. The boy nodded and pushed off the pavement until he was leaning up against Red Rover's right front tire. Now he was ready to drink the entire bottle of water, which he did.

Duncan retrieved another one from the truck and knelt down next to the boy. "What's your name?"

"John Flores. They call me Little John because my dad is Big John."

Riley laughed. "Okay, Little John, where's your mom and dad?"

The boy began to get teary eyed. "Daddy is in Odessa, in the jail. Me and mom were going to find him 'cause they took away our house in Lubbock."

"Little John, where's your mom?" asked Duncan, who immediately scanned the area again to look for another body.

The boy began to sob as he buried his face in his arms. His dehydration didn't stop the tears from flowing down his battered and bruised face. He slowly regained his composure and allowed Riley to wipe his face with the shemagh.

"We stopped here because the road was blocked. Mom was scared because of the bodies, and before we knew it, a truck blocked us in."

In between gasps for air and sniffles, he finished the story. "Mom tried to get back into our car, but one of the men tackled her. It was right over there." Little John pointed toward the front of Red Rover.

"Little John, did they take your mother away?" asked Riley as his face began to turn red from anger.

All the young boy could do was nod his head before pointing toward the east and Patricia.

Riley jumped up out of his crouch, pulled his rifle off his shoulder with a death grip, and stomped up the highway a dozen yards before Duncan joined him.

"Riley, I know what you're thinking," started Duncan as he caught up to his brother. "I wanna hunt them down and give 'em the same treatment these guys got. We can't do that right now. We can't protect the ranch and play lawman."

"What about the kid? Doesn't he deserve justice?" Riley shot back.

"Right now, what Little John needs is a chance to live, and you've given him that."

"How? What did I do?" asked Riley.

"For one, you insisted we come back and pick up that candy-apple-red jalopy. If we hadn't, the boy would've lain there and died. Second, I saw the look in his eyes when you revived him. It was the look of appreciation, brother. We can't help his mother, but we can help him. Let's get him well and safe. Then we'll talk to Dad about finding the boy's father in Odessa. He and I are going to Austin in the next several days. We'll find a way to get him reunited with his dad."

Riley sighed and put his rifle back on his shoulder. Duncan gently patted him on the chest, and the guys returned to Little John, who'd recovered from his emotional breakdown.

"Boys, we need to get this show on the road," said Preacher with a look of concern on his face. "I don't like sitting out in the open like this."

Riley cleared the road of the dead bodies while Slaughter and Duncan helped guide Preacher around Red Rover so they could use the winch to pull it up on the back of the trailer. When the diesel truck had run out of gas, air had gotten into the injector pumps. They needed to return it to the ranch, where they could bleed the air completely out of the fuel lines and injector pumps before the engine would start and run properly.

When the truck was loaded, they piled into the flatbed and started back toward the ranch. Both Duncan and Riley kept an eye on their surroundings, unsure of where the criminals were who abducted Little John's mother.

During the ride back, Little John relayed the events in Lubbock that forced them to leave. The boy recalled what he'd heard his mom say to their neighbors.

Parts of the city were under siege. The military had pulled out to protect the borders, leaving local law enforcement on their own. Little John said a large group had been going door-to-door in their neighborhood, stealing food at gunpoint. Frightened, she had hastily loaded up her son in the car on Christmas morning and headed for Odessa, hoping to reunite with her husband.

Unfortunately, in this world, apocalypse or not, thugs and thieves didn't take Christmas Day off.

CHAPTER 7

December 26
The Armstrong Ranch
Borden County, Texas

Palmer and Sook had taken to one another like sisters. After the excitement of her arrival had worn off and the Christmas festivities were over, Palmer spirited Sook away from Duncan so they could get to know one another. Palmer took her around the ranch and taught Sook the history of her family. Sook marveled at the size of their property and then stared in amazement when Palmer led her through the herd, which had remained on the ranch after the collapse.

Their final stop was the barnyard, where Palmer introduced Sook to Miss Lucy's pride and joy. They toured the banks of the Colorado River, the beaver dam, and the windmill. The entire time, Sook asked questions and Palmer helped her with her English. Eventually, they found their way into one of the barns and settled on some hay bales to talk.

"There is nothing like this in North Korea," said Sook. "Even the government-owned farms are not full of cows and chickens. We rely upon China and United Nations humanitarian aid for our food."

"And fish, right?" asked Palmer.

"Yes, of course. Fish. Until yesterday, I have not had meat in many years. No chicken either. Only fish and lots of porridge."

"Porridge?" said Palmer inquisitively.

"Yes. It is a basic North Korean food. When it is available, we use oats, rice, and wheat."

Palmer smiled and said, "I think you'll enjoy Momma's cookin'. We don't have much porridge or fish, though."

"Good. That is good!"

The girls laughed at Sook's response. Then Sook became melancholy. Palmer suspected she was thinking of the fate of her family.

"Sook, I wish we could tell you more about what happened after the bombs," started Palmer. "They don't let the news people into North Korea, so we do not know for sure."

"I have prayed for my family," Sook said. "My father was so proud to give me a better life. He saw my destiny, and Duncan helped fulfill it. For that, I thank God."

The girls sat in silence for a moment as they shared the emotions associated with the likely death of her entire family.

Sook broke the silence. "I want to be productive. I want to help around the ranch."

"Great," started Palmer. "Miss Lucy will always need help at the house. I am sure—"

"Yes, Palmer. I will help Miss Lucy, but I want to help defend the ranch. I know there will be trouble coming soon. I want to fight, and I am not afraid."

Palmer stood up and knocked the hay off her jeans. She removed her hat, loosened the hair tie so that her blond hair could flow freely, and then addressed Sook's request. "Okay, have you ever shot a gun before?"

"No, but I have good vision and a steady hand. I can make sutures on a body's open wounds without glasses."

Palmer began to laugh, which received a puzzled look from her new friend. "I guess that helps. I will speak to Duncan and my parents. If they say it is okay, I will help teach you, but I am sure Duncan will want to help."

"He is very patient and kind, not like the young men in North Korea," said Sook. "They did not respect women, especially the soldiers. The soldiers did not understand *no*."

Palmer probed Sook's eyes, hoping that she hadn't been attacked or sexually assaulted at some point in her life. Her eyes became steely and somewhat cold.

"I hope they never—" started Palmer until Sook raised her hand and shook her head.

"Not me, but others my age. My father taught me taekwondo as a very young girl. I am very good. Duncan will tell you."

Palmer retook her seat on a hay bale and crossed her legs under her. "Is that like karate?"

"Karate is a Japanese way to fight. It uses hands and not feet as much. Taekwondo uses hands, but involves more kicking, jumping, and spinning."

"Wow, and you can do that?"

"Yes, I will show you," said Sook as she stood and moved to the middle of the barn. She immediately became a different person. Her face was focused and her eyes were emotionless. She jumped slightly and turned her body sideways to Palmer. With her knees slightly bent, she shifted her weight to her rear leg.

"Are you gonna kick me?" asked Palmer apprehensively.

Sook didn't respond, but rather stepped forward slightly, jumped into the air and spun, leading with her front leg. Her body looked like a ballerina doing a complete three-hundred-sixty-degree turn, only her leg was raised and ready to strike. She landed on her feet and then crouched slightly, jumping once again with her legs kicking in both directions.

As she landed with her feet only slightly apart, she stared at Palmer and smiled. "Would you like to learn taekwondo?"

Palmer stood up and raised her hands to Sook to give her a double high five. "Oh yes, please. And then we'll practice on Riley!"

CHAPTER 8

December 27
The Oval Office
The White House
Washington, DC

A month after the EMP strike, America was descending deeper into collapse. As many war planners had predicted, the broad-range effects of the dual EMPs were far greater than the nuclear warheads that had struck the cities of the United States. Millions of lives were immediately lost due to the nuclear detonations, with more left dying from radiation exposure.

The deaths across America resulting from lack of nutrition, health care, and proper shelter spread slowly but systematically to all corners of the once mighty nation. A sense of despair had overtaken the American psyche as its government was unable to meet the basic needs of its citizens.

"Madam President," began Chief of Staff James Acton, "to be fair, nobody could've predicted the severity and devastation wrought by the EMP."

"Yes, James, somebody did, but Washington didn't listen," replied President Alani Harman. She sat behind her desk in the Oval Office, staring out upon the South Lawn. "The threat of an EMP was brought to the forefront with the EMP Commission. As is typical, Congress and other administrations voiced a resounding we agree, then did nothing about it. The excuses always revolved around funding. Now, don't get me wrong, I'm not being hypocritical here. I thought the possibilities were far-fetched, and had I been in DC during those years, I would've found lots of places to spend money besides hardening phone lines and such. I'm just pissed because it happened on my watch."

Acton took a seat in a chair next to the bust of Martin Luther King Jr. The man who had a dream would've never dreamed this. He sat quietly for a moment, as he wanted to choose his next words carefully. His anger towards Texas, President Burnett and newly elected Vice President Gregg had not subsided. In fact, as America collapsed before his eyes, he became more committed to getting even with those uppity Texans and their bigger-than-life persona.

He'd been on the right track until he got busted by Gregg over the bridge fiasco. As a result, he'd have to be careful about which tactics he chose in the future. His best option had just presented itself this morning.

"Madam President, you are highly respected around the world," started Acton. "World leaders are not hesitating one iota to lend a hand. The problem on our end is logistics. Without power to operate heavy equipment, we're unable to handle incoming container ships. Even if we could off-load them, we don't have a nationwide distribution network of trains, trucks, or even airplanes to move the supplies to where they're needed most."

"Wow, James. You really know how to cheer a gal up. I don't need to be reminded of the mess we're in."

"There is a potential solution, which has been offered today."

"What?"

"The United Nations, ma'am. They are prepared to send a sizable contingent into Texas, which would be used as a staging area. Then—"

The president held up her hand. "James, why are we even discussing this? Marion will never allow the UN on Texas soil. They rejected the secretary general's offer to join the United Nations with a big, fat *forget it!*"

Acton allowed the president to finish but persevered. "She has also proven she can be bought. I'm hearing their food situation is getting worse. Despite her resounding win, as soon as Texans realize how close they are to starvation, her authority will be challenged."

"You wanna bribe her? With what?"

"Same as before, a cut of the food, except this time, we'll handle—I mean the UN will handle the logistics completely. She gets food for her Texans without lifting a finger."

"I dunno, James. I suppose it's worth a try. How would it work?"

Acton pushed off the arms of the chair and walked toward her desk. He used it as a map of sorts.

"It would work like a hub-and-spoke system, similar to what was used on a smaller scale during the Berlin Airlift in '48 and '49."

After World War II, an agreement was reached to divide and occupy the large city of Berlin into sectors. West Germany was controlled by the United States and its allies. East Germany, which included the nation's largest city, Berlin, was controlled by the Soviet Union. Berlin, however, was divided as well by a wall into West and East Berlin. West Berlin was an island surrounded by Soviet territory and occupation.

As was often the case, cooperation between the two superpowers broke down over economics. The Western Allies introduced a new form of currency, the deutsche mark, into West Berlin. In response, Moscow ordered a blockade of all transportation routes into West Berlin. They also built a fence, and then a solid block wall, to prevent East Berliners from fleeing to the more prosperous west sector.

To overcome the loss of transportation routes, the Berlin Airlift was designed. Air Forces from seven Allied nations brought nine thousand tons of food, supplies, and fuel into West Berlin for further distribution to their citizens. The airlift circumvented the Soviet blockade and allowed West Berlin the opportunity to prosper. The Soviets, infuriated by the maneuver, could not stop the two hundred thousand flights into West Berlin airports for fear of angering the global community. The practice continued, and then, upon the urging of President Ronald Reagan, Mikhail Gorbachev *tore down that wall.*

"Please explain," said the President.

"We'll make the deal sweet for Burnett," started Acton, who refused to use the designation *president* as it related to the Texas head of state. "She doesn't have to lift a finger. All she needs to do is allow the United Nations access to her commercial airports, which are sitting dormant anyway. For example, Amarillo could service our Western states. DFW could service the Midwest and Northeastern states. Houston would be the hub for the South."

"What if she objects to the UN troops on Texas soil?"

"We'll have the secretary general come up with adequate assurances that his forces and aid workers would be restricted to the airports themselves," replied Acton, knowing full well that would never work in practice, nor did he want it to. "Again, her job becomes easier and her people get a cut of the food. Now, if she wants to become a citizen of the world like the rest of us, she can join the UN, pay dues, and get further aid to her people."

The president stood and smiled. "James, it might just work. This will certainly accelerate our recovery effort. Should I make the call to Marion?"

Oh, no. Leave that to me.

"No, Madam President, I'll make the necessary arrangements and keep you posted."

CHAPTER 9

December 27
The White House
Washington, DC

Acton casually exited the Oval Office and entered the corridor of the first floor of the West Wing. Prior to the collapse, the halls would've been filled with senior advisers and their staff, who occupied the offices on both sides of the corridor leading from the Oval Office to the Chief of Staff's corner office.

If it had been raining cats and dogs in that hallway, Acton wouldn't have noticed. This plan was going to work, he was sure of it. By filling a dire need of the Texans, Acton could induce Burnett into an unforced error. Getting UN personnel on the ground in Texas was like the velociraptor sticking its beak through the swinging doors in the *Jurassic Park* movie. Once that beak was in, you couldn't hold back the monster attached to it.

He strutted through his secretary's office, a temp he was stuck with until his regular aide could be located in Reston, Virginia. He was pounding away on a keyboard and didn't acknowledge Acton as he entered. Annoyed, Acton rapped his knuckles on the man's desk.

"Get me Mohammed on the phone, now!" Acton spun and turned toward his office.

"Which one?"

Acton stopped dead in his tracks and shook his head. The only thing that prevented him from blasting this guy out of the West Wing was his euphoria over a plan coming together. "The Deputy Secretary General named Mohammed. You can't miss him. His name is Mohammed Mohammed. Either way you read it, his name is in the same spot in your Rolodex."

"I don't have a Rolodex," the young man replied sheepishly.

"I spoke to him an hour ago! Figure it out and don't tell anybody about this call. Got it?"

"Yes, sir."

Acton poured himself two fingers of whisky and quickly downed it. Unlike the president, who needed her wine as a crutch, Acton enjoyed his whisky as a means of celebration. His self-congratulation session had to be delayed while he set the plan in motion.

His secretary tapped on the door and stuck his head in. "Sir, I have Deputy Secretary General Mohammed on the line for you."

"Close that door," barked Acton, still annoyed. "And close your door also. Nobody gets in, not even POTUS, got it?"

"Yes, sir."

Acton took a deep breath and lifted the receiver. "Deputy Secretary General Mohammed, thank you for taking my call."

"You're welcome, Mr. Acton," came the reply. "Is there something we failed to cover in our phone call?"

Acton smiled. "No. Actually, I have good news. The president and I discussed this matter at length, and she has suggested an excellent resolution that can benefit everyone."

"Okay, I'm ready to hear President Harman's proposal."

Acton laid out the suggested offer to be made to Texas regarding the logistics and the sharing of supplies. Then he supplemented the basis of the deal with the subterfuge portion of the plan.

"Now, Mohammed, you and I have seen eye to eye for many years. I don't believe we need to revisit the many times I have helped you advance your career."

"Nor do I need to remind you of the accommodations I have granted you in return," replied Mohammed.

"Agreed. I think we also agree that an independent Texas, a nation that refuses to join the United Nations and the new world order, is bad for business. This type of independent, nationalistic activity will encourage others like it. Do I need to remind you of that debacle in Spain with Catalonia? The Spaniards massacred their own people to prevent that secessionist movement."

"James, your Texas has already seceded, and President Harman has publicly acquiesced."

"She was encouraged to do so under false pretenses and coercion for the sake of the American people. This arrangement with Texas will help the American people, but it will also help overturn a terrible injustice to the United States."

"I don't understand how the United Nations can help you with that," said Mohammed.

"Here's how you can help. First, please assign Ruby Carlton, the special envoy to the African Union. She is a Texan and took the position to advance her family's oil interests in the region. She also can be trusted by Burnett.

"Second, I am going to provide you a list of international journalists to embed with the relief workers. There is no greater way to right a wrong than to shed the light of day upon the wrongdoing. It's time for Texas to enjoy the media attention and a little transparency.

"Finally, Burnett will insist upon UN personnel being confined to the airports where they are assigned. Toward that end, UN peacekeeping forces will be assigned to keep your people confined and, ostensibly, to keep the locals from interfering in your operations. This will reduce the manpower required of the Texas military."

Deputy Secretary General Mohammed paused without responding. Acton stopped talking as well, assuming the Saudi was making notes.

Finally, Mohammed spoke. "May I assume that the peacekeeping forces will have further duties should the situation arise?"

"Absolutely," replied Acton. "I want you to send in UNPROFOR, the UN Protection Force. You know, the one that doesn't exist. It's time for them to exist again."

Chapter 10

December 28
The Mansion
Austin, Texas

President Burnett gathered her top military and homeland security advisors together to discuss the proposal she received from the United Nations. On the surface, she was pleased that the international body she despised had appointed an envoy with whom she was familiar—Ruby Carlton. The Carlton family had been generous contributors to the Bush campaigns in the past, which resulted in Carlton's rise to become the ambassador to South Africa and her subsequent position with the UN.

Despite her modest level of trust in the proposal based upon Carlton's representations, the president had serious misgivings about implementing the proposal. This morning, she'd be looking to her chief strategists to decide if accepting the offer was viable.

The president started by polling the jury. "Before we get into the details of the proposal and the pros and cons, let's go around the table and give me an up or down vote based on the concept. Monty, you're first."

"I don't like it," said Vice President Gregg. "I have zero trust in the UN or Harris. This also has that globalist Acton's fingerprints all over it. He's an open-borders guy and very pro-UN."

"That's a resounding no," said President Burnett with a smile. "Kregg?"

Adjutant General Kregg Deur had always been an apolitical voice within the president's inner circle. He was a get-down-to-business kinda guy who tried not to let personalities get in the way of progress.

"Madam President, speaking strictly from a Homeland Security perspective, we would be inviting a foreign military to conduct business on Texas soil. We're not a member of the UN, and therefore the protective forces they offer must be considered potentially hostile. However, we could put in containment measures of our own to prevent UN personnel from leaving their boundaries. You know, the airport property."

"Is that a yes vote?" asked the president.

"Yes, with qualifications. If we are in a position to say no to the proposal as structured and not be in violation of your prior agreements with Washington, then I say negotiate further."

"Kregg, can you devise a security plan that contains the UN personnel to their temporary bases?"

"Yes, ma'am."

President Burnett went around the table and got the opinions of her other cabinet members. The executive branch of the Texas government, when it was still a state, included a variety of commissioners who ran for office. As the transition was made from state to nation-state, each of these cabinet members were elevated to similar positions within the new government.

The consensus was in favor of making the deal in order to access the food shipments, although several members suggested a temporary arrangement until the container ships could arrive to supply Texans with their basic necessities.

After an hour-long discussion, President Burnett agreed to a sixty-day airlift from the United Nations to help Texas get through the harshest parts of winter. Further, by March 1, she was assured the dredging project would be complete, which would reopen the Port of Houston to normal shipping activity.

In the meantime, the midstream operation suggested by Gregg, coupled with their share of the UN supplies, would help feed their citizens and hopefully quell the increasing unrest within Texas. President Burnett was a politician, and reelection was already on her mind.

"Okay, thanks, everybody, for your input," said the president.

"Kregg, I'll need you to work up a proposed security and monitoring plan. Ruby Carlton refers to this as the North American Airlift. My loyal voters will be infuriated that I'm allowing those baby-blue helmets into Texas. I have to convince them the benefits of food and supplies offset their temporary, limited presence here. Most importantly, I have to convince folks that we're gonna keep them caged in. I'm counting on you to make it happen!"

"Yes, Madam President," said Deur as he stood and then nodded to Gregg. "Mr. Vice President."

Gregg nodded a reply and then turned to President Burnett. "Marion, I don't like it. We're makin' a deal with the devil."

"Monty, we're in a pickle here. Our borders are being pushed to their limits. I'm convinced that a quarter of the remaining living Americans have descended upon Texas. I can visualize their faces pressed against our fences, a bunch of sad puppy-dog eyes, begging to enter the promised land. We ain't the promised land. If Texans knew how dire our food situation was, we'd lose control."

Gregg sat back in his chair and reached for a Werther's wrapped candy out of his pocket. "Want one?"

"No, thanks."

"I promised my wife I'd cut back on the cigars, so I placate myself with these things. It was a stupid promise."

"Monty, other than your natural inclination to disagree with anything that might have Washington's stamp of approval on it, can we make this work?"

"I think so, assuming Deur can contain them. We'll have to monitor their inbound and outbound flights to make sure nothing unauthorized comes in."

"Like what?"

"Marion, we have no way of knowing what the real intentions of the UN airlift are until we see their personnel. The most important agencies of the UN include monitoring and evaluation units. They're gonna be like a bunch of spies milling about. Now, that said, if Deur can contain them, then he can control the flow of information sent back to Brussels and Washington."

The president was puzzled and then seemed to grasp the situation. "Are you talking about media? Do you think they might use this as an opportunity to allow news reporters into Texas?"

"Absolutely. The worst kind. The kind who have an agenda wholly contrary to ours."

CHAPTER 11

December 28
The Mansion
Austin, Texas

Major and Duncan left early that morning for the three-hundred-mile drive to Austin. Normally, the trip would take just over four hours, but with speed limits being a thing of the past, Major buzzed down the mainly four-lane highway at eighty to ninety miles per hour. Without the ability to communicate with President Burnett's office, the guys hoped she would make time to see them. If not, they'd opt for the adjutant general instead.

The ride was uneventful except for signs of the apocalypse. Cars were abandoned on the sides of the highway due to lack of fuel. The small towns along the route, from Wingate to Winters and Bangs to Bozar, were largely abandoned. Signs of looting were evident at homes outside the town limits, but there was no evidence of the types of atrocities Major had witnessed in Gail.

Entering Travis County, which apparently had been declared to be a state within the Republic of Texas based upon the temporary signs erected at the old county line, things began to change. There was very little vehicular traffic except for military and law enforcement.

What struck Major and Duncan the most were the large numbers of people just milling about. The jobless. The American economy had been built on consumer spending. Likewise, most Texans held service-oriented jobs that fed off each other's consumption.

Consumerism rested on the assumption that the economy would grow and grow forever. Once the appetite for and the ability to consume faltered, the house of cards collapsed. After 9/11, President

George W. Bush implored repeatedly—in response to every crisis, it was a citizen's patriotic duty to go shopping. Spend your money. *Keep the house of cards afloat.*

As the two rode through the streets of Austin, what they observed was reminiscent of the Great Depression. People standing around or walking aimlessly from point to point. Long lines at temporary government food-distribution centers. Tent cities outside hospitals as people waited to get treated for illnesses associated with dehydration, malnutrition, and dysentery.

The house of cards was collapsing, but hey, the power was on.

*****

"Major Armstrong, what a very pleasant surprise!" President Burnett jovially greeted her longtime friend and consistent donor. It wasn't often that an uninvited guest could meet with the president of any nation without having to go through the pomp and circumstance afforded a person in power. She appeared genuinely glad to see him.

"Madam President," began Major as he shook his head and smiled. The reality of Texas being its own country and his friend Marion as its president just hit him. "Well, what can I say? Congratulations!"

She gave him an impromptu hug, which lingered for nearly half a minute, the sincerity of which did not go unnoticed by Major. Despite the politician's façade, he suspected the president was under intense pressure.

"Duncan, is that you? You're the spittin' image of your daddy when he was your age."

"It's nice to see you again, Madam President," said Duncan as he shook her hand. He too received a hug, which caused him to lock eyes with Major. Major gave a slight shrug and furrowed his brow. He wondered if they'd come at a bad time.

The president broke their embrace and led them both into her office. She left her door open for a minute while her aide brought them three glasses of sweet tea. After they were alone again, the door was closed and the president relaxed.

"Major, don't get me wrong, I think what we've accomplished here is extraordinary. Seriously, it will be written about in history books and analyzed for years to come. But I've gotta be honest, there are times I really miss riding horses out at the Four Sixes Ranch."

"I totally understand, Madam Pres—" started Major before he was cut off.

"Stop that, both of you. I'm surrounded by butt-kissers who madam this or madam that. I admit, it was flattering at first, but if I can't let my friends call me Marion, I might forget who I am."

The guys agreed, and the mood in the room immediately lifted. Major relayed to the president how ranch life had changed. He tried to avoid the negatives of what had happened in Gail and with the intruders at the ranch. The president of Texas had enough to deal with.

She opened up to them about the country's food shortages. President Burnett disclosed the proposal made by the UN, and Major was honest with her as to his opinion. Politically, the additional food supplies would be very popular with the majority of Texans. Ideologically, her core constituency would freak out. But, he added, without normal media operations and conservative talk radio to rake her over the coals, it was unlikely most Texans would know the logistical arrangements she'd agreed to.

The conversation turned to Duncan and the reason for their unannounced arrival. As he began to provide her the backstory on how he had returned to the U.S., the president's aide tapped on her door and entered.

"Madam President, the vice president needs you for one moment."

"Good, please send him in. I'd like him to meet a couple of old friends."

Gregg marched into the room, which was customary for him, and began to address the president when Major and Duncan rose out of their chairs to greet him.

"Oh, my apologies, I was unaware you had guests," said Gregg with an air of formality.

Major studied his demeanor. The confidence Gregg had exuded when he entered was quickly replaced with an ashen, almost withdrawn look when he first noticed their presence.

He extended his hand to shake Gregg's. "Mr. Vice President, it's an honor to see you again. We met here, at Marion's secession announcement. I'm Major Armstrong."

"Yes, um, of course. That was an eventful evening."

"It sure was," added Major. "You were here with another gentleman. What was his name?"

An innocent question, so Major thought. Major had made a career out of reading people. Body language told him a lot as he interrogated suspects and dealt with the criminal element. Gregg's eyes darted back and forth between everyone in the room. For some reason, Major had struck a nerve.

"Oh, of course. Billy Yancey, a fellow Texan and supporter of the president," replied Gregg. He quickly moved to change the subject. "Who is this stout young man?"

"General Gregg, my name is Duncan Armstrong. I proudly served you for three tours in the Middle Eastern theater and later with special operations. It's an honor, sir."

"A pleasure," said Gregg, who started to back out of the room.

"Monty, did you need something?" asked the president.

"No, Madam President. It can wait."

"Mr. Vice President, if I may," started Major, "the matter we need to discuss with the president could use the benefit of your military expertise. What my son has observed could have a profound impact on national security, for both Texas and the United States."

"Oh?" said Gregg inquisitively.

"That sounds quite ominous and foreboding, Major," said the president. "Monty, please join us."

He nodded and took up a seat to the side of President Harman's desk. Major saw him wipe his palms on his pants as he sat down. *He's nervous.*

Duncan was instructed to begin and spent the next ten minutes relaying the details of what he'd seen. Gregg took in the information and occasionally asked a question, but mostly he appeared to be uneasy. His demeanor stood in stark contrast to the evening when Major had met him in the ballroom of the Mansion.

After the discussion was completed, the president assured Major and Duncan she'd pass the information on to her Homeland Security team, who'd increase security patrols along the nation's western border with New Mexico.

A few pleasantries were exchanged, Gregg excused himself, and the Armstrongs left for their truck. As they walked out of the entry toward the front lawn, Major leaned in and whispered to Duncan, "The new vice president seemed mighty nervous."

"Yeah, well, he should be."

CHAPTER 12

December 28
Austin, Texas

Major and Duncan swiftly, but casually, made their way to the truck without speaking. Both had sensed the tension in the room during their conversation with the president and Gregg. In case they were being observed, they avoided any conversation that might be misconstrued. They were several miles away from the capitol grounds when Major broke the silence.

"Son, the former Secretary of Defense was clearly nervous from the moment he saw us turn around. You woulda thought he'd seen a ghost."

Duncan didn't respond right away as he continued to process the brief encounter. Another quarter mile down the road, he pounded the passenger window three times with the back of his fist.

"Son!" shouted Major. "You need to start talkin' to me, now."

Duncan stopped clenching his fist and shook his hand to relax it. "Dad, he knew exactly who I was. He may not have known me if we passed one another on the sidewalk, but when he saw you and looked at me, his eyes gave it away. He knows!"

"You mean the assassination attempt?"

"Dang straight, Dad, and probably a lot more."

Major laughed. "That man was as nervous as a long-tailed cat in a roomful of rocking chairs."

Duncan managed a chuckle, but his mind was clearly racing to a certain conclusion. "Yeah, he was. Listen, Dad. I've never met the man in person, but I've seen him on TV many times. He's calm, collected, and the consummate military man. What I saw today was a politician squirming under pressure, constantly eyein' the exit door."

"Well, I watched his eyes, son. It's something I've done throughout my career, and it's served me well, not to mention kept me alive on a couple of occasions. When I met the former Defense Secretary at Marion's coming-out party, as I like to call it, he had that same shifty look. As soon as I introduced myself, his eyes got squirrelly, and he started looking from me to that Yancey fella."

"I'm surprised they'd be seen in public together," said Duncan dryly. He rested his chin on his fist while staring out the passenger window as they cleared the city limits and hit the open highway back to the ranch.

"Do you know the guy?" asked Major.

"Oh yeah, but we only met once," replied Duncan. "His name is Billy Yancey. He's a Texan and a butt-buddy of the general, um, vice president. Whatever. Anyway, his official title is head of the Political Action Group within the National Clandestine Service."

"That's a mouthful," quipped Major.

"All you need to know is that he's former CIA. The PAG, as the Political Action Group is called, conducts psyops, cyber warfare, and creates economic chaos to effectuate regime change. They're real active in Latin America although they've been known to manipulate elections in Europe as well."

"You mean like that Russian meddling garbage from years ago?" asked Major.

"Dad, what the Russians did on Facebook and Twitter is child's play compared to what Billy Yancey has orchestrated in the name of American national interests. Trust me, I know. I've been right in the middle of it."

Major slowed the truck, as a group of six people were blocking the road ahead. They had broken out the window of an abandoned car and were looking for anything of value. He gave them a wide berth and picked up speed again.

"Son, would he have been involved in the orders to assassinate Kim Jong-un?"

"Are you kiddin'?" said Duncan with a sarcastic laugh. "It was probably his idea. Here's the thing, Dad. I'm not gonna argue with their goals or my orders. In a way, I'm to blame for shootin' the wrong guy. Every sniper has the final say on any mission. It's his trigger finger that sets things in motion."

"Kim inserted a body double into the equation," interrupted Major. "He must have been tipped off."

"Trust me, I've played this through my mind a thousand times. It was either a double-cross by the sister, or she simply got cold feet. My beef isn't with the North Koreans. It's with the guy who called off our extraction. They left us for dead, Dad, and someone has to be held to account."

Major, unaware that his speed was approaching ninety, suddenly caught himself gripping the wheel with white knuckles. "Do you think Gregg and Yancey know something?"

"More than that, Dad. The way Gregg acted today, he may have been the one to give the stand-down order."

Major slowed to a more reasonable speed as he and Duncan processed their conclusions. Under the circumstances, it was probably best to let it go. They needed to focus their efforts on protecting their family and the ranch. On the other hand, he knew his son to be a principled man who was like a dog with a bone. Once he'd set his mind on something, there was no shakin' him from it.

"Duncan, even if you could find evidence, what would you do with it?"

"Eye for an eye, Dad."

CHAPTER 13

December 29
The Armstrong Ranch
Borden County, Texas

Palmer and Sook decided to host a gathering in the barn for the first taekwondo lesson. Riley, who insisted upon learning the Korean martial art, was most likely to be a punching dummy. Duncan sat next to Cooper on top of a picnic table that had been pushed to the side. Major and Lucy found a spot on the other side of the barn on top of some rectangular hay bales. The center of the barn was reserved for Palmer, who took on the role of master of ceremonies, and Sook, who'd been officially proclaimed to be the instructor of the Armstrong Ranch *do-jang*, the term used in Korean martial arts to refer to their training hall.

"Good afternoon, students," Sook said with a bow. After a few giggles from the group, as they were still enamored with her accent, they responded, "Good afternoon."

"Today, I will teach you about the Korean form of martial arts—taekwondo. During World War II, before Korea was separated, our country's martial arts experts combined karate and Chinese martial arts like kung fu to create our own technique. Taekwondo is about more than fighting. It is also about the human spirit. You will learn this first."

Palmer joined Riley at the side of the barn so Sook could be the center of attention. Everyone focused on her words, clearly taking her lessons as seriously as the person imparting the knowledge.

Sook continued. "As students of taekwondo, you must, at all times, observe the basic tenets of this art. These principles are basic means of treating one another with respect during training and in life.

"First, practice courtesy to one another. Be polite to one another as you would ask a stranger to be polite to you. Politeness and courtesy are required in everybody's life to maintain a harmonious society.

"Second, one must be able to know the difference between right and wrong. You must have the power of conscience that if you are wrong, you must feel guilt. This tenet is known as integrity. Without integrity, you will have no self-respect.

"Third, I want you to remember an old saying from the Orient. Patience leads to virtue and merit. One can only make a peaceful home by being patient for one hundred times. In your training and in your life, happiness, prosperity, and achievement will be the reward given to the patient person who is willing to persevere in pursuit of perfection.

"Fourth, all of those who practice taekwondo must remember this is the art of self-defense. It must always be used as a last resort, which requires you to maintain self-control. Taekwondo is the most powerful, and deadly, of the ancient arts. A loss of self-control can be dangerous for the stronger, and deadly for the weaker.

"Fifth, all students of taekwondo must be modest and honest with their fellow man. When you are confronted with injustice, you must deal with hostility without fear or hesitation. You should approach your adversary with an unconquerable spirit, or you will become the conquered. With this spirit inside you, you can pursue your goals with inner peace and strength. You will not fail."

Everyone nodded their heads, but it was Riley's reaction that caught them off guard. He broke up the reverent moment with spontaneous applause and a Texas-sized *yee-haw*. When nobody joined in, the ever-emotional Riley, who stood the most to gain from the tenets of taekwondo, dropped his chin to his chest and stepped backwards toward the outside wall of the barn.

Sook understood Riley's enthusiasm. In a way, her recital of the tenets of taekwondo weren't unlike what she envisioned a minister saying to her in church. The principles had deep philosophical meanings for those who practice the art, but also for those who were looking for guidance in their life.

Clearly, what she said to the group was especially helpful to Riley. He might not learn the techniques, but he had a grasp of how to apply them to his life. Sometimes, that was more important than learning how to fight back.

CHAPTER 14

December 30
Carlsbad Caverns, New Mexico

After the initial snowstorms that had greeted Joseph Manuel Holloway and his band of North Korean gang members during their drive to Carlsbad Caverns, the skies cleared, bringing warm sunshine. Their spirits were high as more North Korean operatives from the Lightning Death Squads found their way to deep rocky caverns hidden high above the Chihuahuan Desert.

During the last several days, Holloway had endeared himself to the Korean forces by first bringing them gifts, which he had procured from the National Guard Armory in Roswell. But it was his tales of battle in the Middle East and the conversation of training techniques of the Afghan soldiers that gained him respect.

While the Lightning Death Squads were well trained and committed to their cause, they'd never seen actual combat. The Kim regime and the million-man army it boasted had never invaded a foreign land nor had it engaged any enemy in combat. There wasn't a combat veteran among them.

Holloway warned their newly appointed general of the North American invasion, Kyoung-Joo Lee, that his men's training was second to none, but their reaction in an actual firefight was suspect.

As a result of their frank conversations, Lee took Holloway into his inner circle, much to the chagrin of his North Korean commanders. They were fighting an ideological war, one bent on revenge and born out of jealousy. While not being overtly critical of Holloway for fear of execution by Lee's orders, the men certainly slighted the only American within their ranks at every opportunity.

Holloway subtly made Lee aware of this. He didn't mind being ostracized by the Koreans. He remained focused on the prize—leading an advance team into Texas so he could partake of the spoils before these locusts destroyed everything in sight.

"General Lee," Holloway greeted Lee respectfully as he approached the commander and spread a map out on the cave floor. Hundreds of candles flickered around them as some of the soldiers slept on the rock floor while others talked among themselves about girls, home, and what the future would bring.

Lee, who'd spent ten years in Canada training operatives before finding ways to assist them across the border into the U.S., had mastered the English language and was able to converse with Holloway fluently.

"Go ahead, Holloway," he responded.

"Thank you, sir. As you know, the goal was to destroy the heartbeat of America with the electromagnetic pulse bombs. The nuclear attack was unexpected, but successful, although it did not finish the job. America still has a pulse and it is Texas."

Lee nodded in agreement. "This is why Dear Leader has ordered us to attack Texas and force it into darkness like the rest of America."

"Exactly, but our time is growing short. Each day, our scouts report that the Texans are increasing their security forces along their western border shared with New Mexico. I believe we must begin to assess our plans of invasion."

Lee straightened his back somewhat, indicating to Holloway that he needed to tread lightly on the new general's turf.

"When the time is right, we will invade." Lee bristled in his response.

"General, may I suggest that an advance team, led by me and my handpicked men, should enter Texas. We should determine the most accessible route for your soldiers. We can assess the weaknesses of the enemy and communicate the information to you by satellite telephone. Knowledge is power, General, and without the benefit of air and satellite reconnaissance, we must obtain information about the enemy the old-fashioned way—with boots on the ground and eyes wide open."

Lee pondered Holloway's suggestion for a minute, picking up the map at one point to get a closer look at the topography and its borders.

History had molded Texas to form the unmistakable shape with its sharp angles of the Panhandle, sweeping curves along Mexico as it followed the Rio Grande, and the jagged edges formed by the Red River and the Gulf of Mexico.

Only a handful of roads stretched into the state from Roswell to their north, in the direction of West Texas, and the Mexican border to their south.

"You will not be able to cross the border in our vehicles," said Lee. "Our scouts have confirmed double fencing with prison razor wire preventing access. Now, the patrols have increased along this entire boundary."

Returning his attention to the map, Lee ran his fingers along the western part of Texas from El Paso due east, until a harsh right angle sent the border north to form the Panhandle.

"Yes, General, I have those reports as well. However, there is an exception that we can exploit."

"Where?" asked Lee as he handed the map back to Holloway.

Unbeknownst to Lee, Holloway had sent two of his men on a twenty-mile trek through the Lonesome Ridge Wilderness area of the Guadalupe Mountains. They found the terrain to be too treacherous for fencing at the Texas border. There were no roads, but walking paths and four-wheeler trails were abundant. After a full day of travel, Holloway's scouts learned that they'd entered deep into Texas without knowing it. There were no fences, no border guards, and no signs of life in the national park except for deer.

"Here, through the mountains, only twenty miles to our southeast," replied Holloway as he pointed at the map. "We wouldn't be able to use our vehicles, but I feel certain we could find suitable transportation once we've entered their territory."

Lee pondered Holloway's request and stared into the candles.

Holloway knew Lee was anxious to begin his operations around the country, not just against Texas, but also at strategic points elsewhere. He was stymied by the lack of communications with the leadership in Pyongyang. Since the dropping of the nuclear bombs, he'd expressed his concerns about moving forward with the absence of direct orders from Dear Leader. Holloway knew this proposal would give Lee the feeling that he was accomplishing something while waiting for further instructions from his superiors.

"You will keep me informed of your activities, with details of your location and encounters, is that understood?" demanded Lee.

"Yes, sir."

"Holloway, you must not engage the enemy. You are on a scouting mission only, do you understand?"

"Yes, sir. Scouting only."

Holloway shielded his face from the flickering light exuded by the candles and smiled.

"Tomorrow, assemble your team and the weapons you'll need for the mission. I want to meet with them before your departure. You will travel under cover of darkness tomorrow evening."

Time to play!

CHAPTER 15

December 31
The Armstrong Ranch
Borden County, Texas

Duncan retrieved Palmer's first rifle from the gun case, a Mossberg 702 semiautomatic Plinkster model chambered in .22 caliber. Their dad had purchased it for her when she turned ten years old. At first, Palmer had loved the balanced feel and the easy-to-reload aspect of the ten-round magazine. Then after incessant teasing from Riley about the pink-and-black camo pattern, she wanted something new. Duncan worked with her until she was ready to graduate up to a Remington 700 bolt-action hunting rifle.

He pulled one of the several hunting rifles to be used by Palmer today, and then he reached for the Daniel Defense DD5V1. The powerful AR-10-style weapon was a nice addition to the Armstrong arsenal. He wanted to send a few rounds down the range to try it out, although very little would dissuade him from using the Barrett for long-range shooting which had served him well in North Korea and Arizona.

Palmer and Sook were waiting at the front door. Palmer had backpacks filled with ammo, magazines, and a weapons tool kit in case maintenance was required. She also had her new H&K VP9 that was purchased for her by her mother. Palmer needed some practice time with her new handgun as well.

"Are we ready?" asked Duncan as he slung the Mossberg over his shoulder and cradled the heavier AR-10.

"Wait," interrupted Lucy from the kitchen. "There's one more thing."

Duncan turned, and his mother approached them carrying a paddle holster, which contained her H&K handgun that matched Palmer's.

Lucy walked up to Sook and presented her with the weapon. "Honey, you are my daughter too. I have worn this weapon on my hip with pride and comfort knowing it will protect our family. I want you to have it because you and Palmer are practically sisters. Sisters should watch over and protect one another."

Sook took the weapon and held it in both her hands as if someone had just handed her a newborn baby.

"Momma, that's so sweet," said Palmer as she quickly gave her mother a hug.

"Thank you, Miss Lucy," said Sook with a tear in her eye. "I will protect my sister, and all of my new family, with my life. It is my promise to you."

The women hugged again, and Duncan stood back as he took in the emotional moment. It was a rite of passage in all their lives. Sook had become a member of the family for many reasons, but Lucy's relinquishing of her beloved sidearm showed confidence that the young woman could now be counted on to protect them as well.

After excusing himself to retrieve a box of fifty rounds for the nine-millimeter weapons, and the new Omega suppressor, Duncan led his students by horseback down to the ravine on the far east end of the ranch.

This natural formation acted as a barrier to anyone attempting to approach them from the east. When the heavy rains came in the spring, or with thawing snow, the ravine's dry creek beds would be full of muddy water flowing down into Wildcat Creek toward Lake J. B. Thomas. The high walls of the ravine kept the sounds of gunfire within it, decreasing the likelihood of any residents around the lake hearing them.

It was a cool morning on New Year's Eve. Sunny, with calm winds, the forty-two-degree temperatures were invigorating. They tied their horses to a small lean-to shed, which served to protect them from the sun during the summer. The building covered a picnic table on which Duncan spread out the weapons and organized them from most to least powerful.

Sook had very little knowledge of weapons, and although it wasn't likely she'd be called upon to use the Barrett or the Daniel Defense rifles, Duncan felt she needed an overall understanding of what the various weapons were intended to do.

"Sook, the first thing you should know is that each of these guns is like a tool," Duncan began as he used his fingers to point as he spoke. "For example, this table is built using nails. A nail is driven in with a hammer. That is what a hammer is used for. If I wanted to break the table, I would use a very heavy hammer called a sledgehammer. It has a long handle and a much bigger head."

"Yes, I understand," said Sook. She touched the buttstock of the Barrett. "Sledgehammer. I have seen the sledgehammer work."

He handed her the Mossberg .22-caliber rifle. "Feel the weight."

"Yes. Light weight."

Duncan took the Mossberg away and handed her the Remington. "Try this."

"Yes, the same." She nodded and returned the rifle to Duncan.

Then Duncan handed her a .22-caliber bullet and the .308 round used in the Remington. "The .22 is a hammer. The .308 is a sledgehammer bullet."

"Both rifles weigh the same," interrupted Sook as she held the two bullets side by side. The .308-caliber bullet dwarfed the .22 in both length and girth.

Duncan took the bullets back and continued. "That's right, Sook. Every firearm and its ammunition has a different purpose just like a tool has its own unique function. Today, I want to teach you how to handle a gun safely, treating it with respect, so when the time comes, you can use it as a tool to defend yourself and all of us. Okay?"

"Yes, sir, General Duncan," said Sook with a laugh as she stood at attention. Palmer joined in and stood next to Sook before giving her oldest brother a snappy salute.

Duncan took the playful ribbing and then got down to business. Palmer retrieved Oakley ballistic protection sunglasses from the backpack. Duncan taught Sook everything from how to load ammo in the magazines to proper stance and technique.

After an hour of practice, Sook was routinely hitting the wooden targets built by Duncan and Dallas years ago. He pulled her farther away as she began to nail the center of the painted rings on the plywood board. He was impressed.

"Sook, you do have a good eye," he said as she finished her one-hundredth round from fifty yards. For training purposes, especially with the .22 rifle, more than fifty yards was unnecessary. He planned on bringing her out for a second time to determine if she'd retained what he'd taught her and to see if today's excellent shooting was merely beginner's luck.

"Okay, my turn," announced Palmer as she checked her magazine and then jammed it into her sidearm.

"All right, Palmer, but let me mention a few things to Sook as you go because this is all a learning experience," said Duncan. "After you empty a mag, I want you to add your new silencer. You'll find a noticeable weight and balance difference that will require some adjustments."

Palmer holstered her weapon and marched downrange to set up new targets. While she did, Duncan gave Sook an overview.

He picked up Sook's new H&K and released the magazine into his hand. He checked the chamber to insure it was empty and handed the weapon to Sook, handle first.

"Very light. I like this," she said.

Duncan began. "There are many things to learn about handling a sidearm. We'll talk about proper grip and sight alignment, but the key to successful performance is pulling the trigger. That sounds like a simple concept, but the part you control is the trigger pull. You must not jerk or flinch when you squeeze it. The key is to pull it slowly so the barrel remains pointed exactly at your target. That takes a lot of practice."

"Palmer has lots of practice?" asked Sook.

"Sook, she is the best in the family, besides me, of course. Riley and Cooper always wanted to shoot their rifles. Palmer enjoyed learning how to draw her pistol from her holster, shoot accurately, and quickly remove an empty magazine to replace it with a full one."

Palmer returned back to their side with a strut of confidence. "Watch this, Sook."

She stood perfectly still, and suddenly, with her knees locked, and feet at hip width, she quickly drew her sidearm out of the paddle holster. Her hands were steady and she began firing.

Palmer threw three rounds down the range, nailing the first target in the center before repeating the action on two other targets close by. Despite having a round remaining in the magazine, she dropped it to the ground and swiftly pulled a backup and slapped it into the bottom of the nine-millimeter weapon's grip. She repeated the process, once again nailing the three targets with three bullets each.

When she finished, she paused momentarily to admire her work, flipped the safety back on, and slid the sidearm back into its holster.

Before she could turn around, Duncan, who was grinning, said, "Show-off."

Palmer laughed. "You wanna give it a try? You don't have to do it as fast as me, so you don't embarrass yourself in front of your girlfriend."

"Very funny, Palmer," said Duncan as he fist-bumped with his sister. "That's very impressive, obviously. But after years of practicing that shooting routine, you should have it down perfect. Here's something you and I, together with Sook, are going to work on. First, you're not gonna let that spent magazine hit the ground to pick up later. We can't run down to the gun store and buy more. If we lose our magazines in a gunfight, our guns will become worthless."

"What should I do?" asked Palmer.

"We'll practice dropping those magazines and sticking them in your pants or a vest. That's the least of my concerns, however."

"What else?" asked Palmer.

"Well, there's a second thing I wanna mention," replied Duncan. "Until now, the family has trained for hunting purposes or to show off their skills, like you just did. It's time we learn what it's like to be in a real firefight—fire while moving, seeking cover, and reloading on the fly. Daddy and I know, but y'all have to realize that targets don't stand still, and they shoot back with the intent to kill you."

CHAPTER 16

December 31
Ector County Detention Center
Odessa, Texas

"Little John," began Riley as he steered the four-door pickup through the south gate of the Armstrong Ranch. He looked into the rearview mirror to the young man they'd rescued the day after Christmas. With the help of Antonio, who sat next to him in the backseat, the young man had overcome the trauma of losing his mother to the *banditos*, as he called them. The time also allowed his body to heal from the beating and lack of nutrition. "We're hopin' to reunite you with your daddy. Will you buckle up your seat belt and promise to do everything we tell you?"

"Yes, Mr. Riley," he replied. "My daddy is a good person. Mommy said he made a stupid mistake and had to be punished."

Major, who rode up front with Riley, turned around and spoke to the young man. "That's true, Little John, daddies make mistakes sometimes. I hope your daddy can be released to take care of you. I'm gonna do my best, okay?"

"Yessir," the boy replied halfheartedly. His life had been full of disappointment, and it was understandable that he'd lack hope.

Major waved to the hands as they shut the gates behind them. He unconsciously gripped the barrel of his rifle, which sat between his legs and the passenger door. He regretted not asking the president for a formal letter of pardon for Mr. Flores. He wasn't sure of the offense for which he was serving time, but since he was being held in the Ector County system, it was most likely minor in comparison to those inmates who would've been shipped off to a state prison facility.

In Texas, minor offenses most likely received a sentence of eleven months and twenty-nine days, which placed them within the charge of the county where they were convicted.

Major hadn't heard any news of what was happening in Odessa since the collapse. He knew the sheriff of Ector County well. Jimmy Griffin was the son of a Texas Ranger. Sheriff Griffin, when he was a deputy, had come under investigation by Company E in El Paso. Because Griffin's father was a Ranger, he and all of Company E had to recuse themselves from any involvement or contact with the investigators on the case. Company C in Lubbock, and Major personally, oversaw the investigation to avoid the appearance of impropriety.

Many years ago, then Deputy Griffin had initiated a traffic stop on Highway 385 south of Odessa in a rural part of the county. He had set up a routine speed trap due to complaints by residents in the Pleasant Farms community. As it turned out, the primary culprit was the teenage son of the county treasurer. The boy had been given a new Dodge Challenger boasting nearly seven hundred horsepower, or roughly double what a seventeen-year-old teenage boy should be pushing.

Deputy Griffin, after an eleven-mile chase, stopped the young man and arrested him on multiple charges, including speeding, reckless endangerment, and resisting arrest. Because of the boy's age and his relationship to the country treasurer, Griffin elected to discard the bag of marijuana found in clear sight on the front seat of the car.

He'd done the boy a big favor, only to be repaid later when the father and son filed a complaint against Griffin for excessive force in an attempt to negotiate the vehicle-related charges away. The charges came at a time when America was hypersensitive to law enforcement's handling of criminals. As a result, the Texas Rangers were asked to look into the case.

Major, who found that the kid had been roughed up a little

because he was high and mouthy, decided on his own to protect Deputy Griffin by claiming there was insufficient evidence to warrant any charges against the deputy. He'd most likely saved Griffin's career, and as a result, he'd ascended to the position of sheriff of Ector County.

Odessa was a city with a population of one hundred twenty thousand, although it had grown together with nearby Midland to combine to a metropolis of over a quarter-million people. Major gave Riley directions that took the travelers on a loop that encircled the city. They could avoid the populated areas and enter the city from the south.

This was Riley and Antonio's first opportunity to see the impact the collapsed power grid in America had on Texans. Similar to Austin, there were indications of widespread unemployment and despair. As they slowed to approach the Ector County Detention Center, the faces of the downtrodden came into focus.

Blank expressions and hollow eyes were the norm. Only a few playing children and the occasional dog wagging its tail were the exceptions.

The detention center was heavily guarded by police wearing tactical gear and carrying automatic weapons. Major was somewhat puzzled by this, as he didn't see any immediate threat to the complex from outsiders.

He provided the guards at the Grant Avenue gate his credentials and instructed them to contact Sheriff Griffin to announce his arrival. He said he'd be glad to explain the purpose of his visit if necessary.

The guard was gone for a few minutes and then returned Major's identification. "You can pass, sir. Do you know where the sheriff's office is located?"

"I do, thank you."

He pointed Riley toward the parking lot of the first building, a single-story structure that contained the administrative offices of the sheriff. The larger two-story buildings to the rear contained the jail cells.

The group entered the facility, and Major instructed them to wait in an adjacent empty waiting area. After speaking briefly with a uniformed deputy behind a glass reception window, he waved to Little John to join him. Riley attempted to come along, but Major told him to wait.

"Stay with Antonio, son," said Major. "I imagine this is a conversation that the sheriff would prefer happen between the two of us."

Twenty minutes later, after a stern reminder of favors granted and reciprocal favors returned, Major walked out of the back offices with a smile, Little John, and a deputy escort.

Riley was the first to join them. "How did it go, Daddy?"

"Very well, son. This young man is going to take us to where Little John's father is working today. The sheriff agrees that Mr. Flores has served his time well and is worthy of getting released due to his good behavior."

Riley reached down and picked up Little John, who was smiling so big his eyes closed shut.

"Little John, whadya think of that news?" asked Riley.

"It sounds like Christmas," he replied.

Major shook his head in sadness. Children shouldn't have to experience the devastation Little John had been through, much less at Christmastime. He was glad they'd saved the boy and given him a ray of hope in a horrific world.

CHAPTER 17

December 31
Music City Mall
Refugee Center, Unit One
Odessa, Texas

After the four loaded up in their truck, they were escorted by two Ector County sheriff's cars to the nearby Music City Mall. The million-square-foot regional shopping mall had been leased by the military department to become the first refugee center to handle local Texans together with those new refugees brought into Texas as a result of the agreement with Washington.

After clearing a security checkpoint, they were led to a parking area, which consisted primarily of sheriff's department vehicles and food trucks bearing names like Sysco, Kraft, and Mission. At the main mall entrance, more guards stood behind concrete barriers to prevent any type of vehicular assault on the entrance.

At the two side entrances, chain-link fencing was placed to create a corridor where people were funneled to be processed for entry. Families stood in line, holding blankets, suitcases, and personal effects. They'd left their homes hoping they'd be fed and kept alive.

The irony was not lost on Major. In a nation that thrived on shopping at the malls to fill their homes with material goods, when the collapse arrived, they turned to those same malls to keep them alive.

As they waited to be cleared for entry, the group stopped to admire the ten-foot-tall, eight-hundred-pound granite tablet with the Ten Commandments engraved on it. The owner of the mall, Jack Huntsman, had erected similar monuments in his businesses located around Texas. In an interview with the *Dallas Morning News*, he was quoted as saying, "In times of turbulence in the world, this is our way of sharing peace and the Lord's love. We all need more of that."

Major grimaced as the group was led past the tablet. He wished Huntsman had erected more of his tablets in places that really mattered, like Congress and the White House, not in front of shopping malls.

Entering the mall, they were struck with the downfall of humanity. All of the mall businesses had rolled down their steel security screens, which prevented the refugees from entering the now-closed businesses. People were packed in like sardines, most lying in rows on the floor sleeping. Many others stood along the rails of the mall's second level, staring at the crowds below them. To say that Refugee Center Number One was full to capacity would be an understatement.

"This way, please. Flores is one of our inmate food servers," said the deputy who'd escorted them from the detention center. "Because he's a short-timer, he was allowed to remain in this facility instead of the jail. Each day, he assists with meal distribution, after which he is allowed to roam freely throughout the mall. He gets fed better than the others, so he reports for duty like clockwork."

Major took Little John by the hand as they pushed through a crowd of new refugees being processed. Each person received a blanket, a ziplock bag of basic toiletries, and a Gideons Bible.

"Is my daddy here with all these people?" asked Little John.

"Yes, little man," replied Riley. "They're going to find him now and bring him to you."

The entourage stood off to the side near the glass elevator and waited as instructed. Little John stood by the rail overlooking the ground floor, where people milled about as they began to form their lines for the six o'clock dinner serving. It was only two fifteen.

With his hands and face pressed against the glass, his eyes scanned the mass of people bouncing off one another as they positioned themselves to form a line. When the elevator started to rise from the lower floor, Little John's eyes grew wider, and then he began to cry from excitement.

His father walked back and forth in the slow-moving elevator like a caged animal looking for a means of escape. He was nervously looking for his only son. When they made eye contact, Major became emotional as he recalled the feeling on Christmas Eve when he first saw his three youngest, and then Duncan, the day they returned to the ranch. Deep down, he'd had faith they'd make it home safely, but a lingering doubt regarding their return had nagged at him that he'd hidden from Lucy and Preacher.

Little John broke away from the group and politely pushed his way through the sea of adults. He made his way to the elevator and stood next to the doors as they slowly opened. His father never made it out of the elevator cab. The young man ran into his father's legs, crashing them both backwards into the elevator.

Major fought back tears as the reunion not only touched his heart, but everyone within the mall who could see into the glass elevator. Nobody knew the story, but they certainly appreciated the reunion. Father and son were together again.

As Major regained his composure in order to tell Mr. Flores the further good news of his sentence commutation and that he was a free man once again, he also gathered the courage to deliver the bad news about his missing wife. Major tried his best to offer words of hope and strength, but both men were realistic.

Further, Little John and his father would not be invited to Armstrong Ranch. Regrettably, the risk of the unknown was too great to expose Major's family to these strangers. It was a tough decision to make, especially under the circumstances of the tearful reunion between the two, but it was one of those difficult choices Major would have to make many times during the apocalypse.

CHAPTER 18

December 31
Carlsbad Caverns National Forest

Holloway was growing impatient and was anxious to move forward with his own agenda. He stood by patiently as Lee gave Holloway's men a pep talk about avenging Dear Leader and advancing the goals of the DPRK. He didn't care about any of that, and he knew his men didn't either. Nonetheless, as soon as they were on the trail to the Texas border, he planned on speaking with his team at the first opportunity to confirm their allegiance to him, and their self-interested goals. If he was unsure of someone within his ranks, he'd shoot them on the spot. He doubted it would come to that.

They started out on foot, as planned, along the trails and gravel roads of the Carlsbad Caverns National Park. Lee's own scouts made trips several times a day to the Texas border where the roads passed into the former state. Security had been beefed up, and the roads were becoming clogged with refugees. His commandos and Holloway's team would only have one means of access—through the mountainous, tree-covered terrain. Holloway considered the logistics of sneaking Lee's men into the state over the winding, treacherous path. He made a mental note to find a better alternative, once again proving his worth to the new general.

They began the twenty-mile trek after Lee's final words of wisdom were imparted upon them. The men, all of whom stayed in good physical shape despite their penchant for partying, walked at a steady, fifteen-minute-mile pace as they followed a trail map taken from the Carlsbad Caverns tourist center.

They utilized a compass to keep them on a due south direction, which would hopefully allow them to enter Texas unimpeded through the park. If they were greeted with any resistance, well, that was what their newly acquired M16s were for. Holloway, while utilizing the raid upon the armory in Roswell to gain the respect of Lee, also made sure his team would be well equipped.

When Lee advised Holloway that his team would only be allowed one weapon per man because of their shortages, he made sure to assign all of them 1911-style, .45-caliber sidearms. The stopping power of the .45s would be a perfect complement to the stash of twenty M16s he'd tucked away in the woods as they'd driven up the side of the mountain to the caverns. Retrieving the weapons and ammo delayed their route south by an hour, but the reward was well worth the effort.

As the men found the trail headed due south into Texas, Holloway walked along with different groups to gauge their attitudes and levels of commitment. He told them they were headed into battle, one which might result in their deaths. But he promised them a far greater reward than the pride of fighting for their Dear Leader, who was holed up deep underground nice and safe with his beautiful concubine wives.

His men would get to keep the fruits of their labor. They would fight to kill, but also to keep what they fought for. Like any conquering army, he told his elite group of killers, to the victor go the spoils. He'd fought for his country and watched his brothers-in-arms die or get maimed for their efforts. He reminded his new brothers that he'd never abandon his men like his country had abandoned him. Holloway promised them a better life, one with riches and women and land in the wide-open countryside of Texas.

Man by man, he received their loyalty, not knowing that he'd soon put their levels of commitment to the test against their own.

CHAPTER 19

December 31
Carlsbad Caverns National Forest
Lonesome Ridge
Near the Texas Border

Holloway took the lead as the team made their way to a canyon overlook that rose several thousand feet above the dry riverbed below. They would now begin their winding descent along a trail that had been used by smugglers for decades.

Before the border wall was built between Texas and Mexico, illegal aliens snuck into the state to the east of El Paso and made their way into the Guadalupe Mountains where the border patrol didn't conduct searches. The well-worn path could be seen making its way down to the bottom of McKittrick Canyon. The footing was treacherous, and Holloway debated whether to make the trip in the darkness.

He scanned the trail with his binoculars and determined they could reach the bottom before darkness took over. Advising the men of the task, they picked up the pace and followed him down the winding trail.

An hour later, Holloway brought his men to an abrupt halt. He heard voices up ahead. He lowered himself to a crouch and advised his men to pass the word up the trail. They needed to create a kill zone, one in which his men held the high ground and the low ground, forcing the approaching group into a space where there was no escape from their fire.

His instructions were succinct. Kill everyone without hesitation, but not each other by accident. Friendly fire was a problem in warfare.

Holloway took up a position above the trail behind a rock outcropping. He would allow the approaching group plenty of time to fall within the middle of his team. He would watch for additional people below this group, or for any who might try to escape.

He positioned himself where he was fairly well hidden, and he studied the approaching group through his binoculars. He passed the word to his top lieutenant, who carefully worked his way through the trees to pass along the instructions.

Five men. All armed. Terminate.

What he didn't point out was that three of the men were fellow members of the Lightning Death Squads. Like their Mexican escorts, they wore drab khaki-colored pullover tunics, sombreros, and dark-colored pants. Their faces, however, were unmistakably Korean.

Holloway wanted the men dead because he wanted what they were hauling on the back of two burros—weapons, and lots of them. They were destined for Carlsbad Caverns, but Lee's attitude about equipping Holloway's men still angered him. As a result, three commandos would have to be sacrificed for the benefit of his crew.

The M16s, which were stolen from the armory, were not equipped with optics. Therefore, they would not have the benefit of identifying their targets as Koreans, only men moving along the trail. The M16 had two adjustable sights, front and rear. He had not taken the time to train his men on sight adjustments, as he planned to do that after they arrived in Texas. He hoped that twenty rifles could take down five unsuspecting targets with ease.

The air was still as the group of three commandos chatted among themselves. They reached a particularly steep incline, and the commandos moved slightly ahead of the two Mexicans, who focused on urging their burros forward.

The explosion of gunfire in the direction of the trail caught Holloway by surprise, resulting in his dropping the binoculars to the rocky surface below him and shattering the left lens. The gunfire stopped as soon as it started. He quickly grabbed up the field glasses and saw the damage.

"Big deal. I only need one side anyway." He laughed to himself after making reference to the open eye socket where his left eye once resided. He looked through the binoculars and saw the three commandos lying in a heap on the side of the trail. Their bodies were riddled with bullets.

The Mexican men were standing between the burros with their hands raised. Because of their short stature, they were protected from the gunfire unless his men let loose and killed the pack animals too.

"Hold fire! Hold fire!" Holloway yelled. He realized the two Mexican smugglers might have valuable experience to help them on their journey.

Holloway hustled down the side of the mountain, kicking rocks and debris as he made his way to the trail. His men closed on the two frightened Mexicans, one of whom had wet his pants.

With their hands high in the air, they trembled as they begged for their lives.

Holloway knew a little Spanish, *just enough to be dangerous*, as he often joked. Not that he needed his little knowledge of Spanish to be dangerous.

"*Tranquilo! Siéntate!*" hollered Holloway.

The two men immediately complied, closing their mouths and dropping to the ground on their butts.

"So what do we have here?" he mumbled as he approached the burros. "Somebody unpack these animals and show me what we've got for our trouble."

Four of his men quickly approached the stoic animals and began to unload the contents of the burlap sacks. Holloway's grin expanded from ear to ear as the loot was displayed on the ground. He began to reel off the inventory aloud.

"Fifty cal—check. A half-dozen AK-47s, ammo, and lots of magazines—check, check. AR-15s and more ammo—double check. Hey, what's that?"

Slowly, one of his men began to pull the last weapon out of the stash.

"Gimme that!" shouted Holloway.

He was handed a grenade launcher and three Type 69 rocket-propelled grenades. The Chinese copy of the original Russian RPG-7s was more advanced and designed as a modern, shoulder-launched, antitank weapon. Holloway used to call the weapon *pocket artillery* because of its ease of use and significant firepower.

He hadn't held one since Afghanistan, and the feel of the weapon in his hands made him smile. He turned and walked away from the burros as he thought of the possibilities when he was interrupted.

"Sir," one of his men said, interrupting his thoughts, "the three men who were killed were ours. They are North Koreans."

Holloway turned and glared at the man with his only eye. "That's a shame. Please dispose of their bodies by throwing them over the edge into the canyon."

"Yes, sir," said the young soldier.

Holloway turned away, shrugged, and chuckled. "Sucks for them."

Part Two

CHAPTER 20

January 1, 2023
New Year's Day
The Armstrong Ranch
Borden County, Texas

Lucy, like most of us, had her rituals on certain special days of the year. Birthdays were most important to her. As she put it, your birthday was the one day of the year that you were allowed to make it all about you. She and Major had never been New Year's Eve revelers. Even in their younger days, the biggest party night on the planet in their remote part of West Texas involved staying up late, enjoying hot chocolate in front of the fire, and watching Dick Clark do the countdown in New York's Times Square. They got older, the luster of ringing in the New Year wore off, and Dick Clark was replaced with Kathy Griffin, an entertainer whose name was synonymous with vile, in Lucy's opinion.

New Year's Day morning was typically an opportunity for Lucy to reflect on her life and on those she loved. She'd get up early, allowing her husband a rare opportunity to sleep in, and start the coffee. A fire was next on the agenda, and then she'd make a batch of monkey bread, a marvelous concoction made up of sweet, gooey, sinful cinnamon sugar together with walnuts poured atop chunks of biscuit dough baked in an upside-down Bundt pan.

Most years, her mind was consumed with what was in store for her children. Matters of school, coming of age, and unfortunately, fears associated with two young men who chose to fight for their country. On this morn, for the first time in her adult life, she was unable to visualize what a year in the life of an Armstrong looked like.

New Year's Day 2023 was a blank page in an empty three-hundred-sixty-five-page book. Visions of proms, graduations, rodeos, and life on the ranch were replaced with concerns about food shortages, security, and an uncertainty she'd never felt before.

By the end of her second cup of coffee and another helping of monkey bread, Lucy Armstrong became determined to write one page of this year's story at a time. She smiled, thanked God, and prayed for the protection of every living soul within her charge. Then she channeled the great authors she'd read.

A change in the year brings a change in the weather. There is nothing we can do about it but hope the nastiness passes and sunnier days are ahead.

"Happy New Year, Momma," announced Duncan cheerfully as he was the first to enter the kitchen. "I smelled the monkey bread, and it reminded me I was at home."

"Honey, you've been home for a week," Lucy reminded her oldest.

"I know, but I've been consumed with getting settled and going to Austin and, you know, transitioning from one life to another. When I smelled the coffee and the monkey bread, it reminded me of years ago before I went into the service. Well, like I said, it reminded me I was home."

Lucy fixed him a plate of the delectable pastry and started on another batch. There were many mouths to feed under her roof, the most since Duncan had left for basic training. Lucy grinned as she reminded herself that Riley had grown up to account for half a dozen of said *mouths.*

"Duncan, you and I haven't talked much about what your plans are. Your dad has relayed to me some of your conversations, but he seems to adhere to some kind of code of silence with you better than the other kids."

Duncan laughed as he took his first bite of monkey bread. He closed his eyes and shook his head in euphoria. He didn't have to say a word for his mother to know he approved.

"It's called bro code. You know, like you guys have girl code."

Lucy washed her hands in the sink and looked out the window as the sun began to peek over the horizon. A stiff, cold wind shook the house, causing her to shiver.

"Girls always break girl code," she replied with a chuckle. "It's the dumbest *code* ever created."

"Dad and I are different, I guess. We've always managed to hold the code pretty well, unless he spilled the beans on something he shouldn't have."

Duncan was studying Lucy, so she couldn't lie. He had his father's knack for seeing inside someone's head.

"He told me the details of your observations on your trip home. He also revealed your reaction to meeting our new vice president."

"I suppose those are minor infractions, in bro-code speak," said Duncan as he rose to pour himself another cup of coffee. He'd grown up drinking it black and had retained that habit throughout his military career.

"Honey, I know you want to find out why they called off your pickup, but under the circumstances, it's doubtful you can get to the truth. Am I wrong?"

Duncan nodded. "Probably not. Forget what's happened to the world for a second. The information I'm trying to attain can't be found through media inquiries or congressional investigation. In my world, there is no internal affairs to find the truth. We live in the shadows, and the powers that be reside deep within the government. They transcend presidents and politics. More importantly, they protect their own."

"Like a bro code," Lucy added.

"More than that, Momma. I'd call it deep-state code, or, even better, *shut-up-or-die* code. There are names you've probably never heard of—Vince Foster, Seth Rich, Jamie Zapata, Mary Mahoney, Ed Willey. The list is long."

Lucy studied her son's eyes over her coffee mug. "I never took you to be a conspiracy theorist."

"Momma, it's not all conspiracy theory. I wasn't in North Korea because I thought it up on my own. I most likely wasn't there upon orders of the president either. Listen, our spy agencies have a group of longtime insiders who make these decisions. They run things, despite what presidents and congress might believe. Whoever ordered the assassination of Kim Jong-un was the same person who retracted the order to retrieve Park and me from North Korea."

"You could've been killed," Lucy interjected.

"No, I should have been killed," said Duncan matter-of-factly. "It was a combination of skill and luck that got me out of there alive. My partner was not lucky. Somewhere, his mother is sitting alone at a kitchen table, wondering where her son is. And the people responsible for his death are still tucked in bed, nice and comfy, without giving Park, a good man, a second thought."

Lucy sat quietly and absorbed Duncan's words. He was angry and passionate about finding the people responsible. As the rest of the house could be heard stirring awake, she decided to ask one last question. "Duncan, I understand, and I wish your pain could be taken away. Is there any possible way you can move on from this? Can you accept what happened as fate and just let it go?"

"I'd never be able to live with myself if I did."

CHAPTER 21

January 2
The Mansion
Austin, Texas

Following a swearing-in ceremony at the state capitol, President Burnett held a reception for high-ranking members of both parties in the ballroom of the Mansion honoring the formation of the new Republic of Texas. Despite the monumental tasks before them, lawmakers of all political persuasions were anxious to get to work in a bipartisan effort to make life better for Texans. However, the matter of refugees coming into the new country remained a point of contention.

"Madam President, congratulations on accomplishing something those of us only dreamed about," said her new Senate Majority Leader, Connie Miles. The Republican from Flower Mound had been a friend and ally of the president for years.

"Thank you, Connie," the president responded. "While I appreciate today's lovefest, I sense the underpinnings of discontent from those on the other side of the aisle."

"New country, same political issues," said Miles with a laugh. "The biggest issue seems to be finding ways to feed our residents, especially those in the typically high-crime areas within the Houston and San Antonio inner cities. Armed gangs are forming, and local law enforcement is overwhelmed. Your martial law order is being disregarded by crooks and cops alike."

"Are our people standing down?" asked the president.

"Madam President, you know I've always got your back. I'm sure your Homeland Security folks are overwhelmed dealing with the border, but within Texas, societal collapse is approaching. The spirit of cooperation is giving way to a *me first* attitude. We're on the brink, to be honest."

President Burnett saw the Senate Minority Leader, a rabble-rousing flamethrower of a progressive from Austin, heading their way. Austin had often been referred to as a blueberry in a sea of tomato soup. Prior to the collapse, Austin had ranked in the top ten most liberal cities in America behind such bastions of left-thinking political persuasions as San Francisco, Seattle, New York, Chicago, Detroit, Boston, and Washington, DC.

If Austin was the blueberry, Patrick Linkletter, it's rotund former mayor and new Senate Minority Leader of Texas, was its Violet Beauregarde of Willy Wonka fame.

His voice, as boisterous as his belly was round, was a megaphone on the left. There was nothing that Marion Burnett could propose, either before or after secession, that he'd agree with.

Free food for all? His people didn't get their fair share.

A government stipend to stay home and off the street? Mere crumbs from the wealthy oil barons.

Texas has a border and it must be respected? Tear down that wall!

"Madam President, Majority Leader Miles, thank you for inviting this humble servant of the people to this extravagant soirée. I have my assistant gathering my share of the aperitifs to distribute to the hungry outside your beautiful iron fences."

President Burnett bristled at Linkletter's pompous, holier-than-thou attitude. Yet she stifled a laugh at the man's misuse of the word *aperitifs.* He probably thought he was referring to the appetizers, because there were no dessert cocktails served at this midday gathering.

"Well, thank you, Patrick. I was unaware that we made doggy bags available to our guests."

"Hrrmph," grunted Linkletter as he tried to allow the slight to roll off his shoulders. "Madam President, now that the coronation is over, it's time to do the people's business. What are you doing to solve the hunger problem?"

"Hmm, world hunger," started Miles as she stepped in to shield the president. The three leaders of government were starting to draw the attention of several members of the new Congress. "That's a tall order for any administration, wouldn't you agree, Mr. Minority Leader?"

"Surely you have a plan," he insisted, ignoring Miles's deflection.

"Yes, Patrick, I have a plan, and it is being implemented daily. Today, in fact, additional United Nations relief flights are entering Texas for further distribution to our people and to points beyond in the U.S. We are working diligently to marshal our nutrition assets to assist those who need it the most."

"Well, if you'd come out of your palace and walk around your own neighborhood, you'd see that your efforts are not enough," said Linkletter disrespectfully.

Miles bowed up and once again came to her old friend's aid. "What's your plan, Patrick? I've heard nothing but dissent and complaints since this whole thing began. You don't think we all heard the clips played on WBAP radio?"

"I have a duty as the leader of the opposition party to voice the concerns of the people," said Linkletter defensively.

"You've got the rhetoric down pat, Patrick," responded Miles sarcastically. "What's your plan?"

"Okay, since you asked," he replied, then directed his attention to the president. "For one, call on your rich rancher buddies and tell them to fork over some of those cattle assets they're sitting on. I have reports of the big ranchers holding onto tens of thousands of head because they couldn't make it to the auctions before the EMP hit."

"Come on, Patrick, you can't be serious," said the president dismissively. "Our founding principles, just like those of the United States, would be abandoned if we began to confiscate the assets of private citizens for redistribution."

"Oh, sure, hide behind the Constitution while Texans wither away to nothing," Linkletter shot back, emboldened by several of his like-minded lawmakers who'd gathered around the conversation.

Miles, who towered over Linkletter by a good six inches, cowgirled up and stuck her finger in his chest. "You need to show some respect to our president, mister."

"I'll give her the respect she's due when she solves our problems," said Linkletter as he continued. "How about putting all the farms in this state to work? Your side of the aisle stood idly by while out-of-staters like the Koch brothers swooped in and bought up all the small farms and ranches only to convert them into unproductive patches of dirt. Rather than producing, they cut back on operating the farms so they could artificially drive up the price of food staples around the country."

"Patrick, you're being unreasonable," said President Burnett. "We can't even find the Koch brothers, much less order them to begin farming."

Linkletter was on a roll now. "Well, if you can't find them, then they can't object to your taking over their operations under the martial law declaration. It's within your purview. Take over the land, put it to work, and feed your people. Easy breezy, mac and cheesy, in my book."

Several members of Linkletter's entourage began to applaud, which drew even more attention. President Burnett was not enjoying this exchange, nor did she like Linkletter getting the upper hand. All of his points struck a nerve with her as she tried to stay true to her principles while helping Texans survive too. Her adjutant general, Kregg Deur, gave her an escape.

He approached and whispered to her, but loudly enough for all to hear. "Madam President, we have a situation. It's urgent, I'm afraid."

The president bowed her head, frowned, and nodded her understanding. "I'm afraid we'll have to take this up another time. Good evening, all."

President Burnett didn't like leaving the argument this way, and she was not one to shy away from a fight, but the emergency got her out of an unpleasant situation. As she walked away with Deur, Linkletter fired off one final shot.

"What about the refugees? Are you planning on letting them

freeze to death? Do you even know what the body count is?"

She stopped in her tracks and spun around like an angry bear that had been poked one time too many. She strutted back toward Linkletter, who was taken aback by her forcefulness.

"Do the people of Texas you purport to speak for know that you want to let millions of outsiders into our country? Do they know that all of those people want to eat their food? Take their jobs? Live in their homes? Who do you represent, Mr. Minority Leader? Texas or everyone else in the world?"

Linkletter sank within himself as his hypocrisy was exposed. After a death stare, which was caught on camera by a local news photographer, President Burnett turned and left the ballroom without another word.

CHAPTER 22

January 2
The Mansion
Austin, Texas

President Burnett led the way to her office without asking Deur what the situation was. Linkletter's rant did give her an idea, however, one that wouldn't be popular with her ranchers, but it might help everyone solve a problem. As she turned down the hallway, she hailed her chief of staff and instructed her to bring the agriculture secretary to her office immediately.

By the time the president reached her office, she'd forgotten Deur was several paces behind her, trying to keep up. When she moved around her desk to sit, his presence startled her.

"Madam President, my apologies for interrupting you," started Deur as he stood between the chairs in her office. "The first UN aircraft have landed, and the unloading process has begun."

"Okay," she interrupted. "Is there a problem?"

"Madam President, we're processing the personnel first in order to keep tabs on who is entering our country. Many of their passports are not checking out and not in any database. While they all have personnel files from the UN at my insistence, too many are ghosts, so to speak."

President Burnett rolled her eyes and fell back into her chair. She knew this was a bad idea, but she was under the gun and had to do something. "Kregg, what do you suggest?"

Before Deur could answer, the president's chief of staff tapped on the door and announced the arrival of Carlos Fuentes, the Secretary of Agriculture. Fuentes was a descendant of Antonio Fuentes, a San

Antonian born of Mexican parents who fought alongside the Texians at the Alamo.

"Madam President," said Fuentes as he entered the room, "Mr. Adjutant General, my apologies. I understood this to be urgent."

"It is, Carlos, in a way. Please sit down. You too, Kregg."

"Yes, ma'am," said Deur, who appeared frustrated that he was not allowed to speak with the president first. President Burnett brushed this off.

"Carlos," began the president, "this will not be an easy task, but I need you to get on it right away."

"Yes, ma'am, how may I help?"

"I want you to investigate and determine how many cattle are being held in the twenty largest ranches around Texas. Then I want a number of how many of those head would've been taken to slaughter in the remaining months of last year had it not been for the EMP."

Fuentes raised his hand like he was a student in a classroom. "Madam President, without a significant amount of time and resources devoted to your request, I'd never be able to come up with an exact count. May I ask, are you looking for a specific number, or are you seeking a good estimate in order to make a policy decision?"

"A good estimate, please. I want a number that differentiates the ranchers' current herd count from what is customary for them. Then I want you to determine the average net weight they would've brought at auction and the price per pound at the last auction data at your disposal."

"Yes, ma'am, I understand," said Fuentes. "You're looking for a total value, I assume."

"Yes. In addition, I want you to put all of this information into a proposal, one which indicates how many mouths we can feed if we were to purchase the beef cattle from the ranchers at a fair price. Also, calculate the costs of gathering the cattle up, taking them to auction, and ultimately to slaughter. Once you have that number, see the Treasury Secretary and create a budget."

"Then we'll come see you," added Fuentes to close out the president's thought.

"No later than tomorrow, please," she instructed without looking up from her desk, which contained a weather forecast. As a result, she didn't see the look of consternation on the face of her Agriculture Secretary. "That's all, Carlos. Thank you."

"Thank you, Madam President." Fuentes quickly left.

Fuentes left the door open, so Deur got out of his chair and closed it. Curious ears didn't need to hear what he'd discovered.

"I'm sorry, Kregg, continue."

"Madam President, I have a gut feeling that the UN has done this purposefully. There are too many of their representatives that have no records for us to review."

"Whadya wanna do, Kregg, kick 'em out?" asked the president sarcastically. "If we're gonna do that, at least unload the planes first. We'll see how that windbag Linkletter likes that idea."

Unaware of the conversation with Linkletter from earlier, Deur appeared puzzled but continued. "No, ma'am, but I do suggest a quarantine or some type of restriction on their movements. The personnel whose identifications check out may continue with their duties under our supervision. Those who do not are subject to expulsion unless further information on their backgrounds is provided."

"That sounds fair," she said, her mind clearly elsewhere. She shuffled some papers to the side and looked to Deur to see if he was finished.

"This will necessarily delay the off-loading of the aircraft and the distribution of the supplies."

"Kregg, I get it. You gotta do what you gotta do. Why are you bringing this to me anyway? This is Monty's deal. He's the one who should deal with it."

"My apologies, Madam President, but the vice president can't be found," Deur answered.

"What? What do you mean? He's the vice president."

"Yes, ma'am, of course. After the ceremony at the capitol, the vice president eluded his security detail and left in a dark-colored sedan. It crossed through the security barricades and was last seen headed east, away from the downtown area."

President Burnett finally became attentive to Deur. "Kregg, was he kidnapped? I mean, shouldn't we do something?"

"Ma'am, apparently his chief of staff is aware of the vice president's departure. When quizzed about it, he said the vice president needed some private time."

The president sat back in her chair for a moment and recalled her last several conversations with Gregg. He had been distant and had also expressed some difficulty at home with his wife. She thought maybe he needed a time-out, or just an opportunity to hook up with someone to let off some steam. He was in his early sixties. The wonders of modern pharmaceuticals could make that happen, she supposed.

"Kregg, let's not call out the dogs just yet. But if he doesn't turn up by evening, let me know."

CHAPTER 23

January 2
Austin, Texas

"Where have you been?" Gregg snarled at his companion in the backseat of the black Lincoln Continental. Gregg was used to people moving heaven and earth to do his bidding. His new position as vice president of Texas didn't seem to carry the same weight as being the Secretary of Defense of the United States had. More importantly, despite the travails of America following the collapse of the power grid, the deep state was still alive and well. He was just not a part of it anymore.

"Business as usual, Monty," started Billy Yancey, his former comrade in Washington.

"Well, I need you to be a little more responsive when I need you."

Yancey dismissed the driver by telling him to take a walk. After he left, he responded to Gregg's statement. "Now, Monty. Hold up. It was your idea for me to stay in Washington. After that confrontation with Major Armstrong, and when I learned the kid was still alive, it was necessary for me to stick around and keep a pulse on things. I would've been just fine riding out this storm at my ranch."

Gregg took a deep breath and exhaled. Of course, Yancey was right. Even under normal circumstances, their communications and meetings were clandestine by nature. At times, it took them several days to get together.

"Okay, Billy. I understand. Here's why I put out the nine-one-one. I came face-to-face with Armstrong meeting with the president. They have her ear and the ability to waltz right in like it's nobody's business."

"Monty, Armstrong can't tie his orders to either one of us, especially you," said Yancey. "If anything, I'm the one he'd be looking to for answers, but I'm untouchable in Washington."

Gregg was not satisfied. "Billy, from what you've said, he's a good soldier and all of that. But he has to be mad that we left him behind. He'd never buy our phony excuses or justifications for leaving the two of them to die in North Korea."

"Monty, don't you think Armstrong has more to deal with now that he's returned? In case you haven't noticed, we're in the middle of the frickin' apocalypse here."

Gregg thought carefully before he made the next statement. He'd weighed the options in his mind many times, and the conclusions were always the same. Duncan Armstrong Jr. was a threat to his position in the newly formed Texas government. Gregg stood to lose everything he'd accomplished, both present and in his service to America. The guy had to go.

"I want him removed from the chessboard," Gregg finally blurted out. "Whatever it takes, Armstrong's got to go, Billy. He could take us both down. Heck, he has the potential to expose a lot of us."

"Monty, come on. You're being irrational. First off, the family is tight with Burnett. Heck, they're practically neighbors out in West Texas. Second, unless they're idiots, and they're not, we can't just send a team waltzing onto their ranch to *remove him from the chessboard*, as you say."

"Are you out of operatives since the botched deal up at Wichita Falls?" said Gregg sarcastically. "You should've warned me about that, you know."

"Maybe so, but Acton kept the whole plan under wraps, and I was out of the loop until the last minute. If I'd known, I would've done it much differently."

"Well, Armstrong aside, don't let them try that crap again. Our guys have itchy trigger fingers now."

Yancey nodded and looked around for his driver. He checked his watch. "Monty, we've been gone an hour. They'll come looking—"

"Billy, don't blow me off," barked Gregg. "What are you gonna do about this problem?"

Yancey shook his head and stared out the window. "You mentioned trying to recruit him at one point. You know, put him in a position where friendly fire solves the problem for us."

"Yeah, that's still an option, but he might not take the job. He's lucky to be home. I wouldn't do it if I were him. Any other ideas?"

Yancey sat quietly for a moment and tapped his fingers on the passenger door. "We've gotta lure him away from the ranch somehow. Then we can get a shot at him."

"How will you do that?" asked Gregg.

"Armstrong's file makes him out to be an uber-loyal, white-knight type. If we can't get him to come out voluntarily, maybe we can force him out for another reason. Let me think on it. Monty, rest assured, one way or the other, I'll take care of our mutual problem."

"Fine, but hurry. I don't like this hangin' over my head," said Gregg, who was rattled for the first time in his life. That happens when one's chickens come home to roost.

CHAPTER 24

January 2
McKittrick Canyon
The Guadalupe Mountains
Texas-New Mexico Border

As requested, the early morning security team awakened Holloway well before dawn. Yesterday afternoon had been a test for his unit. While the disguises worn by their fellow North Koreans might have prevented the shooters from second-guessing their shoot-to-kill orders, their reaction afterward provided Holloway confirmation that his men would remain loyal to him. There were no grumblings or challenges to his authority. To the contrary, the evening was lighthearted as the group examined the weapons cache they'd found and traded stories of how they planned to use them on the high and mighty Texans. Moreover, the team's unity left Holloway comfortable that he didn't have to sleep with one eye open.

As he gathered his gear for another day of hiking, he thought of the YouTube videos posted from Korean Central Television, or KCTV. Years ago, Kim Jong-un had formed the elite commando unit to be North Korea's answer to Delta Force and the SEAL teams. Holloway would never forget the words of the KCTV announcer.

Once Supreme Commander issues an order, they will charge with resolve to thrust a sword through the enemy's heart like lightning over Mount Paektu.

The commandos trained on Mount Paektu, a mysterious volcanic mountain near the border between North Korea and China. The harsh conditions, rocky terrain, and high altitudes created a brutal environment for the Lightning Death Squads, but it hardened them in a way that most other forces like them around the world would never know.

All of Holloway's men had paid their dues at Mount Paektu. Granted, over the years, they'd become somewhat soft, spoiled by the luxuries and comforts of the American way of life, but the discipline they'd learned at one of North Korea's most sacred spots was paying off as a cold front found its way south into the Guadalupe Mountains overnight. The mild weather they'd experienced after their departure from Carlsbad Caverns was replaced with an icy wind that was broken somewhat by the pine trees that enveloped their campsite.

After a breakfast of MREs stolen from the armory in Roswell, the group began their final descent into McKittrick Canyon. The sun was up and the wind was beginning to howl down the side of the mountain as Holloway led them out of the forest and into a clearing near the bottom of the canyon.

He was greeted with a welcome sign, of sorts. A half sheet of plywood, which had been painted white, was suspended between two four-by-four posts in the rocky soil. Painted on the board with black stenciled letters was a warning—*Republic of Texas: Do Not Enter!* Holloway stared in amusement as the rest of this team appeared in the clearing by his side.

"Whadya think, boys? Should we turn around and go back?"

His guys got a kick out of the sarcasm and began to laugh, with some spontaneously pelting the sign with rocks.

Holloway sneered at the warning sign and then muttered, "Wait'll they get a load of me."

He slapped the sign hard enough to make it shake on its posts as he walked by and listened as each man who followed him did the same. He was twenty yards past when he heard the last thud of a fist pounding the worthless warning, causing it to topple over onto the rocky ground. He managed a smile and picked up the pace.

He was in Texas.

*****

The midday sun warmed their bodies, but the strong northerly winds continued. Now that his team was in Texas, Holloway would focus on finding them transportation. His first opportunity came as they approached the trailhead, the entrance point of the route they'd followed from the top of the mountain to the base.

They came upon a small contact station, which was part of the Guadalupe Mountains National Park facilities. The building resembled a rest area complex on an interstate highway. There were shaded picnic areas, outdoor exhibits showing the various trails that originated there, and a building that acted as a visitors' information center and restroom facility.

What grabbed Holloway's attention the most were the two vehicles parked at the front door and the smoke that floated in the air from behind the building. It was occupied, and the vehicles might be operable. He put his commandos to work.

Holloway ordered his men to surround the building as he continued to conduct his surveillance. Thus far, nobody had appeared in the front of the building although he could make out the faint sounds of muffled voices.

He and his men trained periodically in a remote area of the Chino Hills State Park east of Fullerton. There were several dilapidated cabins, which provided them a training facility to conduct dry-fire exercises. He spent a considerable amount of time learning their forms of visual hand signals, and he also taught the basic commands he'd learned in the service.

His team didn't have the benefit of advanced communications gear such as microphones and headsets installed in helmets. They had to operate old school, using hand and arm signals, which enabled a team leader to keep control over an operation without being detected. The men knew they had to space themselves to maintain a continuous line of sight to one another in order to transmit their messages rapidly over short distances.

The signals were being relayed to Holloway's position. Left hand covering their eyes meant *I see*, which was followed by four fingers. Four hostiles were seen at the rear of the building. The next set of signals came in.

A left arm was held straight into the air with the man's hand shaped like a pistol. This was followed by two fingers raised in the air. Two of the hostiles were holding rifles.

Holloway studied the scene and considered their location. The sound of gunfire would echo throughout the canyon. Ideally, they'd take out their targets by lighting up the place with their automatic weapons. He considered his options for a moment, and then he motioned for two of his men to follow him into the parking lot.

They ran at a low crouch, using the two Chevy Suburbans as shields to prevent anyone inside the building from seeing them. Once they arrived, he sent one man to each side of the entrance and posted them against the stucco and block wall.

He turned to the men who'd filled the void he and his men just left. He held up two fingers and waved them forward. Two men scampered across the parking lot and joined him. He gave them instructions to enter the building, one working the left side and the other working the right. He would go through the center to the rear entrance.

Holloway was the only member of the team who carried a silenced sidearm. It had been part of his gear since he'd left the service and became a mercenary. You simply could not be a successful assassin unless you were able to mask the sound of your gunfire.

His men led the way. Quiet, deliberate, catlike. They entered the building with their rifles swaying back and forth in choreographed unison. Holloway followed, quickly assessing the building's layout, but staying focused on the rear exit to where the hostiles were standing around a fire. He trusted the men to his left and right, comforted in knowing they'd kill anyone who threatened him.

He continued through the building until he reached a plate-glass door. Pressing his back against the wall, he slowly peered around the edge to get a better look. Four men, dressed like hunters in camouflaged clothing, were standing around a fifty-gallon drum, which was spewing flames, ash, and smoke into the air. They were sharing a cigarette and laughing at what Holloway imagined were the same tired old jokes they told on all their hunting trips.

With the men only twenty feet away, he was able to quickly identify the two with the rifles slung over their shoulders. The other two men appeared to be unarmed. Clockwise from left to right, they stood at positions two and three for the riflemen, with one and four being unarmed.

The hunters' lack of awareness turned them into the hunted and easy prey for a professional killer like Holloway.

Holloway readied his Beretta M9A3 pistol. His weapon held a seventeen-round, double-stack magazine of nine-millimeter rounds. He'd only need four. Holloway took a deep breath to relax his body.

He leaned his hip into the push-bar handle of the glass door and burst into the opening. His aim was dead on the money. Bullet holes appeared in the nose of *position two* and the forehead of *position three.* Their bodies stood momentarily suspended in disbelief before they fell over backwards like trees cut down in the forest.

Holloway swung his pistol quickly to the left, sensing that the man in *position one* was reacting faster. He was right, catching the man in the chest with a glancing blow. His body twirled in a pirouette motion as he tried to catch his balance.

The silenced barrel of his pistol swung back to the right, catching the slower of the two unarmed men in a state of frozen animation. His gaping wide mouth expressed his disbelief and made a perfect bull's-eye for Holloway's fourth shot. The round tore through the man's upper palate, ripped through his brain, and exploded out the back of the man's skull.

Holloway turned his attention back to the wounded man, who tried to catch his balance by grabbing the searing hot barrel of fire. His hands gripped the edge, unable to release, as he fell backwards toward the ground. Burning embers and branches fell on top of him and immediately lit up his camouflage coveralls with fire.

The man's screams were deafening as Holloway walked up to his body, which was being engulfed in flames. The heat of the fire began to irritate Holloway's eye socket, which caused him to squint as he enjoyed the spectacle of the man burning alive.

The only reason Holloway considered wasting the fifth bullet on the dying man was to stop the screaming. He allowed himself another few seconds to watch the flames melt the man's skin before he sent the final bullet into his skull as an act of mercy.

CHAPTER 25

January 2
Preston Smith International Airport
Lubbock, Texas

Airport authorities loved to refer to their particular local airfield as *insert-name-of-city-here international airport*, when in reality there was nothing *international* about it. The same was true of the Lubbock Preston Smith International Airport in the Northwest Texas city. Prior to the collapse, all of the LBB inbound and outbound flights were between Texas cities except two—Denver and Phoenix. Of course, after Texas seceded, any flights continuing to those locations, technically, would be international destinations. But flights to those two locales had been cancelled indefinitely: Phoenix because the city was under siege from Mexican drug cartels in a turf war that rivaled Vietnam; and Denver because, well, the city had been mostly destroyed by the hydrogen bomb dropped on nearby Colorado Springs.

Today, Lubbock was truly anointed international status as the first Boeing 737 jets bearing the humongous black-and-white *UN* lettering landed on the runway. Part of the United Nations Humanitarian Air Service, the UN charter flights originated in Europe and were the first to arrive in Lubbock as part of the accord reached with the United Nations to distribute aid to the U.S. and, in part, to Texans.

Like its counterparts in Dallas, Houston, Austin, and El Paso, Lubbock also welcomed the UN Trojan horse orchestrated by Chief of Staff Acton together with his coconspirators at the UN. The tale of the Trojan horse arose from the literary accounts of the Trojan War between Greece and Troy.

After ten years of fighting, which resulted in a stalemate, the attacking Greek forces offered a gift to the people of Troy—a large wooden horse, the recognized symbol of the city of Troy, as a gift.

After wheeling the massive trophy off its ships and up to the gates of Troy, the Greeks sailed away, seemingly giving up the fight. However, after the wooden horse was allowed inside the city, under cover of darkness, elite warriors inside the horse infiltrated the city and destroyed Troy, thus ending the war.

The term *Trojan horse* became an often-used metaphor to mean a trick that allowed the enemy to enter a secured location to cause harm.

The UN flights contained two types of elite soldiers—members of the United Nations Protection Force, or UNPROFOR, and the media. For decades, reasonable minds would argue which of the two was deadlier, the warriors or the press.

UNPROFOR was first used as a peacekeeping force in Bosnia during the Yugoslav Wars between the Yugoslavian government and the ethnic groups of Serbs, Croats, and Albanians. Over the next three decades, the UN secretly diverted humanitarian-designated funds to the UNPROFOR division of the UN peacekeeping forces. Make no mistake, the commandos recruited and assigned to UNPROFOR were not interested in keeping the peace. They were there to quell nationalist-leaning dissent in the host country.

The United Nations and its globalist supporters feared the rise of nationalism around the world. The media labeled those who had strong tendencies toward patriotism for their nation as authoritarian and intolerant. In the minds of the Secretary-General and his deputy secretaries, the success of Texas could not stand. The secession of the Texans was nationalism's finest hour and must be shown to be a failure.

A cold wind swept across the former South Plains Army Airfield as the UN personnel walked across the tarmac to the processing center. As the passengers began to enter the airport, an explosion was heard near the aircraft and smoke began to pour out of the aft cabin doors.

Momentarily, chaos ensued as ground personnel assigned to the airport from Fort Hood raced toward the aircraft with their weapons raised. Many of the UN personnel, especially those who were truly humanitarian aid workers, crushed one another to get inside the airport out of fear.

The military forces that made up the UNPROFOR contingent ran back to the aircraft in an effort to help their comrades. They had not been issued their weapons as of yet, but they didn't hesitate to assist the members of the Texas military.

As people ran haphazardly in all directions, four men and one woman wearing khaki pants and black North Face jackets quietly slipped out of the line and made their way in between the idle blue luggage truck trains that were parked off to the side. Once they were clear of the cover provided by the carts, they swiftly walked along the side of the airport terminal building and ran across a tree-lined walkway toward a tall chain-link fence.

One of the men retrieved a set of bolt cutters from his backpack and quickly cut an opening for them to pass through. Amidst the carefully orchestrated chaos, five elite operatives of the international media entered Lubbock—becoming the second of the new nation's many nightmares to arrive.

Holloway, of course, was the first.

Chapter 26

January 3
Wink, Texas

Holloway led the way in the newly acquired forty-year-old Chevy Suburbans, which had thus far served them well. He was constantly on the lookout for additional, more suitable vehicles. A Cadillac Escalade was high on his wish list. But this part of West Texas was so deserted even the prairie dogs died of boredom, so he doubted many Escalades were around.

Without the aid of a map, he continued to follow the rising sun and headed east until a major road became available. The fuel gauges on both trucks were heading toward empty, and his men, who were packed in like the proverbial sardines, were growing restless.

The Chevy trucks were equipped with two bench seats that allowed for three passengers in the front and backseat. In the rear, four men were sitting with their knees crammed against their chests, unable to move. The old trucks' suspensions had seen better days too. With every pothole came a groan. Every swerve to avoid an obstacle in the road threw bodies against one another.

Holloway needed a small town to refuel and possibly add vehicles to his fleet, and he needed it quick before his Lightning Death Squad mutinied.

After traveling several more miles along the deserted farm-to-market road, a designation that puzzled him to no end but kept his mind occupied as his search for fuel continued, a roadside billboard welcomed them to Wink, Texas, population nine hundred forty.

Below the word *Welcome* was the smiling face of singer Roy Orbison. Known for his odd singing style and famous hits like *Only the Lonely*, Orbison must have written a song about the fair hamlet of Wink, Holloway surmised. In quotation marks beneath his black-haired image and dark glasses were the words—*football, oil fields, oil, grease and sand.*

Holloway laughed to himself as he slowed his approach into the town. *You don't have to be a rocket scientist to figure that out. Just give me some gas, a new car or two, and maybe a piece of tail, and I'll be on my way.*

He pulled to a stop next to the first sandlot-style football field of Wink's residential neighborhoods. Despite being midmorning, there were no signs of life. He spoke to his lieutenants, who rode in the front seat with him.

"I can't go rollin' up in here with two truckloads of Koreans. That might raise eyebrows, don't you think?"

They didn't answer, not that he expected them to. He'd taught them long ago that when the team was on a mission, he was the only one that could be funny, and everyone else was expected to follow orders.

"All right, listen up," he began. He pointed to one man in the backseat and touched the man next to him on the shoulder. "You two, stay with me but hide down in your seats so nobody can see you. The rest of you, join the other group. Keep your ears open. I don't expect any trouble, but if you hear gunfire, send the cavalry and, boys, shoot everything that moves. Got it?"

After receiving everyone's acknowledgments of his orders, Holloway moved closer to the center of town. More people came into view, but they didn't give his vehicle a second glance. The experience was far different from his travels eastward after the EMP. Going through the major metropolitan areas of LA and later Arizona, moving vehicles were rare. He felt like a fox in the henhouse, dressed up like a rooster.

"This is gonna be too easy," he thought out loud.

He was driving closer to the center of town when a blue road sign caught his eye. It read *ERCOT-Wink Switching Station* and was accompanied by an arrow pointing to the right. He slowed and then made the turn. He remembered a news story from years ago following a hurricane, which had devastated the Texas Gulf Coast, that ERCOT crews were standing by to restore power. He made the logical connection. He didn't know what a switching station was, but if there were workers there, Holloway was sure they'd volunteer the information to him.

He drove another mile to the outskirts of the city until he came to a large chain-link-protected area with an open gate. Just inside the entrance was a small brick building with two cars and a pickup in front. Before entering, he stopped and surveyed the grounds. The cold wind prevented anyone from taking a stroll along the transformers and power lines that culminated at the facility.

The tall towers erected to carry the high-voltage power lines that traversed Texas could be seen to his south, east, and west. He was briefly fascinated by the structure and wondered if taking out this substation would have a crippling effect on the power grid of Texas. He suspected the ERCOT employees inside would have answers for him.

"It's showtime, gentlemen. We're gonna pull up to the front door, storm in like we own the place, and scare the hell out of whoever is inside. Do not shoot anybody unless they raise a weapon. We need some information from these people and their vehicles."

Holloway pulled the car up to the front door, grabbed his rifle and exited in a hurry. His two men followed suit, and without delay, they ran to the front door and grabbed the handle to pull it open.

It was locked.

He looked to both sides of the building, wondering if he'd missed the workers milling about.

Nothing.

Holloway couldn't waste any more time, as those inside might have seen him and could be calling for help. He drew his Beretta out of his leg holster and, using the silenced weapon, fired two bullets into the top and bottom of the plate-glass door. Shards of glass exploded inward.

"Go!" he shouted to his men, who crouched beneath the door handle and walked across the broken glass.

The main office area, which consisted of metal desks, chairs and maps covering every wall, was empty otherwise. Holloway quickly moved toward two office spaces on the right, forcefully pushing open a partially closed door until it slammed against the wall. A young woman was cowering in the corner next to a file cabinet, crying and gasping for air.

"Claimed!" shouted Holloway as he chuckled to himself. He'd always wanted to say that since he'd seen that season of *The Walking Dead.*

"I've got a guy in here, too," shouted one of his men.

"The rest is clear, sir," stated the other.

Holloway slowly backed out of the woman's office but kept his gun pointed in her general direction.

"Bring him out!" he ordered.

His men shouldered their rifles and pulled the man out from under his desk. He was trying to cover his head, a natural human reaction when one feared physical harm. Unfortunately for the victim, a forearm over a forehead wouldn't make a hill of beans' difference when a beat-down was administered.

They stood the man up and forced him into the outer office.

"Stand here," said one of Holloway's men as he gave the ERCOT employee a good shaking to drive the point home.

"Watch this one, but don't touch," instructed Holloway calmly as he pointed to the girl, who was sobbing uncontrollably. "Are we clear?"

"Yes, sir."

Holloway walked toward the man and leaned down until their faces almost touched. He wanted the frightened employee to get a good look at his eye, as well as the hole where the other one used to be.

"What's your name?" Holloway growled.

"Edwards," replied the man, who began to breathe rapidly as if he was going to hyperventilate.

"You're weak, aren't you, Edwards?"

The man nodded his head up and down rapidly.

"Good, glad we don't have to argue about that," Holloway continued. "Tough guys have to be treated differently than guys like you. Kudos for honesty, pal."

The man continued to tremble as he tried to turn his head from Holloway's gaze. Holloway holstered his weapon and grabbed the man's chin, straightening his face forward.

"You, pal, are gonna answer some questions, okay?"

"Uh, uh, yes, sir."

"Very good. Now, I want you to tell me about all of these maps, and you'd better tell the truth. My eye knows when you're lying. Are we straight?"

Once again, the bobble-head ERCOT employee nervously nodded his understanding.

The woman in the office began to plead for mercy. "Please, mister. Let us go. You can have our money and cars. Take it all. Please don't hurt us."

Holloway's face became enraged. He grabbed Edwards by the few hairs he had left on his mostly bald head and pulled his Beretta, forcing the barrel into the side of the man's temple. He dragged the man into the open doorway so the woman could see the gun at his head.

"Edwards, are you her boss?"

"Yes."

"What's her name and position with the company?"

"Her name is Naomi, and she's my assistant."

Holloway turned his attention to Naomi, whose eyes were wide with fear. "Naomi, would you like a promotion? Do you want his job? If so, say one more word and we'll terminate this pussy!"

She shook her head violently from side to side, causing tears and mucus to spray against the wall.

"Good, seems like we have an understanding. Now, pal, explain how this whole ERCOT thing works. Here's what I want to know, hypothetically speaking, of course, because I want you to know I am not a terrorist or anything like that. I consider myself to be an opportunist, and in a place as large as Texas, opportunity abounds, wouldn't you agree?"

The man did everything in his power to avoid eye contact, but managed a response. "Okay."

"Edwards, in my hypothetical," began Holloway as he let go of his hostage and began to walk around the room, dragging his silencer along the map-covered walls as he walked, "which of these substations would I have to destroy to bring down the entire power grid?"

He took a seat on a desk in the corner and dangled his legs off the side. He'd expected a quick, concise list of places to go and substations to destroy. What he got was a lesson on how complex and protected the ERCOT power system was. Bringing down the entire Texas grid through attacks on a handful of substations was a pipe dream. Nonetheless, he made the man write down a list of those locations that would do the most damage to the largest population centers.

Then he pressed the man on the grid for Lubbock. Lubbock Power & Light was independent from ERCOT prior to the collapse, but they had cooperative agreements in the event of outages. The man explained the grids had been tied together following the nationwide grid failure, but Lubbock still relied on a series of switching stations like the one in Wink to act as a conduit from ERCOT.

"Bottom line it for me, pal," began Holloway. "Can the Northwest Texas grid be taken down by itself?"

"Yes," replied the cowardly Edwards. In an effort to save his life, he pulled the map for the region and circled the exact locations to be attacked with a black Sharpie.

Satisfied that he had the information he needed and noticing the shadows on the power towers were growing longer, Holloway knew it was time to move on.

But first, it was time to eliminate witnesses. He took the maps from Edwards with one hand and shot him in the head with the other, allowing the man's body to slump inside the doorway to his assistant's office, causing her to shriek.

After shooting Edwards in the head, Holloway gave instructions to his men. "Okay, gentlemen. Check out their vehicles and pick the three with the most fuel. Those are the three we will leave with."

"Yes, sir," they replied.

"Give me a little time in here with Naomi, and I'll be along soon. And, boys, don't interrupt me unless it's the friggin' Lone Ranger and Tonto himself coming up the road. Clear?"

The men nodded and exited the building. Holloway walked into the young woman's office to mark off the third thing on his wish list and studied her trembling body.

She was pregnant. Holloway closed his eyes and ran his left hand down his face from his forehead to his neck. He exhaled.

"Naomi, this is your lucky day," he whispered as he turned around and walked out.

CHAPTER 27

January 4
The Mansion
Austin, Texas

President Burnett faced a dilemma—feed her soon-to-be-starving citizenry or violate all of her core principles by confiscating the food supplies and storage facilities of private companies. She had just received the report created by her Secretaries of Agriculture and Treasury. Working around the clock and using the best information available to them, they'd created a proposal that reached a startling conclusion.

If they acquired all of the beef cattle in Texas, slaughtered them and distributed them to each household, they'd feed the population for five and a half days.

The conclusion, while not surprising to the president, reminded her of the constant debate in favor of taxing the rich to eliminate America's debt and reduce her deficits. If you confiscated all of the wealth of those who paid half of the country's taxes, you'd still have a deficit.

The same applied to the livestock acquisitions. There simply wasn't enough to go around, so the president began to look for other solutions.

Restaurants around the country were closing their doors, mostly due to lack of customers. Nobody could afford to eat out, as the American currency was worthless and the Texas Treasury Department was still experiencing growing pains in establishing a replacement currency based upon the gold standard. In addition, restaurants couldn't serve a full menu.

A typical meal consisted of food delivered from various sources. Fresh vegetables were obtained from a local produce supplier. Dairy products came from regional companies who distributed milk, eggs, cheese, and butter. The rest of the ingredients for their dishes, from canned goods to frozen meats and seafood, came via large institutional jobbers who had large regional warehouses. Those warehouses were stocked by truck deliveries originating all over the U.S., which had come to a screeching halt on Black Friday.

With the restaurants closed, the large warehouses sat dormant and partially filled with canned goods and frozen foods. The large corporations that owned the facilities were located outside Texas and couldn't be reached. The local warehouse managers didn't have the authority to negotiate a sale to the state.

Desperate to supplement the livestock purchase plan, if approved, the president met with her attorney general to amend the martial law declaration yet again. She was going to confiscate the contents of the warehouses and relocate the products to cities where they could help the largest number of hungry Texans.

In exchange, the treasury would issue notes to the corporations to pay them for the foodstuffs at pre-collapse market prices. She planned on paying the ranchers the same way. Texas needed to maintain its gold reserves to support its new gold-backed currency. Unfortunately, that meant the country would go into debt to finance the survival of its citizens.

She could supplement the livestock acquisitions with the excess food supplies to buy Texas another couple of weeks of dredging operations to open up Galveston Bay to shipping. The midstream off-loading plan was still a couple of weeks away, and the dredging would take another month, she'd been advised.

She stood up from behind her desk and walked into the hallway outside her office. It was oddly quiet, as she was unable to find her secretary. President Burnett wanted to speak with her adjutant general to advise him of her decision and to get an up-to-date assessment on their border intrusions, which were on the rise.

She found her way to his office and was surprised to find several members of her staff crowded around a television monitor that was receiving live satellite feeds from CNN in London. The group, including Deur, were so consumed with the report they didn't notice her presence.

"Texas is bigger than life in many respects, John." The female reporter, dressed in khaki pants and a black winter jacket, was standing about one hundred feet from the checkpoint located to the west of Lubbock. To her right stood another reporter with a microphone, respectfully listening to the CNN reporter.

She continued. "The enormity of its area can only be equated to something we know. For those of us in the UK, let me try to give you some perspective. To travel from El Paso in the west to near Beaumont in the east is nearly nine hundred miles. That's roughly the same distance as it is from London to Edinburgh in Scotland and then back again."

"That is a big territory," added the announcer in London.

"John, Texans have bought into this and have always embraced it with their braggadocio that everything is bigger in Texas."

She turned around and allowed the camera to pan the masses of people pressed against the fences, which was causing the ten-foot-high structures to give slightly.

She continued her reporting. "As the crowds seeking refuge continue to build along their border, more former United States military forces are being brought in to prevent a repeat of the debacle at the border north of Wichita Falls recently. I'm told there have been numerous occasions in which the military has fired warning shots and even rubber bullets at the desperate families trying to find a better life in Texas. I believe we have some footage to show our viewers."

The screen cut away to video of the fences bowing in and the soldiers manning the security checkpoint firing over the refugees' heads. When they failed to back off the fence, they were fired upon with rubber bullets, causing some to lose an eye or the fleshy part of their cheeks.

Defiantly, the crowd didn't give up as they shouted, "You can't kill us all! You can't kill us all!"

The screen returned to the reporter, who looked back at the camera lens. "As you can see, John, the Texas government in Austin has created a humanitarian crisis of epic proportions. Those who don't die of starvation or dehydration succumb to the elements as a massive cold front has descended upon the region, bringing bone-chilling temperatures. Back to you."

The studio host quipped, "Something has to give in Texas. They simply cannot allow this madness to continue. Where is their heart? Have they lost their moral compass?"

President Burnett had had enough. "Turn that dang thing off! You hear me? Off! Now!"

The power button on the monitor was turned off, and the Mansion staff scurried out of Deur's office. The president was livid.

"What do they want me to do? I can't feed my own, much less all of those people who didn't prepare for something like this. And where did international reporters come from, Kregg? This is the last thing we need."

"I'm sorry, Madam President," said Deur as his chin hit his chest.

"No apologies. Fix it. Find them! Arrest them! Deport them! Do it now!"

CHAPTER 28

January 4
The Armstrong Ranch
Borden County, Texas

"The radio stations are getting better about reporting what's happening around Texas," said Lucy as she poured Major a mug of coffee. As she reached over his shoulder to set it on the kitchen table, he grabbed her around the waist and stole a kiss. "Get your hands off me, you grubby cowboy."

"You like it." Major laughed as he refused to let go of her. "Let's fool around before the children wake up, you wanna?"

Lucy smacked him upside the head. "They're not young'uns anymore and neither are you, mister man. Besides, I was about to tell you about the weather so you could get a move on."

"What about it? Happens every day. Nothin' I can do about it," said Major dryly as he took his first sip of morning brew.

"They have a forecast now. International news networks are providing information to the Texas AM radio stations, including the weather forecast. Listen to this. Temperatures in Houston hit minus five last night, a new record."

"So much for global warming," muttered Major. "Is snow coming?"

"They said this is a dry front, but as temperatures warm in a couple of days, the wet stuff will begin falling," replied Lucy.

Their conversation sounded like any pre-collapse discussion over morning coffee, until Lucy updated him on the latest news.

"There's more in the news, though," she continued. "The foreign media got cameras inside Texas and began broadcasting from the border west of Lubbock. Major, they said women and children are freezing to death, literally. There are bodies being dragged through the crowd to the rear so more refugees can cram themselves up against the fences. The reporter said those fences may get knocked down any day."

Major sat up in his chair and calculated the distance from Hobbs, New Mexico, to the ranch. It was right at a hundred miles.

"Did they estimate how many people were out there?" he asked.

"Tens of thousands, maybe more," Lucy replied as she finally sat down after shuffling through the kitchen to prep for a breakfast of oatmeal and canned fruit.

Major was about to tell Lucy of his plans to fortify their perimeter security using the backhoe to dig trenches and create mounds of dirt to use as barricades when Duncan arrived in the kitchen.

"Mornin'," he mumbled as he kissed his mother on the cheek. He fixed an insulated tumbler with coffee and flopped in a chair at the head of the table.

"Good morning, son," said Major, puzzled by Duncan's solemn mood. He wasn't his usual chipper self. "You okay?"

"Yeah, Daddy. Woke up with the wrong things on my mind, that's all. What's goin' on?"

"Your momma and I were discussin' the news. I guess the local radio stations tapped into the international news feeds."

Duncan nodded and sipped his coffee. Major decided to let it go until later.

"There's one more thing that is important," continued Lucy. "Marion has modified the martial law declaration."

"Great," said Major sarcastically. "What now?"

Lucy hesitated, glanced at Duncan, and then turned her attention back to Major. She gripped her coffee with both hands and explained, "The food situation is reportedly dire around Texas. After six weeks of being cut off from the outside world, those who didn't prepare are out of food. The government supplements they were receiving have dried up."

"No surprise there," said Major. "We knew this would happen. The only reason it was delayed a month is because the power is still on in Texas. Had it not been for that, people would be dying of starvation all over the place."

"What about the deals they announced with foreign nations and the United Nations to bring in food?" asked Duncan.

"It won't be enough, son," replied Major. "You can't ship in enough food to feed twenty-some million Texans. You sure as heck can't feed all of those refugees surrounding us either. I hate to tell folks *I told you so*, but there's a reason we've prepped for a situation like this."

Duncan turned his attention to his mother. "How did she amend the declaration, Momma? You seem like you don't wanna say it."

"Turn off your secret-agent senses, please," said Lucy with a nervous chuckle.

"Spill it," was Duncan's reply.

"Marion amended the martial law declaration to allow confiscation of the livestock from the twenty largest ranches in the state, um, country."

"What!" Major exclaimed. "She thinks she's gonna take our cattle?"

"Not for free," replied Lucy. "The government will issue treasury bonds equal to the value of the livestock they take based upon the last auction values. It'll be like an IOU, except backed by the Texas gold repository."

"That's a load of crap," said Major as he slammed his empty coffee mug on the kitchen table. "Those steers are worth ten times what they were before the EMP. And that's cash value. You can't put a price tag on their worth as a food source to everyone on this ranch. If we run out of food because we sold the cattle to the government for a fistful of papers, a lot of good their dang gold will do us."

"I agree, Major, but I don't know what we can do about it," said Lucy.

"We refuse, that's what we'll do," said Duncan. "Do you really think the president is gonna enforce that order against you guys?

What's she gonna do, send in a battalion from Fort Bliss to take them?"

"Maybe, maybe not, son," said Major, who'd calmed down somewhat after running several options through his head. "Here's why I call BS. They won't be lining up at the Four Sixes Ranch herdin' Marion's horses into a trailer for slaughter unless folks are ready to eat chewy horse meat."

"Double standard, I know," said Lucy. "I wonder if the order applies to the Slaughters' dairy cows? They produce multiple foods that we can use. An IOU doesn't feed the families on this ranch."

The trio sat in silence for a moment while they processed the ramifications of the president's order.

Finally, as the sounds of the rest of the family heading downstairs could be heard, Major spoke up. "I'm not gonna wait 'til they're knockin' on our front door. There's a snowstorm comin', and we don't have time to sit around hand-wringing about it. I'm gonna get Preacher and head into Lubbock. Let's see what the slaughterhouses can do for us."

"Yeah, they can't confiscate our food," said Lucy. "I like the plan. Let me get some breakfast goin'."

Major pushed away from the table and stood. "I've lost my appetite, Miss Lucy. I'm gonna go find Preacher."

"Me too, Momma," added Duncan. "Can I ride with y'all? You might need an extra rifle."

"Yup, come on," replied Major.

The two men gave Lucy a kiss on the cheek and headed out the door as the rest of the family arrived in the kitchen. Duncan paused to hug Sook and kiss her on the cheek. He whispered in her ear, and she replied by saying, "Be careful." Like Miss Lucy, Sook was growing accustomed to her man bolting out the door, on a mission, with a rifle in his hand.

CHAPTER 29

January 4
Lubbock, Texas

Major explained to Preacher the need for urgency as he drove northward toward Lubbock. Preacher was skeptical as to whether President Burnett would actually enforce the order against the Armstrong Ranch, but he also saw signs of desperation in issuing the modified declaration in the first place. Preacher also was curious to see how Lubbock was faring under the circumstances. The city had already been descending into societal collapse a few weeks ago, especially on the west side of the metro area.

If their regular slaughterhouse, Plains Meat Company, which was located in the heart of downtown, was too dangerous to approach, they'd opt for the next best option, which was a small retail butchering operation known as Five Star Quality Meats. The company had taken over the operation from a company called Klemke's Sausage Haus years ago. Located southwest of Lubbock in a community known as Wolfforth, the area would be safer, but Preacher doubted they could handle more than half a dozen or so steers at a time. They decided to try Plains Meat Company first.

As they approached Gail, Major told Duncan about what he and Preacher had discovered on their prior trip this way. Duncan took in the information and readied his rifle, just in case.

The drive through the small town was surreal, as Gail had become a ghost town. Whether it was the weather or fear, nobody could be seen outside. The businesses had been boarded up, as had the government buildings. The sheriff's office and the county jail were also boarded up and covered with no-trespassing signs. The apocalypse had claimed another victim.

The remainder of the ride was uneventful as Preacher picked up speed and sailed along the desolate county roads. The scene resembled a Mad Max movie as he dodged abandoned, fuel-starved vehicles and the occasional tumbleweed sent flying by as the winds swooped across the high plains at gusts approaching thirty miles an hour.

Every once in a while, the four-door Ford SUV would shake, causing its passengers to sit a little straighter in their seats. All of the men were on edge as they approached Lubbock.

Unlike before, when local law enforcement had manned checkpoints at major highways entering town, the roads were abandoned except for the occasional vehicle moving from point to point. The weather had become the group's ally, as folks remained inside to avoid the wind chill, which sent temperatures to just above zero.

"Major, looks like I-27 is open again," said Preacher as he pointed toward the on-ramp. I don't see any National Guard trucks blocking the way, do you?"

"Nope. I say go for it. Take the Broadway exit, and we'll circle under the highway. It'll make it less likely we'll encounter trouble that way."

Preacher slowed as he entered the on-ramp to avoid more stalled cars and the concrete barriers left behind by the Guard. Thus far, they hadn't encountered another moving vehicle. As they took the elevated exit, the Fairgrounds came into view.

Major pointed straight ahead. "Preach, look up ahead. It's empty."

"What's empty?" asked Duncan.

"Son, not long ago, after the EMP, the Fairgrounds were overflowing with National Guardsmen and active-duty military," replied Major. "The interstate was closed to civilian traffic, and this whole downtown area was used as a staging area. They've apparently pulled out."

"I'm guessin' they put them all on the border," added Preacher.

Lubbock was Major's old stomping grounds. Driving past the

deserted government buildings he used to frequent saddened him. One of his favorite restaurants, Triple J's Chop House, had burned to the ground. Nearby, vandals had spray painted the bronze, lifelike statue of Lubbock native, musician Buddy Holly.

Major hummed one of Holly's songs as they passed the still-smoldering restaurant, mouthing the lyrics to *That'll Be The Day.*

Preacher made a few turns to wind his way around the Lubbock County Jail complex. As he turned onto Main Street, he slammed on the brakes, bringing the truck to an abrupt halt. There was a large crowd gathered around the entrance to the jail.

"Whoa! We don't want any part of that," hollered Preacher as they observed the angry mob attempting to enter the jail.

"Preach, slowly back up and keep goin' up Buddy Holly Avenue," instructed Major. "I don't know what's goin' on, but I see people with baseball bats, knives, and huntin' rifles. Somethin' has happened in Lubbock to piss all of those people off."

"No doubt," muttered Duncan from the backseat as he pulled the charging handle on the AR-15 he'd chosen for the day. "Should've brought the Barrett."

"Take the second right by the body shop," instructed Major, who remained focused on the crowd until Preacher cleared the intersection. "We'll park on the back side and sneak around the sidewalk."

"Daddy, we're not gonna be able to sneak a cattle truck past a mob like that. Seriously, we'll have to kill them all, and the ones we don't take out will come back to the slaughterhouse later and steal our meat."

"We may have to post guards until they're done," said Major.

Preacher began to laugh.

"He's not kidding," added Duncan.

"Oh, I know," said Preacher defensively. "I was just thinkin' about how we've gotta pack heat in order to pack meat."

The guys got a chuckle out of Preacher's ditty. He found a place to park, and the men exited the truck. Duncan insisted upon approaching the slaughterhouse first, instructing his father and

Preacher to wait behind.

He quickly moved around the corner and worked his way toward the entrance, using telephone poles and parked vehicles as cover to shield him from the mob just two and a half blocks away.

Major crouched down and leaned around the corner of the building to follow Duncan's approach. Preacher covered their backs.

Major knew it was a no-go when Duncan entered the slaughterhouse from street level rather than taking the short flight of concrete steps to the front door. That meant the roll-up door had been breached or left open.

A few minutes later, Duncan came running back toward them, crouched down to lower his profile. He shook his head as he locked eyes with his father.

"Completely destroyed inside," he announced as he slipped around the corner of the storage company building on the corner. "Looters took what they wanted and destroyed the rest of the place."

"Plan B," said Preacher as he tapped Major on the shoulder. Without another word, the men loaded up and began the more treacherous drive across Lubbock to the area supposedly ravaged by refugees and residents alike.

Preacher followed Major's directions and made his way onto the Marsha Sharp Freeway. At one point, they were fairly high above the city on an overpass when Major asked that Preacher pull over. Ordinarily, pre-collapse, parking on the side of the freeway carried a death wish with it. Traffic was always busy as commuters headed out of downtown Lubbock to the jam-packed bedroom communities of Coronado, Bowie, and Wester. They stopped and exited the truck to take in their surroundings.

Their observations shocked them. Smoke billowed from buildings in all directions as fires burned out of control. Even with basic governmental services available, albeit on a reduced basis, police and fire units could never keep up with the demand. The sustained winds didn't help either.

"Unbelievable," said Major as he looked toward Texas Tech University. Several high-rise buildings had been burned out. "I don't understand what could've caused all these fires other than looters."

"Carelessness, too," added Preacher. "The power is on, but that doesn't stop folks from doing stupid stuff to keep warm."

"I hear gunfire, too," said Duncan. "I bet most folks are armed in Lubbock. They're either defendin' or takin', but one thing's for certain, bullets are involved either way."

"Let's go," said Major as he kicked at a side-view mirror that had been knocked off someone's vehicle. "I've seen enough of what used to be Lubbock."

"Daddy, hold on a minute," said Duncan as he laid his rifle in the backseat and retrieved the binoculars. He returned to the concrete guardrail and looked to Levelland, which was located due west of Lubbock. "Look at all those people walking this way."

Major took the glasses, studied Route 114 for a moment, and then passed them to Preacher.

"There are thousands of them," muttered Preacher as he took a long look before lowering the binoculars. "There aren't that many folks living in those little towns. Gotta be refugees."

Major shook his head and began walking back to the truck. "Why is Marion letting that many folks into Texas? Look around us. Lubbock can't satisfy and sustain its own population."

"I don't know, boss, but we gotta get goin'," said Preacher as snow flurries fluttered in the air. "If we're gonna slaughter any steers, we've gotta git 'er done soon."

CHAPTER 30

January 4
The Armstrong Ranch
Borden County, Texas

Major brushed off the cold and entered the ranch house after their day trip to Lubbock. The warm fire caused his face to tingle as he greeted his wife, who was monitoring the news. They had the AM radio stations reporting, and Riley showed them the shortwave frequency bands that produced the most conversation. Not all of them were part of the militia groups. Many were preppers from around America passing along both observations and rumors.

She stood and gave him a kiss before leading him to the hearth in front of the fire. He declined a cup of coffee, instead choosing to unwind and relay the day's events to Lucy.

"This smaller slaughterhouse is not the greatest option, but we've made a deal with them," he began. "They can handle eight of our big boys per day. We'll truck them up there, have our hands wait until they're butchered and processed, and then drive home the same day."

"What's it gonna cost us?" asked Lucy.

"We offered up a dairy cow for each trip," replied Major.

"Will the Slaughters be okay with that?"

"Yeah, if he wants to eat our beef. I'll need one of his men each day, and two of ours will accompany Antonio. Preacher will make the first run tomorrow to make sure the deal is kept."

Lucy turned off the radio and set it on the cocktail table. She gestured for Major to sit on the seat, and she helped him remove his boots. "Major, are you sure this is necessary? It's gonna use up a lot of diesel, put our men at risk, plus expose some of our valuable assets like the cattle and the trailer."

"We talked about that on the way back," he replied. "The only way to avoid this is to see Marion again and get a waiver. I'm sure I'll have to stand in line behind a dozen other ranchers. We'll provide Antonio several different routes between here and there so nobody can establish a pattern of activity. Also, he'll be under strict orders to abandon the cattle and get themselves back to the ranch in the event of trouble. We've got more cattle, but good men and the trailer are in short supply."

"What about the diesel?" she asked.

"We're gonna have to go in the other direction for that," replied Major. "When we were in Odessa, I spoke with one of the deputies, who told me Arnold Oil Company in Midland was supplying a lot of the ranchers who were their regulars."

"Not us," interrupted Lucy. "Remember how they screwed Pops over years ago?"

Major grimaced and nodded. "Yes, of course I do, and my reaction was the same when the deputy mentioned their name."

Arnold Oil Company was founded in Corpus Christi after the end of the Depression. Over time, they expanded throughout Texas and continued with the Arnold family operating their locations for many years. During the boom of the oil industry in the eighties, the grandchildren of founder Gene Arnold began to sell off their locations to larger corporate interests.

Major's father, Pops, enjoyed handshake deals with Jim Arnold for decades but lost the benefit of the company's promises after the sell-off. An annual prepayment of twenty-one thousand dollars for diesel at a greatly discounted rate per gallon was not honored by the new company because there was nothing in writing.

In the meantime, Jim Arnold had suffered a stroke and was unable to confirm the arrangement to anyone. The failure to memorialize the transaction in writing was partly Pops's fault, but it stuck in the craw of the Armstrong family for years. The falling-out had been somewhat bitter and was remembered by Major. He wasn't sure if the new proprietors were aware of it, or cared at this point.

"Well, Miss Lucy, I may have to go down there with hat in hand. More and more businesses are shutting their doors due to lack of customers and an unstable currency. Marion is having a heckuva time getting her gold-backed dollar off the ground, which has resulted in a barter system. Our deal with the slaughterhouse is a great example."

Lucy patted him on the legs after he propped them on the table. "Make the deal and get our tanks filled. Let's get our freezers stocked with meat too. But, Major, we've got to stop venturing out of the confines of the ranch. It's becoming too dangerous out there."

"I know," mumbled Major as he leaned his head against the back of the sofa. He closed his eyes for a moment as Lucy continued.

"I'm not just referring to places like Lubbock. From what I'm hearing on the news and the shortwave, the fences are gonna give soon. We're gonna be crawlin' with hungry, desperate folks who have nothin' to lose."

CHAPTER 31

January 5
Interstate 20
Wickett, Texas

"Go big or go home, boys," said Holloway to his men as they crammed inside a roadside truck stop in the small town of Wickett, between Odessa and El Paso. Two days prior, he'd observed a convoy of food trucks, which had crossed their path, headed east on Interstate 20 toward Odessa. They were fueling their four vehicles at a small convenience store when he noticed them roar by, escorted by a military Humvee at the front and rear. He asked the clerk, who was being held at gunpoint to prevent him from notifying anyone about Holloway's men, if he knew where they might be headed.

The man was frightened but volunteered what he knew. He told his captors about the mall in Odessa being used as a large refugee center. The food supplies were most likely being sent there or up to Lubbock, where the city was in dire straits.

Holloway waited until the vehicles were topped off, considered this new information, and decided to take a chance. People were creatures of habit, and the government was guilty of being regimental as well. The trucks would be back, and the next time, he'd be ready for them.

The first step they took was to create a three-car crash on the interstate near the off-ramp to the town of Wickett. This would force any vehicles off the highway temporarily so they could bypass the wreckage. Some cars might even choose to purchase fuel while they pulled off, making them easy targets for Holloway's men.

The two days spent at the Main Street Market and Truck Stop

proved most advantageous. They secured another seven vehicles, which they promptly loaded with fuel. They confiscated all the supplies of any travelers before piling their dead bodies in a dumpster behind the truck stop.

Wickett had no law enforcement protection, so Holloway was not concerned with being discovered. The routine was a simple one. If a vehicle entered the Main Street Market, it never left the parking lot.

When his lookouts roared down the exit ramp, he knew it was *game on.* He pulled all his men in from their sentry posts and positioned them around the bottom of the exit ramp. One of his truck drivers fired up a tractor-trailer rig and got into position. When given the signal, he would proceed southbound on the two-lane road traveling under the interstate. At just the right moment, he'd spring the assault on the convoy.

Some of his men had practiced this routine in Winslow, Arizona, before they were derailed by a sniper who came out of nowhere. This time, Holloway kept his men positioned around the off-ramp, instructing them to monitor the highway and the high ground. The stakes were too high this time for some do-gooder to get in his way.

Holloway positioned himself down an embankment with half a dozen men. They used short bushy trees as cover. If the convoy was similar to the one two days ago, he would have an opportunity to score a Humvee. If it had a Ma Deuce mounted on top, he might just wet himself with excitement.

The sound of the diesel truck utilizing its Jake brake to slow down brought him out of his daydream. He inched his way under the tree, silently cursing the rocks that jabbed into his kneecaps. The lead Humvee, a soft top, stopped short of the wreckage.

"He's probably assessing the situation," Holloway mumbled to himself. "There's no way around it, pal, so come on down. Trust me, the price is right."

The driver inched forward, and the passenger waved his arm out the window and pointed down the ramp.

Here we go.

Holloway was only slightly disappointed when he saw the single

Sysco truck sandwiched between the two escort vehicles. He had an army of twenty men to feed, and two truckloads of provisions would last them a month or more. This was an opportunity that wouldn't likely come again, but he wasn't going to complain. Especially when he saw the second Humvee roll right in front of him, barely fifty feet away from where he and his men lay on their bellies.

He held his breath and waited. The signal would come at any moment, and his men would pounce out of their positions and take the convoy down before they knew what hit them.

The convoy was barely rolling down the ramp when the sound of metal crashing into metal could be heard. There were no tires screeching as brakes were being applied. The driver of the lead Humvee was unable to honk his horn to warn away the oncoming Peterbilt.

For a split second, Holloway mused about the joke that he'd heard as a child, which asked *what is the last thing a bug sees when it hits the windshield?* He tried to imagine what the Humvee driver was thinking when the Peterbilt T-boned his truck.

His musings caused him to miss the action. With catlike speed, his team raced toward the eighteen-wheeler and the rear Humvee. A soldier had climbed into the turret and had his head shot off, literally. His arms were draped over the roof of the truck, and his head was obliterated.

The rest of the personnel assigned to the convoy didn't fare much better. They were quickly eliminated. The only injury to Holloway's team was the man assigned to drive the Peterbilt rig into the lead Humvee who was injured when his head crashed into the steering wheel, knocking out two teeth.

Grinning from ear to ear, Holloway approached his new ride. He opened the rear passenger door and dragged the headless soldier's body out of the Humvee and onto the asphalt. He quickly crawled up through the turret and grabbed the handles of the powerful machine gun. Visions of his days in Afghanistan filled his mind as a wave of excitement overcame him. Fortunately, the wetting himself part did not.

He ordered his men to quickly clear the wreckage and strip the soldiers of their weapons and uniforms, regardless of how bloody they were. Everything could be useful at some point. He walked down the exit ramp and circled his hand in the air, telling everyone to get their vehicles and prepare to pull out.

Holloway had a route picked out that would lead them north toward Lubbock. He'd chuckled as he'd looked at the podunk towns on the Texas map like Patricia, Lenora, and Gail. What was with these people? he mused. Did they name their towns after their wives?

CHAPTER 32

January 6
The Armstrong Ranch
Borden County, Texas

Duncan and Cooper ambled along the Colorado River as they took their afternoon shift on perimeter patrol. The guys made small talk, mainly about Duncan's military experiences in the different theaters of war he'd been assigned to. He and Cooper agreed there would be a time that the battle would come to the ranch. The guys appreciated all of the efforts put into security by Preacher and Major, but at some point, they knew they would be tested by a real force, not just the wandering refugees and hungry Texans who happened to stumble upon Armstrong Ranch.

"Here's the first thing you notice about a gun battle," began Duncan. "They're totally chaotic. Training helps overcome that, but mostly a firefight is unpredictable and unorganized. You improvise a lot. It's not choreographed and planned like you see in the movies."

"In the movies, the scenes move very fast, it seems," added Cooper.

"That's because they're scripted," said Duncan with a laugh. "Live combat isn't like that usually. Whether I was working with my guys in a unit, or it was just me and Park in the middle of an operation, we would take our time to maneuver and even experience a lull of five or ten minutes to slowly position ourselves to gain ground on the enemy. You just don't charge against an objective at top speed. On the battlefield, with your full kit on, even the adrenaline coursing through your veins can't prevent you from getting winded."

"The bullets, however, move lightning fast, don't they?" asked Cooper.

"Yeah, that's for sure. When you hear the gunfire, the wall in front of you could be getting riddled with rounds meant for your body."

They rode through the trees and stopped to observe the beavers dealing with the frozen river. The dam started by Major and the ranch hands had held up well thus far. The beavers had supplemented the initial construction and created a perfect dam. The frozen, still water created an ice skating rink except where the beavers were normally active. They didn't hibernate in the winter, but spent most of their time inside a beaver lodge constructed of twigs and mud on the bank of the river, which extended into the water. This enabled them to have an opening through which they could access their food cache at the bottom of the river. Like most wild animals, beavers were preppers too.

Duncan continued. "Here's another thing, these things usually happen at the end of a long day. It never fails that your unit might be at the end of the patrol, hot, sweaty, tired, and suffering from a loss of concentration. You're trying to watch your buddy's six, the L-T is trying to communicate and coordinate movements, and then boom, an IED goes off, or a mortar round hits nearby, or automatic weapons unleash a barrage on top of you."

"Wow," said Cooper.

"Yeah, wow. I mean, you go into sensory overload and your body starts pumpin' adrenaline like it's nobody's business. All of this is hittin' you at the same time, yet you gotta focus on your job or you'll die."

Cooper moved ahead slightly to pull a branch up to allow Duncan to duck and cross under. "What's goin' through your head during all of this?"

"Coop, it's like havin' a bunch of little birds chirpin' in your ear at the same time. Where's the enemy? What weapons do they have? Does my unit know where I am? Am I in cover? Is it good enough cover to keep my tail from gettin' shot off? What's my ammo count?"

"Holy crap!" exclaimed Cooper.

"Oh, that's just part of it," Duncan continued. "Once you get oriented, in the back of your head you wonder if any of your guys have been hit. Is my unit moving without me? Did someone just yell my name? Don't forget to breathe. You know, it's hectic as hell, to say the least."

"Sounds surreal, totally different than what you see on TV or in the movies."

Duncan laughed, although the conversation wasn't intended to be funny. "That's why I can't watch the Hollywood version of war. They glorify it to the point of absurdity. There is nothing you could watch that would ever give you the feeling you get when you're trying to kill another human being who is working his tail off to kill you. Nothing can prepare you for a gunfight except training with the people you plan to fight with, and die with, if necessary."

The guys entered a clearing as they headed west along the water when they both noticed a vehicle coming in their direction at a high rate of speed. Duncan quickly dismounted and pulled his rifle out of its scabbard. Cooper followed his lead, and the two readied their weapons. Although the truck was from the ranch, they were always on edge, prepared for all contingencies.

As it got closer, they lowered their rifles as they saw Antonio waving his arm out the window. Everyone who drove vehicles on the ranch had been told not to use the horn to avoid drawing attention to the property. Duncan called it *sound discipline.*

"Mr. Duncan, you're needed back at the ranch house right away," said Antonio as he slid to a stop. "You take the truck."

"Antonio, did something happen? Is everything okay?" asked Duncan.

"Yes, sir, I think. The Army is here to see you. Two men in uniforms with stripes."

Duncan looked to Cooper and shrugged. Antonio took his place on patrol, and Duncan headed back to the house, except at a much calmer rate of speed.

CHAPTER 33

January 6
The Armstrong Ranch
Borden County, Texas

The first thing Duncan noticed when he arrived was that the vehicle was a black Chrysler 300 with blue-and-white U.S. government tags. This was an indication these visitors were officers, possibly high-ranking, from Fort Hood. The U.S. tags didn't surprise him. He doubted the Texas prison population was cranking out license plates at this point. He walked slowly past the vehicle and glanced into the front seat. Stuck between the passenger seat and the armrest was a thick file folder with his name, social security number, and old military unit typed on it. He immediately wondered if these men knew of his post-military activities. Either way, he was gonna play it close to the vest because he smelled a rat.

Duncan casually walked inside and took off his jacket and hat. He hung them on the wall next to his father's. However, he kept his leg holster and sidearm on. *One never knows.*

As he entered, he could hear chairs scooting on the well-worn wooden floors in the kitchen. He was about to meet his unexpected visitors.

It took him a split second to realize he was going to be greeted by a full-bird colonel. His eyes darted around to make sure there were no military police waiting in the wings. Something must be up, and he was immediately on the defensive.

"Commander Armstrong, I am Colonel Sanderson with the Texas Quick Reaction Force headquartered at Fort Hood. I'd like you to meet Captain Jon Harris, whose unit is made up of elite military personnel like yourself."

Duncan snapped a salute and they returned it. He still hadn't spoken.

"We apologize for this appearance without notice, but we had no other way of reaching you. Captain Harris has remedied that situation by providing your parents a satphone and charger. Your family will now have communications access to me or Austin, as necessary."

Why would that be necessary?

"Thank you, sir," said Duncan. "How can I help you?"

"May we sit," said the colonel as he glanced toward the sofa and back toward Lucy, who stood near the kitchen door with Major.

"Sure, anywhere you'd like," said Duncan. The group headed to the family room and suggested the two visitors take the sofa. After some small talk, Duncan brought the conversation back to his original question.

"Colonel, I'm sure you didn't come here to make small talk, with all due respect, sir. How can I help you?"

The colonel laughed. "Your file indicated you were a straight shooter, in more ways than one," he began as he provided Duncan a wink, which set off alarm bells throughout his body. They knew about his special ops. "The TX-QRF is the Texas military's version of a SWAT team. We serve at the pleasure of President Burnett and are available on a moment's notice to address security concerns that might threaten our national security."

"I am familiar with the TX-QRF through news reports of the incident at Midwestern State in Wichita Falls," interjected Duncan. "I heard it was a nice, clean operation."

"Yes, it was a success without loss of innocent lives," said the captain. "Commander Duncan, you have been referred to us by the highest levels of our new government as what can best be described as an incredible asset. We need men like you to protect Texas and everything required to make our new nation function without outside interference. Would you be willing to discuss this with us?"

"I'm listening," replied Duncan.

"We are prepared to provide you your own unit, with a team

handpicked by you," continued the captain. "The TX-QRF is establishing a regional headquarters in Lubbock, and your close proximity, coupled with your father's knowledge of the area, would provide us a leg up on any potential situations that might arise."

Duncan sat up in his chair as he processed everything that was said. "I have a duty to protect my family now. I already have a unit here at Armstrong Ranch. Besides, I don't need a job to make ends meet."

"We understand that, Commander," broke in the colonel. "There are other intangibles that we're prepared to offer you, and your family, for your assistance. For one, as a high-ranking member of our new military apparatus, and technically a part of the administration's protective detail, your family will be exempt from certain provisions of the martial law declaration, whether presently in place or later enacted."

"The cattle confiscation?" interrupted Lucy.

"Yes, ma'am, although, without quibbling, the ranchers are being paid for their livestock," responded the captain.

Lucy was about to fire back her opinion of that when Major gently rested his hand on her knee to subdue his sometimes fiery wife.

The colonel continued. "We will also provide you a Humvee with a full-time aide and a choice of weapons, as well as your choice of confiscated weapons from our stockpiles to be used here at the ranch."

"You said our unit would be based in Lubbock?" asked Duncan, before adding, "Lubbock is already a war zone, Colonel."

"That it is, and we hope our increased presence there will help calm things down. You will be stationed at the Army National Guard facility on East Regis Street, adjacent to the airport. We are planning on supplementing your operation with several elements out of Fort Bliss and Fort Hood to help deal with the refugee crisis that has escalated significantly in the last two weeks. This will include choppers and other forms of air support as logistics allow."

They spoke for another fifteen minutes as Duncan tried to flesh out who, specifically, had suggested him for this task. He knew it was

Gregg, and he enjoyed watching the colonel squirm to avoid confirmation.

They eventually said their goodbyes. Duncan promised them an answer within several days, and the vice president's front men left.

Within seconds of the car leaving the ranch, Duncan and his parents were rehashing the conversation. He wanted to consider the offer for two reasons. One was the benefits provided to his family and the ranch. The trips to Lubbock to slaughter cattle grew more dangerous by the day. Also, adding to their arsenal was huge.

Second, this would give him an opportunity to get on the side of the Texas military apparatus to learn what he could about Gregg, Yancey, and the reasons he was left behind in North Korea.

Both of his parents were adamantly against it. They thought they'd lost Duncan once and were not going to lose him to a fight that wasn't necessarily theirs. Duncan was still unsure until Palmer and Sook returned from the barnyard. He looked at her beautiful face and remembered what they'd been through to get home. He made his decision without speaking another word about the offer.

No.

PART THREE

CHAPTER 34

January 7
Patricia, Texas

As nightfall approached, Holloway's Humvee led the way as they sped away from Wickett, using country roads and deserted highways to zigzag northward toward Lubbock. He knew the National Guard in Odessa would be concerned about the convoy's disappearance within hours. One phone call, and this desolate part of West Texas would be carpeted with choppers looking for the tractor-trailer rig filled with food.

He studied the map and identified an area halfway between Lubbock and Midland-Odessa. The towns in this part of West Texas were small and therefore conquerable. They could easily conduct raids into the surrounding midsized cities and then disappear into this barren wasteland of oil rigs and scrub brush.

The convoy was speeding northeast on County Road 115 when the driver swerved slightly to avoid dead bodies on the side of the road. The big rig behind them wasn't as deft, choosing instead to plow over the rotting corpses, slinging blood and body parts under the truck and onto the convoy's trailing vehicles.

"Patricia," mumbled Holloway. "Sounds like a nice place to lie down for the night. Slow them down. I want to think this through."

The driver slowed, and Holloway exited the truck. He studied the map and walked slowly down the highway to think. They needed to hide the truck or off-load it and send his men to ditch it somewhere. More importantly, they needed a base of operations. A location that was centrally located, not only for his personal purposes, but near enough the western border that he and his unit could assist Lee and the rest of the Lightning Death Squads into Texas.

"The quaint hamlet of Patricia might just fit the bill," he said aloud as he walked past his Humvee and approached the eight trucks and cars that now made up his unit's fleet. He waved them all out of their vehicles, and they hustled to gather around him.

"Here's the play, gentlemen," said Holloway. "This little town may only have a dozen houses or so in it. There's also a high school about a mile past it. Nobody's gonna give a rat's ass about Patricia, Texas, but it suits us perfectly. Here's what we're gonna do."

Holloway broke his men into the pairings that best suited their talents. One wheelman coupled with a shooter. The plan was a simple one. Race into town. Bust into homes. Kill everyone, no exceptions. They would take over the town and find a place to hide the truck.

"Everybody got it?" he asked before instructing them to *cowboy up*, which drew laughter from his band of Korean murderers and thieves.

Holloway left the Humvee and its fifty-caliber machine gun to guard their rear as well as the prized food truck. He took the wheel of a four-door Ram pickup and led the charge at nearly eighty miles an hour. The first stop, Patricia Farmer's Cotton Gin, was his target. He waved the rest of this men forward into the town.

Each team of two rushed ahead, seeking a residence or a business to attack. Holloway and his partner moved swiftly and efficiently through the cotton gin operation, but found it to be uninhabited, just as another group had learned two weeks prior. He looked at the enormous drive-thru Quonset-hut building used to load and unload cotton. It could hide four rigs like their food truck.

Holloway sent his partner to retrieve the Humvee and the eighteen-wheeler. While they were catching up to him, he walked through the quiet gravel parking lot toward the highway, intently listening for the sound of gunfire. The big rig was secured and hidden upon its arrival. Then Holloway headed farther into town to find out why his men didn't engage any of the locals.

As he passed the houses, his men stood in the front yards and waved, some holding their rifles high in the air as a salute. In the ten minutes it took him to walk slowly through Patricia, he realized there were no hostiles to engage. The town had been abandoned.

Holloway stood in the middle of the two highways that intersected the tiny community. He slowly spun in a circle, taking in his surroundings. As the sun disappeared to their west, he realized they were now the locals.

"I want perimeter security established at all four of these roads entering town. Patrols need to be set up around the clock with double coverage on the cotton gin. Be ready. These Texans are gonna be pissed when they see the mess we left back there."

He motioned for his two top lieutenants to join him. His mind was racing at the possibilities of having this location to hide his activities. It was well off the beaten path. There was a high school down the road, which might yield more food and living space for Lee's men as they rallied before being sent elsewhere.

"First thing in the morning, I want you to take two guys over to the high school," began Holloway. He turned toward the east and squinted, but the coming darkness prevented him from seeing far. "Clear the area, go inside, and let me know how many men you think it can house. I'm thinking about bringing Lee and his commandos here. When you're finished, we'll head into Lubbock and get a lay of the land."

"We'll need more vehicles and fuel," interrupted one of his men.

"That's high on the priority list," said Holloway. "I also want to identify the substations to be taken down."

"Maybe they have an armory?"

"Probably do, and it's on the shopping list too," replied Holloway. "First, get the men in place and settled. Tomorrow will be a big day."

CHAPTER 35

January 7
The National Mall
Washington, DC

The snow had just begun to fall when Yancey exited the Town Car and walked toward the Reflecting Pool, which was mostly frozen over. The glorious monuments of the nation's capital, the Lincoln Memorial and the Washington Monument, rested silently, without power.

Through a herculean effort coordinated by the Capital Police and the National Guard, much of the chaos in Washington had been subdued. A large swath of the city from the Potomac to the U.S. Capitol complex, as well as the streets surrounding the White House, had been cordoned off. The most important buildings that housed the United States government were protected and their electricity powered by massive backup generators.

Yancey continued to work out of the CIA headquarters in Langley, Virginia, but was summoned to the White House by Chief of Staff Acton. At the last minute, he was advised that Acton would meet him away from the White House, on this bench across from the Reflecting Pool next to the JFK Hockey Fields.

As he approached, Acton spoke first, choosing to dispense with the preliminaries. "I've been doing some thinking, Billy. I may be wrong, but I doubt it. You see, this whole secession thing has bothered me from the moment I learned of it. Monty's unexpected disappearance into Texas with the lame excuse of appeasing his wife didn't make sense. Now, in hindsight, it all fits. Monty Gregg is knee-deep in this betrayal of our nation, and he's standing in the way of our country's recovery from the EMP."

Yancey listened as Acton spoke, somewhat relieved that the ire of the president's chief advisor was directed elsewhere. He exhaled and nodded, choosing to hold his words until pressed by Acton.

"Billy, I'm prepared to bring treason charges against Monty for his role in the Texas secession and for his role in the assassination attempt of Kim Jong-un."

Yancey perked up and fought back the reaction that his body so desperately wanted to release. *Run!*

Acton turned his body to look Yancey in the eye. "You didn't think I'd find out about something this big? Well, I guess if we'd continued business as usual around here, you and your goon squad could effectively hide the truth or eliminate those who wanted to come clean. You couldn't pull off a mission like that one without underlings to help. After the collapse, your control of the situation collapsed with it."

"I don't know what you're referring to."

"Shut up, Billy, or I'll drag you into Leavenworth along with your deep-state buddy," said Acton with a raised voice. "I'm not here to have you arrested or snitch on your pals. I'm here to offer a deal, make an alliance, in effect, that furthers my agenda and saves your hide in the process."

"I'm listening," said Yancey. He'd switch to the winning horse to save his hide.

"You went to Texas for a while when Monty left Raven Rock," continued Yancey. "I doubt you were involved in the secession movement, although, with your background, you'd be a valuable counselor on such matters. What I want to know is whether you've returned to Washington to do your job for the United States government, or are you Monty's *do-boy* on the inside?"

"Okay, you've been reasonable, so I'm going to be straightforward," replied Yancey. "I considered the Texas option but not as a part of their government. They don't have a use for a man of my talents. I might have been consulted now and again, but mainly, I planned on retiring and riding out my years watching the world collapse around me."

"What brought you back to DC?" asked Acton.

"Assuming, for sake of argument, that there was an assassination attempt on a certain dictator, which may or may not have triggered a big mess, loose ends existed that could blow up in everyone's faces, regardless of culpability. I decided it was my duty to sweep the floors, so to speak, before some media mope stumbled across something."

"I get it, and I commend you for that," said Acton. "Be that as it may, I have a problem, a thorn in my side, that I need surgically removed. I need a win for my president, and you're going to use your considerable talents to effectuate the change necessary to give her that win."

"What do you want me to do?"

"Let's start with Monty," replied Acton. "I need him out of my way so that he can't act as Burnett's shield. Do you have any ideas?"

Yancey thought for a moment. "Well, let's just say he's asked me for a favor that I'm about to implement. Perhaps I can use that to our advantage and possibly as leverage."

"What is it? Some kind of quid pro quo?" asked Acton.

"Sorry, don't forget rule number one of any White House senior advisor—*plausible deniability*."

CHAPTER 36

January 8
Midland, Texas

The weather had cleared and warmed enough to begin melting snow off the roads. Major and Preacher readied the trucks to make the eighty-mile drive into Midland, where the Arnold Oil Company was located. When he woke up, he and Lucy retrieved one of his caches of gold from behind the house.

Within a small notebook she kept with her most of the day, Lucy had a series of treasure maps, as she called them, written down in sufficient detail that any member of the family could follow them.

Over time, she and Major had converted cash into junk silver and gold coins. They'd envisioned a grid-down scenario in which currency had become worthless and a barter economy rose out of the ashes. If such a new economy never came to pass, then they always had the ability to convert their precious metals back into paper currency.

In the meantimc, prior to thc collapsc, thcy'd thought it prudent to hide their silver and gold throughout the ranch in the event they were overrun. Initially, they'd marked each spot using the global positioning satellite apps on their smartphones. But as they learned more about the electromagnetic pulse threat, they'd opted for the old-fashioned paper and pencil method.

To store their gold and silver, Lucy used old paint cans and oxygen-absorber packets. The paint cans provided a good seal, and the oxygen absorbers slowed the tarnishing of the silver. Once the can was secured, she dug a hole at least two feet deep and buried the can. Then she marked exact distances between permanent landmarks, whether it was a tree, a building, or large rock, in order to remember its location.

Finally, to frustrate any unauthorized prospector from finding her stash with a metal detector, she implemented diversions designed to confound the thief. All around the stash location, she buried empty steel cans and any kind of trash made of metal, including nails. Someone with a metal detector would hopefully get frustrated digging up garbage before they got to the bull's-eye where their barter currency was buried.

During the days following the collapse, many forms of barter came to mind, from cattle to ammunition. Unless absolutely necessary, Major wanted to avoid bartering their food resources. Under no circumstances would he agree to barter guns or ammunition, which would provide a stranger the tools necessary to kill his family. That was just plain stupid.

Their gold and silver resources were not unlimited, obviously, but would help them as they continued to survive until the world righted itself. Having access to fuel was a critical part of their survival.

Two of their three-hundred-gallon tanks were empty. Using heavy-duty chain and steel hooks, the backhoe lifted the tanks into the air and set them each inside a pickup truck. To secure the tanks, the ranch hands used the same chain and four-inch-wide tie-downs used on their flatbed trailers when hauling rolls of hay.

They needed two trucks to accommodate the weight of the tanks when filled. Diesel weighed around seven pounds per gallon, compared to just over six pounds for ethanol-free gasoline. Once the trucks were loaded, they began the trip to Arnold Oil located northwest of Midland.

Major and Preacher drove the lead truck while Duncan and Sook followed behind. The two hadn't spent much time together other than during Duncan's firearm-training sessions. Duncan was very impressed with her ability to handle a sidearm, especially in close-quarters combat scenarios.

Her slight frame still made it difficult to handle more than one shot with a long rifle due to its recoil. He'd just started training her with the AR-15 that morning when Major asked them to travel to Arnold Oil.

The group traveled the backroads, working their way to the west through Vealmoor and Ackerly, then turning south toward Midland when they reached Route 349, a few miles south of Patricia. This took them directly toward Midland and Arnold Oil.

The ride was uneventful, but the bartering between Major and the general manager was not. The first thing that Major noticed was the level of security around the facility. Two military vehicles were stationed at the ten-foot-tall chain-link gate to the parking area. Two guards stood behind concrete barriers with their weapons at low ready, while another man was stationed at the front door. A fourth Guardsman was walking the perimeter of the fenced utility yard, which contained a single metal prefabricated building and an office.

After Major provided the guards his identification and the group agreed to check their weapons, they were allowed to drive in.

Arnold Oil was not a gas station that was ordinarily open to the public. It was a wholesale jobber, selling fuel to small gas stations in the region and to the larger ranches that could handle deliveries of a thousand gallons or more.

Before the collapse, off-road diesel fuel ranged from $2.09 a gallon if five hundred gallons was purchased, and that amount was reduced to $2.01 a gallon for a thousand gallons or more. On-road, or highway-use, diesel was a dollar more per gallon.

After the collapse, the price had increased fivefold. Major was astonished when he was told the price.

"Ten-fifty a gallon," he started. "Is that the price for everyone or just the Armstrong family?"

The salesclerk, who had been around since the days of the feud, had immediately recognized Major when he walked through the door. He'd been arrested in a car-theft ring many years ago by Major's Company C. Although the kid had innocently worked in the chop shop that split the vehicles into much more valuable parts, he'd still had to go through the system in order to provide testimony on behalf of the government.

"Mr. Armstrong, I promise you, this is the price now," the young man responded. "I heard it's gonna go up soon. You got here just in time."

"Lucky me," mumbled Major as he did some calculating in his head to determine the cost in gold. This was the first time he'd exchanged gold for a commodity such as diesel fuel. If the price of fuel had gone up fivefold, surely the price of gold had as well. "What's the total for six hundred gallons?"

The clerk banged on his calculator and wrote the price on a receipt pad. "Sixty-three hundred Texas dollars. Needless to say, we don't accept U.S. money anymore. Do you have Texas dollars?"

"No, but I brought gold and silver," replied Major. "What's the price in silver?"

"Well," the clerk began to answer. He pointed to a chalkboard behind him. "Here's this week's exchange rate based upon the Texas Treasury advisories. The spot gold price is currently thirteen thousand three hundred twenty-four Texas dollars per ounce. Spot silver is a little more complicated to calculate. One thousand dollars' face value is currently going for one hundred eight thousand dollars. That's assuming, of course, that your thousand in face value was equal to seven hundred fifteen troy ounces."

The hyperinflation was astonishing. In just a short period of time, the value of precious metals had skyrocketed. Major started scribbling some calculations on a notepad in front of him. He needed a calculator to determine how much he owed.

"Mr. Armstrong," interrupted the young man, "I'd be glad to help you with that and give you some perspective. I saw your reaction to the price of diesel, and I'm guessin' you were comparing that to before the attack. While diesel has gone up five times, silver and gold has risen nearly ten times in value. The fact of the matter is, in Texas anyway, there is a greater supply of diesel than there is pure silver and gold. You're actually getting a very good deal."

Major tilted his head slightly and glanced at Preacher, who shrugged. Major reached into his jacket and pulled out a small pouch of gold American Eagle coins and Preacher handed him a canvas bag, which pulled together with a drawstring.

"Well, I guess I am. So will you fill us up?"

"Of course," the clerk began to reply as he punched some numbers into his calculator. "I'll assume that you're paying with silver 'cause we can't make change for any gold coins."

"Yes," said Major, still dumbfounded by the value of his silver and gold. He couldn't imagine what he'd purchase with a one-ounce gold bar that used to be worth twelve hundred dollars and was now valued at well north of twelve thousand.

"I'll need sixty-one dollars and a dime, face value, please. Please make sure your coinage is pre-1965. I'll be required to double-check while the fuel is being dispensed."

"Okay," said Major as he and Preacher began to count the coins. While the clerk left his post to instruct his men to fill up the tanks, Major leaned over to Preacher and whispered, "Can you believe this?"

"No, boss, but congrats on a dang fine investment," replied Preacher. "Maybe we should do some shoppin' before the price of gold drops back to normal."

"Yeah, we'll talk with Lucy about it. I've got a lot of things on my wish list, like more weapons, ammo, and men to protect the ranch."

They continued to count the money, unaware they were being watched through a security camera above their heads.

CHAPTER 37

January 8
Midland, Texas

Duncan wheeled out of the parking lot, careful not to turn too abruptly and cause strain on the top-heavy fuel tank strapped in the pickup bed behind them. Before he could catch up to the bumper of Major's truck, a four-door Nissan with the right front fender missing pulled out of a side street and rode close behind his bumper. Duncan didn't like the sudden appearance of the car and sat a little taller in his seat. He had to constantly remind himself that Texas was increasingly dangerous too. The former state might be an island in a sea of darkness, but it was also isolated from the rest of the world and potentially lawless. Texans would have to step up in order to prevent falling into the type of societal collapse being exhibited beyond their borders.

Duncan followed closely behind his father, constantly checking his mirrors, watching the driver's every move behind him. He asked Sook to also focus on the passenger seats of the small truck. If a head popped up or a rifle barrel revealed itself, Sook was told to fire her sidearm at them.

The three vehicles drove along for two more miles until the Nissan pulled off a side street where a fork in the road appeared. Duncan followed the cloud of dust, which headed on the county road parallel to them. Eventually the car, which was traveling much faster than they were, disappeared. Relieved, he decided to address the offer made by the colonel and the TX-QRF with Sook.

"Sook, my family is divided on whether I should take the job in Lubbock," started Duncan, who thought he'd made a decision until the family had approached him afterwards. "Really, it is up to you and me to decide."

Sook shook her head. "No, Duncan, only you can make this choice. My concerns are for your safety. This makes the decision full of emotion, not made of clear mind."

Duncan chuckled as he thought of the number of family decisions that were made every day based upon raw emotion rather than logic. It seemed to him that no decision could be strictly logical so long as it might affect someone you care for.

He reached across the armrest to hold her hand when he heard the high-pitched whine of a dirt bike. His head looked to his rearview mirror first and then on both sides of the truck. Then he took another look to their right.

Approaching them from the south were at least five dirt bikes zipping across the flat desert ground as if they were on air. From the angle of attack, it was impossible for him to gauge the speed of the bikes, but he saw they were closing fast.

"Sook, take my rifle," he ordered. "Do you remember how to operate it?"

"Yes, but my aim is not good yet!" she shouted in an adrenaline-fueled voice.

"Doesn't matter," he continued. "You just have to scare them away. But, Sook, before you shoot, make sure the barrel is outside the window. The gunfire is very loud inside the cab of the truck."

"Okay!" Sook quickly rolled down the window and pointed the weapon toward the riders. Before she prepared to shoot, Preacher was firing upon them with his shotgun. Duncan imagined the resulting decibels in the other truck was close to concussion levels.

As they got closer, the dirt bikes scattered in different directions. The scene was all too familiar to Duncan. The approaching fast boats in the Gulf of Oman had used the same technique, only they had been trying to force a mistake on the part of the crew of the USS *Jack Lucas*.

The bikers shot ahead and behind their two trucks. Duncan was looking all around when Major suddenly lurched forward in a burst of speed. He was gonna try to outrun the bikes.

Duncan wished they had communications gear so he could tell his father that this approach was a bad idea. They weren't sure of the attackers' intentions, but one thing they didn't need was to draw them directly to the ranch. Unless they successfully killed them all, the bikers could return to Midland and bring their buddies once they feasted their eyes on Armstrong Ranch.

The better course of action was to stop and take on the attackers head-on. Duncan punched the gas and pulled alongside his father. He waved at him until Major saw him in the driver's side mirror. Major slowed to let him pull alongside.

"Daddy, we've gotta turn off or we'll lead them straight to the ranch," shouted Duncan through the passenger window.

Major and Preacher talked back and forth just as Sook exclaimed, "They're back!"

Suddenly, the dirt bikes were immediately behind them and were firing at the trucks. Small-caliber bullets ricocheted off the bumper and tailgate.

"Follow me, but I need to put some distance between us. Watch for a left turn ahead!" shouted Major as he sped in front of Duncan.

Duncan looked in the rearview mirror and saw the much faster dirt bikes close on them. If they were gonna turn, he'd need to give them some space to do it. He let off the gas to let Major pull ahead fifty yards.

"Sook, pull the charging handle and release the safety like I showed you."

She quickly complied and didn't wait for his next instruction. Hanging her left shoulder and arm out the truck's passenger window, she methodically fired several rounds at the lead bike, whose rider immediately responded by hitting the brakes.

Duncan smiled and nodded at both Sook's taking care of business and the rider's obvious show of fear. They didn't have their heart in this and certainly weren't prepared to risk their lives during the attack.

Two of the other riders seemed unfazed, however. Shots rang out once again as the riders fired handguns in their direction. One of their rounds found a target. Barely missing the diesel fuel tank behind the seat, a single round found the glass window in the backseat of the pickup, shattering it from end to end and sending small pieces of safety glass throughout the cab. Sook shrieked, then got angry and sent six rounds in the bikers' direction.

"Hold on!" shouted Duncan as he jammed on the brakes, sending Sook backward toward the dashboard with a thud.

His hard left to keep up with Major threw Sook around the cab some more, but she kept control of her rifle. The tail end of the truck swerved a little in the loose gravel, and the top-heavy diesel tank tested its straps, but they held.

As he accelerated toward the Knott Farmers Co-op, he realized he'd lost sight of his father and Preacher. It was impossible for them to speed that far ahead, Duncan thought to himself. The whine of the motorcycles reminded him that there was no time to think. *Just do!*

He sailed past the steel sheds, which were usually filled with seed and fertilizer. The dirt bikes were gaining on him.

"Should I shoot them?" asked Sook, yelling over the sound of the wind blowing through the cab.

Before Duncan could answer, Major and Preacher ran from behind a grain truck into the middle of the road behind him. Standing shoulder to shoulder, they opened fire on the approaching motorcycles. The attackers never had a chance.

Their attempts to stop their progress on the gravel road caused three of the men to lose control and slide past Duncan's allies. Major and Preacher remained focus on the greater threat—the two men who kept their heads and control of their dirt bikes.

They ducked, attempting to make their target smaller, but they were no match for the deadly aim of the shooters they faced. Hit center mass in the chest, their bodies were elevated into the air, riddled with bullets. Blood flew in all directions as gravity brought them back to earth to a certain death, cracking their skulls if the bullets hadn't done the job of killing them already.

In unison, Major and Preacher turned and shot the three other cyclists, who rolled to a stop on the road, pinned under their bikes, with bones and bodies disfigured. Apparently, there was no need to interrogate them as to their intentions because a few well-placed shots to their heads brought the assault to an end.

Duncan exhaled as he brushed the broken glass off the front seat and onto the floorboard of the truck. He looked over at Sook, who provided him a calm smile. She returned his rifle. Duncan carefully picked glass out of her hair and wiped a smudge of blood off her cheek where a piece had grazed her.

He could no longer act surprised and amazed at her calmness in the face of danger. He'd come to expect it and could only assume she was brought up to be prepared for situations like this one.

Major and Preacher approached the truck. Major opened the door for Sook and helped her out. She immediately gave him a hug and then leaned back to hold her hand high. Sook had learned to appreciate the meaning of a high five—a job well done.

"Nice shooting, guys," said the seasoned operative. Duncan was patting Preacher on the back as they walked back toward the dead bodies.

"Idiots," was the only response Major could muster. He looked around the co-op. "Seems pretty deserted."

"Like everything else," added Preacher. "You reckon there's anything here we could use?"

Major looked around and started walking toward the main office. "Since we're here, we might as well take a look. I could use some ammonium nitrate."

Preacher started to laugh. "For fertilizer, or are you plannin' on makin' bombs, boss?"

"Yeah, maybe a little of both."

The two guys walked off, and Duncan looked at the five dead bodies in the road.

"Whadya want to do with these?" he asked, pointing toward the mangled bodies.

"Leave 'em, son," replied Major without stopping or turning around. "Buzzards gotta eat too, you know."

CHAPTER 38

January 8
The Red River
North Texas

President Burnett, Vice President Gregg, and Adjutant General Deur left Austin early that morning to take a tour of the Red River, which created the border between Texas and Oklahoma, and then a short portion of Arkansas. The view from the sky was surreal.

On the Texas side of the river, patches of snow dotted the landscape, which consisted of fields full of green but dormant grasses, stands of trees, and lakes filled with water from the melting snow.

On the Oklahoma side were the tent cities filled with masses of humanity that had been accumulating there for nearly two months. As their Piasecki X-49 SpeedHawk helicopter flew overhead, they drew little attention from the weak and diseased refugees. Rarely did one of the poor souls look skyward, much less provide a wave or a gesture.

Farther away from the water's edge where they had gathered, plumes of smoke rose into the air from the funeral pyres created for the deceased. From their altitude, it was difficult to determine if a body lying on the ground was sleeping or dead.

The inhumanity of it all tugged at the president's heartstrings. Mile after mile, the scene was the same. From Wichita Falls to Denison to Texarkana, where they turned south toward the Gulf of Mexico. A humanitarian crisis of epic proportions was on full display.

Yet in President Burnett's mind, it was beyond her control. Those suffering below her belonged to America and, thus, were another president's problem. She didn't know how she'd be judged in American history books someday, but in Texas, she firmly believed Texans would understand her motives and thought processes.

"The areas along the Red River are firmly under control," said Deur as the trip continued. "The border situation is more complicated along Louisiana."

"What's the situation along Shreveport following the nuclear detonation?" asked Vice President Gregg. "Have the prevailing winds kept the radiation from encroaching onto Texas soil?"

"Yes, and based upon our team's calculations, the nuclear fallout is no longer an issue," replied Deur. "With the cooperation of the Louisiana governor, we created a medical zone at our mutual border. The medical supplies obtained from the CDC stockpile in Dallas, used by our emergency medical teams, were able to treat many thousands of Shreveport area residents to protect them from the harmful effects of radiation poisoning."

President Burnett pressed her face against the window and looked beyond Shreveport where Barksdale AFB was once located. A crater could be seen where Interstate 20 crossed the Red River into the city. A massive radiation-filled lake had been created, temporarily halting the flow of water southward. The environmental impact of the nuclear bomb striking the center of the Red River would last decades.

"The governor has expressed his thanks many times for our efforts in helping his citizens," said the president. "Here's some interesting news, which is strictly confidential, of course. Louisiana, upset with Washington's lack of assistance to their state, is considering leaving the United States via their own secession movement. In fact, they've made overtures to me about joining us."

"Really?" asked Gregg.

"Yes, Monty," replied the president. "In fact, there is a movement from several other states including Mississippi, Alabama, Georgia, and Florida to secede as well. They've contemplated forming their own country, but Louisiana has suggested they join us."

"I don't know how Texans would feel about that," suggested Gregg. "Politics would play a big factor in it. You might create an usversus-them mentality if you expanded your territory to the east."

"Oh, trust me, I've considered that, Monty. However, consider this. If we controlled Louisiana, we'd control virtually all the oil refineries in North America. Plus, the mouth of the Mississippi River empties into the Gulf at New Orleans. All riverboat transportation from the American Midwest would have to cross our territory. We could command quite the transportation and energy juggernaut."

Gregg shrugged as he looked toward the ground and saw the refugees stacked up against the double-fenced rows as they approached the Sabine National Forest. "That's more border to control, as well," he mumbled.

Deur interjected his thoughts. "Easier, actually. Our eastern boundary would be the Mississippi River. That's much easier to protect than what you see below us. I mean, it's doable."

"I don't know," Gregg continued to question the consideration of the proposal, if it even came to fruition. "Look at those fences. They're bending. My fear is an orchestrated effort, an attack of some kind, that could blow them wide open. We need to assign more troops to this eastern border."

"I agree, which is why I scheduled this flight with both of you," started Deur. "I'm going to redeploy our resources to border control, especially along the east side. The Red River is secured, as is the area bordering Mexico all the way to El Paso."

"What about West Texas and the Panhandle?" asked the president.

"We pulled our units out of Lubbock a month ago and sent them into Amarillo to protect the Panhandle," replied Deur. "Unfortunately, the city of Lubbock suffered, as our own turned on one another when the security forces pulled out."

"What are you doing about that?" asked Gregg.

"We're establishing a quick reaction force in Lubbock, headed up by Major Armstrong's son if he accepts the offer. He's a decorated vet with extensive training in this area."

Gregg gulped and then asked, "He hasn't accepted the position?"

"Not yet," replied Deur. "I've heard that he's been through a difficult time as he returned to the States and then back to the family ranch. We didn't want to push him."

President Burnett spoke up. "We need all Texans to stand strong and step up when they're needed. It's gonna get worse before it gets better. Should I call the young man into Austin to discuss it with him personally?"

"No, ma'am, not yet," cautioned Deur. "Let the offer ride for now. There are other pot sweeteners that we can offer, if necessary, to induce him to take the job."

"Okay, I've seen enough," said the president. "Take us back to Austin."

Deur gave instructions to the pilot and the SpeedHawk chopper raced across The Woodlands north of Houston back toward Austin.

President Burnett leaned back in her seat and closed her eyes. Big changes were in store for Texas, and she needed to rally the people behind her.

"Gentlemen, I need to address the nation. We'll call it my first State of the Union address. I'll give the speech to a joint session of Congress. We'll broadcast it over the radio networks and repeater towers across the country. It'll be unifying, uplifting, and act as a call to action for everyone to do their part."

"I believe that's a great idea, Marion," started Gregg. "We need everyone to pull together until the first of February when our food deliveries can make it into the Port of Houston. The country could use a boost, in my opinion."

"Thanks, Monty. Say, weren't you going to take some time off?"

"Yes. With your permission, I'd like to take a week at my ranch sometime after our address."

"Absolutely, Monty. I understand your predicament. Listen, I work from home, so it's easy for me to find a place to relax. You have a wife that needs you. Spend some time. Reenergize your mind and body. We'll all need it for the final stretch."

Gregg smile and nodded. He appeared tired. "My wife enjoys riding horses at the crack of dawn. It's been years for me, but I suppose now that I'm back in Texas, I should see if this old war horse can still ride without gettin' bucked off."

CHAPTER 39

January 8
Lubbock, Texas

The warming weather was welcomed by Holloway and his men as they entered Lubbock piled into three vehicles. He'd left seven men and a top lieutenant behind to guard their new stronghold in Patricia. He and a dozen men brought the least useful cars into the city with an eye on trading up. High on their list were four-door SUVs and pickups, preferably full of gas. It was a shopping trip where the only currency traded was bullets.

Before they began their quest to enhance their fleet, he wanted to identify the electricity substations that would be attacked when the time was right. According to the now-deceased engineer at the ERCOT station in Wink, the relationship between Lubbock Power & Light, LP&L, and ERCOT was complex. So complicated, in fact, that Holloway had considered keeping the smart guy as a hostage just so he could explain it again, if necessary.

However, the map the man had provided, coupled with Holloway retaining what he'd learned rather than getting distracted by the young girl, helped him with the primary task at hand—preparation for the collapse of the Texas power grid.

LP&L was owned by the City of Lubbock and initially integrated with the Eastern Interconnection power grid. Through advance planning, LP&L had reciprocal agreements with ERCOT to share electricity to help each other with peak power requirements. The load and transmission network was integrated into ERCOT's, which enabled Lubbock to draw power from ERCOT in the event of an outage within the Eastern Interconnection.

To accomplish this, LP&L built three power generation and transmission facilities around the city. The locations were identified as North, located north of the city; Wadsworth, located east of the city; and New Oliver, located to the south.

Holloway and his teams spent the first part of the morning locating the three power-generating stations. When the coordinated attacks on the Texas grid began, his team would have three targets, whereas the other Lightning Death Squads would have just one. After surveilling the last power plant, the consensus of the men was they'd need explosives or an additional rocket-propelled grenade launcher for the three Type 69 RPGs they'd taken from Lee's men. He pledged to give that some more thought. They moved on to the next order of business, which was locating and assessing an assault on the National Guard Armory.

Holloway and his men's capabilities couldn't be placed into a single box. They were adept at roadside hijackings, as they'd proven in Wickett with the military convoy. They were highly successful in their raid on the Roswell National Guard Armory. The taking of the whole town of Patricia, albeit an empty one, gave Holloway the confidence he needed as they began their raids of Lubbock.

They stopped at a convenience store, refueled their cars, and picked up a few things, including a map, an old *Homes Real Estate Guide*, and an *Auto Trader* magazine. They thanked the sole salesclerk and his woefully outmatched armed guard, shot them both in the head, and then left.

As they made their way into Lubbock to the Army National Guard facility, Holloway devised a one-stop shopping plan that would minimize their exposure while in the city and accomplish their purpose.

Holloway took his eyes off the map for a moment and immediately ordered his driver to stop. As they rounded a bend in the road, the airport came into view, as did dozens of military vehicles pulling into the back side of the National Guard property.

"This is not going to work, boys," said Holloway as he gestured with his hand for the driver to pull ahead. "Take the first left up here on MLK and just keep driving south. We only attack soft targets, and there's nothing soft about what I see in front of us."

They drove a few miles away from the airport, and when they came upon South Loop 289, Holloway pointed his driver in the direction of the west on-ramp.

"Where to?" the driver asked.

Holloway folded the *Auto Trader* magazine open and pointed to an advertisement for Pollard Friendly Ford. "Their ad says they've got over fifty crew cabs on the lot. I can't think of a better vehicle, can you, guys?"

"Four-door pickups?" asked one of the men in the backseat.

"You bet," replied Holloway. "Including one of those Texas-sized King Ranch trucks for yours truly."

"Do you think they'll be open? Look around, this place looks a little like South Central LA except these dudes are mostly Anglos."

Holloway patted his M16 and grinned. "This rifle guarantees us private shopping and zero-down, zero-percent financing. Right?"

The three-car caravan turned off the highway, circled under the overpass, and eased past the Valero gas station, which had been closed down. The windows were broken out, and the small gas station had been looted. Adjacent to the Valero was Pollard Ford, and Holloway immediately grinned as he saw evidence that the advertisement didn't lie.

There were rows upon rows of shiny new Ford trucks facing forward and ready for acquisition. The dealership's lot was surrounded by heavy-duty chain to discourage anyone from driving onto the property, not that Holloway intended to.

Vehicular traffic was practically nonexistent, and only a few pedestrians milled about. The *new homeless*, as Holloway called them, who traveled from one closed business to another. Although the new homeless were not truly homeless, as they most likely lived in nearby Lakeridge Country Club or the prestigious Reserve at Ravenwood. They were dressed nicely in their Sheplers western wear and Tony Lama boots. Even the red Target shopping carts they pushed gave them an air of superiority over their truly homeless counterparts, who opted for the smaller Dollar General models. Hungry and desperate was a common thread the homeless, new and old, shared.

One thing was certain, nobody was in the market for a ridiculously priced sixty-nine-thousand-dollar pickup truck, except Holloway, of course.

They spent thirty minutes watching for a security guard to patrol the perimeter of the car dealership. A single guard, wearing his Sentry Associates uniform, drove between the rows of vehicles in an E-Z-GO golf cart. He only appeared once before disappearing to the rear of the building near the repair shop.

Holloway dispatched his men one at a time to take up positions around the building. He donned an eye patch, which he rarely used except on those rare occasions he needed to look respectable. He topped off his façade with a cowboy hat found in the home in Patricia that he'd taken for his own.

Once the men were in place, Holloway approached the plate-glass doors at the front entrance of Pollard Ford. He cupped his eye and looked through the windows into the showroom. There was no movement of any kind.

He pounded on the door, hoping to get someone's attention. If they opened the door, his task would be made easier and more sly. He'd slit the throat of the unsuspecting fool who gave him access.

Nobody responded. He pounded again, this time with a little more force. If they didn't answer, that was fine because he knew they were in the rear of the building, where a gunshot could be masked.

Again, there was no answer, so Holloway walked through an open breezeway connecting the showroom with the repair shop intake center. When he rounded the corner, he found the security guard leaning against the E-Z-GO, smoking a cigarette. Holloway quickly drew his sidearm and pointed it at the guard's head.

"Hello, friend," said Holloway in a deep voice. Holloway's imposing size caused the man to slide away and drop his cigarette. His right hand slid down toward his holster, which Holloway immediately noticed.

"Not a good idea, pal," growled Holloway as he used the barrel of his pistol to direct the man's hand away from the butt of the pistol. "Whether I kill you depends on the answer to the next two questions. Do you understand?"

"Um, yeah."

"Are you alone?"

"Yes."

"Do you have access to the keys to these trucks?"

The older man nodded his head up and down.

"Very good, Cletus," said Holloway.

"But my name isn't—" stammered the old guy.

"Cletus! I don't care what your name is, old man. You're Cletus today, got it!"

The old man nodded his head up and down vigorously, then got weak in the knees.

"Stand up!" shouted Holloway, and the old man regained his composure. Holloway lifted his right arm and circled his hand in the air. His operatives would pass the message down the line and be by his side in minutes. "Let's go, Cletus. Open up for business, and we'll get this over with quickly, fair enough?"

Once his men were inside the dealership, Holloway located the lockbox that contained the keys to the new trucks. He had twelve men with him, and he planned on leaving with twelve new trucks. He sent two guys onto the lot to identify the dealer stock numbers for the trucks located in the inner row adjacent to the building. He also instructed them to get the number for the King Ranch special edition in gold that was parked next to the Texas flag.

He devised a risky plan, which could work as long as the local law enforcement had more important things to do than investigate missing vehicles from a car lot. Holloway would pull the truck closest to the street over the sidewalk and onto the service road. The other eleven men would follow him in new trucks.

Because they were only a few miles from the outskirts of town, they would park this first *purchase order*, as Holloway called it, and then pile into one truck and immediately make another run until they'd exhausted their window of opportunity. To expedite matters, they matched the keys with the vehicles to take on subsequent runs.

Upon their return, it was simply a matter of jumping out of the back, choosing a truck, and heading out towards the Woodrow neighborhood where the other vehicles were stashed.

Holloway knew that this might be the most important aspect of the preinvasion planning to assist Lee and his commandos. By obtaining several dozen vehicles for his commandos' use, they could move into position on the western border and move swiftly from the chaos they created.

"I think we're ready," said his lieutenant as the men gathered around. "Each guy has a truck assigned, and the backups are already identified too."

"Good work, gentlemen," Holloway said with a smile. He accepted the keys to his new truck and began to walk toward the front door.

His lieutenant called after him, "Whadya want me to do with the old guy?"

"Take him in a back office and kill him," replied Holloway.

"Hey, I thought you said you wouldn't kill me!"

Holloway laughed. "I said I wouldn't. I never said he wouldn't. Sorry, Cletus."

CHAPTER 40

January 9
Armstrong Ranch
Borden County, Texas

The more hospitable weather enabled the members of the Armstrong Ranch to incorporate hunting into their weekly routine. Although the frequent trips into Lubbock had greatly increased their available meat supply, the Cryovac packaging enabled them to store the meat in favor of other readily available sources. Lucy and Major were beginning to think long term now as the prospects of food supplies dwindled and the threat of cattle confiscations loomed large.

For the first hunt, Cooper and Riley led a group that consisted of Duncan, Palmer, and Sook. Each of them held the reins of a horse to carry their kills out of the valley on the east side of the ranch, where they'd hunt for the day.

They made their way past their shooting range and into the woods adjacent to Lake J. B. Thomas. Once known for its deer hunting, the population had been decimated by a recent outbreak of epizootic hemorrhagic disease, which was transmitted by small flies.

"How did it happen?" asked Duncan as they ambled along toward the flat ground ahead.

Cooper provided an explanation. "Landowners along the lake would mow down their crop fields at the end of the growing season so the deer would come out into the fields. This past year, they noticed the deer didn't come out as usual, and some of the guys began walking through the woods that border our property and the small farms. They found dozens of them lying dead throughout the woods."

"Flies carried the disease," added Palmer.

"Flies, midges, and mites," said Riley, who explained further. "Hundreds of deer were killed off in our area alone. When Texas Parks and Wildlife were notified, they sent a whole team out here to capture the deer and treat them before they died. They relocated them to other parts of the state where the disease hadn't shown up yet. Any deer that they missed died."

"Very sad," said Sook.

"Well, the good news is the disease does have an expiration date—the first frost," said Cooper. "The midges, or no-see-ums, as we call them, can't survive the freezing temperatures. The plan was to repopulate the woods with deer this spring, but I'm thinkin' that's not gonna happen."

They rode along as the group approached the trails that entered the woods. Ordinarily, they could hear four-wheelers running the trails or along the edge of the lake. Today, only the occasional red-tail hawk could be heard searching the ground for food. Unlike most birds, many raptors, including red-tails, did not migrate during the winter months. They didn't necessarily stay in the same nest from year to year, but these woods appeared to be one of their favorite habitats.

Riley changed the conversation. "After deer huntin' season, we'd turn our attention to wild pigs. Especially in cold weather."

"Why in the cold?" asked Sook.

"The cold weather causes the hogs to eat earlier in the day and consume more food," started Riley in response. He was the most experienced hunter of the Armstrong siblings. "That exposes them longer because they come out to forage earlier and more often, giving us hunters a better chance."

"Here's another thing," added Palmer. "Most wild hogs breed in the spring or fall. They carry their baby pigs for just under four months, which means a lot of young pigs are weaned and competing with the older hogs for food. The competition is stiff, and the hogs tend to focus on food rather than safety."

"And we don't have to quickly return to the ranch with our kill," said Riley. "The meat won't spoil as fast in this cold weather."

"Whoa," said Cooper as he brought his horse to a stop. "Let's tie off here and enter the woods at this point. If we follow these trails in, the underbrush gets thicker and heavier as we get closer to the muddy areas along the lake. The melting snow gives them soft ground to root around, but the dead brush in the winter gives us a longer line of sight."

They secured their horses outside the perimeter of the woods and then divided into teams. Duncan and Sook would take the trail thirty yards toward the canyon wall. Cooper and Palmer would move farther east, which was closer to the lake. Riley would take the most difficult trail, *right up the gut*, as he called it. This trail was more overgrown, but it was most likely to have nests, which would include young pigs. Riley once said if you think a mama grizzly is ferocious, you've never walked headfirst into a feral pig protecting her young.

They were all making their way into the woods when all of a sudden gunfire could be heard, and it wasn't coming from their rifles.

CHAPTER 41

January 9
The Reinecke – Slaughter Outpost
South side of the Armstrong Ranch
Borden County, Texas

"Where's that coming from?" asked Riley as he backed out of the woods. Duncan and Sook were running in his direction, holding their rifles with both hands, with eyes darting in all directions. Cooper arrived by Riley's side first.

"That's coming from the other side of the ravine," said Cooper, who pointed toward the southwest.

"Coop, are you sure?" asked Duncan. "Gunshots can play tricks in an open landscape like this."

"I'm pretty sure, Duncan," replied Cooper as gunshots rang out again.

"We gotta go, y'all," urged Riley.

"Okay, I'll follow Coop's lead," said Duncan. "Riley, come with us too. Girls, can you get the extra horses back to the ranch?"

"We wanna come with you guys," protested Palmer, speaking on behalf of Sook, who nodded in agreement.

Duncan walked up to them and explained, "We need the horses protected, and if we're wrong about the location of the gunshots, we need you guys to help defend the ranch until we can get over there."

Several more gunshots could be heard, which prompted Palmer to agree. "Okay, come on, Sook."

"Saddle up, boys," shouted Cooper, who was the first to mount his horse and tear off toward the ravine. He took a more southerly route, which took them past the shooting range and around the back side of the Reinecke Operating Unit.

"Hurry, Coop," yelled Duncan. "I think two of the Slaughters' ranch hands are working our perimeter security today. It'll be Chris and the women against whatever's attacking them."

"Hah!" shouted Cooper as he dug his heels into the side of his horse. His horse immediately responded, breaking into a gallop and streaking up the trail until the oil and gas wells came into view.

When all three guys arrived at the top of the plateau, the Reinecke complex came into full view. Slaughter was pinned down behind his truck in front of the caretaker's house. He was being fired upon by two sets of shooters. Two men were hidden by a small pickup, and another couple were standing behind a broken-down International Harvester tractor closer to the house.

Duncan took the lead and slowed his horse so he wouldn't attract the attention of the shooters in front of them. They made their way behind a pumping well, which was inoperable, but provided some cover.

"Okay, guys, it's time to go hunting," said Duncan as he dismounted and tied his horse off.

"Here comes the cavalry," announced Riley as he lowered himself to the ground and pointed behind the Slaughters' house.

Several riders were coming from the direction of the Armstrong Ranch. They were still too far away to identify.

"I see them, but I don't like their angle," said Duncan. "If they come around the house, they'll be sittin' ducks. We gotta take these guys out first."

Duncan moved behind the concrete base of the well and found a comfortable place to rest his .308 rifle. He adjusted his scope. Cooper and Riley positioned themselves on either side of their older brother. They all studied the targets through their scopes.

"I'll take the two behind the tractor," said Duncan.

"Gimme tall and lanky in the plaid shirt," said Cooper before he chuckled. "That leaves the fat one for Riley. He's the biggest target."

"Very funny, Coop," grumbled Riley. He adjusted his scope and brought the target into his crosshairs. "Shoot to kill?"

"That's what Daddy said," replied Cooper.

"Ready, guys?" asked Duncan.

"Yeah," the guys replied in unison.

"I'll count it down," said Duncan. "Three, two, one."

The staccato sound of the gunshots might have tricked someone's mind into thinking a machine gun was firing upon them.

Low-powered handguns like a twenty-two were considered subsonic, meaning they had muzzle velocities less than the speed of sound. Rifle cartridges were considered supersonic, which allowed them to travel a substantial distance before being detected through the rifle's report.

This explained why the three male targets were struck before the fourth attacker, a woman, attempted to react, not that it mattered. Duncan was capable of pulling the lever and chambering a round before her mind could process what was happening to her.

He never hesitated to shoot under some sense of valor that required him to give this woman a break. She hadn't offered to give the Slaughters a break when she shot at Chris and his wife, together with the two other women inside their home.

Like the first round that had penetrated her friend's skull, blasting through and through, followed by his brain matter, she received a single shot from Duncan's rifle, quickly bringing an end to the attack.

The guys mounted their horses and rode into the Reinecke complex. Preacher and three men had arrived on the scene just in time to see the shooting skills of Duncan and his younger brothers. He instructed the men to confiscate the weapons and dispose of the dead bodies in the middle of the nearby field.

After the emotions died down, Mr. and Mrs. Slaughter thanked the guys for coming to their rescue. Slaughter was about to run out of ammunition, and the women were not very good shots. Their only real benefit was to lay down cover fire, and they weren't entirely comfortable with that.

Duncan used this as a teachable moment. "Listen, just because you have a weapon doesn't mean it will be able to protect you when the time comes. You guys have got to train. We have .22-caliber rifles we can give you with thousands of rounds to practice with. All three of us are teaching Sook how to shoot as well. You're always welcome to join us."

They promised to take him up on the offer and thanked him once again. Just as the Armstrong contingent were about to mount their horses and head back to the ranch, more gunfire could be heard.

"Now what?" asked Cooper.

"That's comin' from the ranch! Let's go!" shouted Riley.

CHAPTER 42

January 9
The Armstrong Ranch
Borden County, Texas

Palmer and Sook had almost arrived at the ranch house when the gunshots could be heard again, but this time it was toward the river. Palmer hesitated for a moment and looked around the barns. Nobody was here. She glanced at the ranch house, and the gunfire hadn't raised her mother's attention. Then she realized the shots were coming from the barnyard.

"Sook, let's go. Momma's in trouble!"

Sook dropped the lead ropes, which strung together two of the horses, and dug her heels in to chase Palmer toward the barnyard. The two women lowered themselves behind their horses' necks to reduce the wind drag as they kicked up soft dirt alongside the driveway.

More gunshots were heard, and Sook spontaneously shouted, "Hurry!"

Palmer smiled and urged her horse to go faster. She had her sister by her side.

When they arrived, Palmer saw her mother's horse tied to a fence post alongside her father's. Across the chicken coop in the other barn appeared to be three men, who periodically stuck their heads through a window and shot toward her parents.

Palmer was incensed. She pulled the horse up well short of coming into view of the shooters in the barn, whose focus remained on her parents.

"Come on, Sook," whispered Palmer as she slid off the side of her horse, keeping it between her and the barn. Sook dismounted and retrieved her rifle from its scabbard. She had shown remarkable progress up to a range of two hundred yards although she had a tendency to squeeze the trigger a little too hard.

What Palmer had in mind was much closer combat. "Sook, do you see those steel water troughs by the fence?"

"Yes," replied Sook as her eyes gauged the distance from their position to the troughs, and over toward the barn.

The two of them instinctively ducked as one of the attackers leaned out the barn window and fired wildly toward her parents. She noticed neither of them returned fire.

"I think my parents are low on ammo, so they're biding their time until help arrives," said Palmer.

"We are the help," said Sook succinctly with a look of determination on her face.

Palmer nodded and smiled. "This is the plan. I'll cover you while you run to the water trough. Lie on the ground and stay hidden but watch for the shooters to stick their bodies out the window. Okay?"

"I can shoot them."

"Yes, but wait until I'm in position." She and Palmer crouched down beneath the bellies of the horses. She pointed toward the back of the barn. "When I get into position, I will put my thumb up like this."

"Okay, thumbs-up."

"Exactly. The next time they stick their body out the window, shoot them. If you miss, that's okay. Just keep firing into the side of the barn. It will distract them."

Palmer handed Sook her rifle. "Take this. When you are out of bullets, use my gun."

"What will you do?"

Palmer patted her holster. "I have everything I need right here. Sook, remember, keep them busy and focused on you. I'll take care of the rest."

Sook nodded, and after taking a cautionary look toward the barn, she ran across the open area in a crouch while carrying both rifles and then quickly crawled on all fours behind the galvanized trough. Palmer felt comfortable sending her behind the water container. The ballistic protection was excellent, and the shooters didn't have a good line of fire at her. If they attempted to lean out the window to improve their angle, either her father or mother would have a clean shot.

Palmer pulled her sidearm, readied it for firing, and ran in a circuitous route toward the back entrance of the barn. When she arrived at the corner, she was relieved to see the double doors were pulled open.

She took a moment to catch her breath, and then she gave Sook the thumbs-up. Now it was up to the marauders to make their move.

Palmer eased up to the open door, crouched to the ground, and slowly peeked around the corner of the door. There were three men at the far end of the barn. One was sitting on the ground clutching his shoulder, which was bleeding so badly his shirt was completely covered with blood. His head dipped up and down as he approached unconsciousness. The other two men hid beside the open barn windows with their rifles ready. They each had a knothole in a barn board to watch for movement from her parents.

Palmer was only twenty yards away from the men, an easy shot on the range. However, as Duncan had taught her, a real gun battle is much different than firing upon stationary targets. If she was going to end this standoff, she'd need to close on the shooters as soon as they were distracted. She readied her sidearm and watched.

A minute passed, during which time she wondered why they didn't have additional backup. *Did everyone go to protect the Slaughters, leaving my parents alone to fight off three against two?*

She put that out of her mind and studied the men's body movements. The injured man had passed out or died and fallen over into the hay. The man on the left seemed to have an itchy trigger finger. He readied his rifle and quickly made his move to the open window while his partner watched.

Palmer trusted Sook and immediately sprinted toward the men. She was three or four strides in when Sook opened fire on the man.

She missed, but she followed instructions. She immediately began to pepper the barn with round after round. It was all the distraction Palmer needed.

As the men cowered behind the bales of hay, Palmer shot the first man once in the chest, then she quickly adjusted her aim and took down the other man with a shot to the chest. As she learned from her training, two subsequent head shots were necessary to finish the job. Finally, as she continued to sprint toward her targets, she fired two rounds into the body of the previously injured man who appeared dead from his wounds.

"Clear! Clear! Momma! Daddy! It's over!"

Both of her parents came running around the side of the barn and joined Sook as they rushed toward Palmer. Palmer engaged her safety and holstered her weapon. She opened the side door of the barn to let the others in.

Because he was a father, Major ran past her with his weapon ready. He looked around the barn, including the hayloft above the three dead men. Then he came back to join the celebration.

"Wow, look at you two!" exclaimed Lucy as she joined the girls in nervous exuberance. "Daddy and I could see through the cracks in the barn board as you ran to the back of the barn. We thought about shooting but didn't, knowin' you had a plan."

"The plan worked," said Sook, who immediately earned a hug from Lucy.

"It sure did, dear," said Lucy. "Palmer, are you okay?" Lucy showed genuine concern toward her daughter who'd just killed two men.

"Look," said Palmer, who ignored her mother's question and pointed toward the ranch house. "Here come the boys. There was a shoot-out at the Slaughters' place. Daddy, we live in a dangerous neighborhood, it seems."

"Palmer, our neighborhood has gone to the dogs," he said with a laugh, not realizing how true that statement was.

CHAPTER 43

January 10
Klondike High School
Near Patricia, Texas

Holloway fired up his shiny new King Ranch Ford pickup and picked up his lieutenants for the short trip over to the local high school. Klondike High taught kids from two adjacent counties, Martin and Dawson, which were just to the west of Borden County and the Armstrong Ranch. In West Texas, the high prairie stretched as far as the eye could see, with only an occasional residence or ranch on the horizon. A high school the size of Klondike stood out and made a much bigger footprint than the small dwellings in a town like Patricia.

A plan was developing in Holloway's mind, which could provide for the entry of the North Korean commandos and provide them a base of operations to conduct their activities. As a country, Texas was larger than France and twice as large as Germany or Japan. This would only be the first stop for the commandos, but Klondike High could handle the influx of hundreds of Korean commandos before they were dispatched around the state.

The night before, his men had cleared the facility and stationed two roving patrols to ensure no interlopers made a move on their new headquarters. Holloway's men had not seen another living soul in the area since their arrival, but the patrols would give his men a sense of purpose while they waited for their comrades.

Holloway had to check himself as well. He was anxious to begin his raids into Lubbock. During their four trips back to the Ford dealership, in which they secured over forty trucks for the DPRK commandos, they'd taken different routes through the wealthy southwest neighborhoods of Lubbock. He salivated over the half-million-dollar homes, properties that would sell for a couple of million in Los Angeles. He'd already begun planning his raids into Lubbock, then Midland-Odessa, and maybe as far north as Amarillo.

But he had to be patient so he didn't awaken the sleeping giants to his south—the former United States military installations at Fort Bliss and Fort Hood.

As he walked through the high school's buildings and pointed out things that might help their future endeavors, his mind wandered to the next phase of their operations. First, he needed to place a satellite phone call to Lee. The two hadn't spoken in days, and Lee appeared ready to make his move. He'd lost all communications with Pyongyang, or wherever Dear Leader was hiding out. They were on their own, and that suited Holloway just fine. He'd earned his way into Lee's good graces, and his next move would allow him to write his own meal ticket.

The current bunch of North Korean military leaders proclaimed themselves to be experts at war despite the fact they'd never really fought one. This was a nation that spent every waking moment in a defensive posture but prepared to attack one particular objective—South Korea. Both nations wanted reunification, the argument was over which side would control the government. Their battle, if it was in fact under way after the nuclear strikes, portended to be a brutal affair with an incredible number of lives lost on both sides.

Holloway's approach to the attack upon Texas would be different. If he were advising Lee, he would remind the new general that he was woefully outgunned. They would have to focus on their objective, which was to take down the power grid, send the new nation into chaos, and then sneak out the back door without getting killed. Knowing Lee, there would be secondary objectives on the new general's mind, none of which appealed to Holloway.

He wandered into a geography classroom and studied a large map of the world that hung on the wall next to a chalkboard. Scrawled across the board were written the words *Happy Thanksgiving*. It was a reminder to Holloway that the blackout of the power grid had taken place nearly eight weeks ago. Coupled with the nuclear attacks, he wondered how many millions of North Americans had died as a result.

As he continued his walk through the main classroom building toward the administration offices, he realized Lee had probably lost sight of the fact that the mighty million-man army wasn't coming. If the primary objective was to overtake America in order to plant the flags of Iran and North Korea on American soil, then they were going to need some help.

If the plan was to further bloody the nose of their sworn enemy, then they could certainly do that, but then what? This was what puzzled Holloway about those who fought ideological battles and wars. What did the conqueror gain? Bragging rights? Smug indignation? The ability to say I brought a great nation or person down?

Holloway liked his approach to war better—to the conqueror go the spoils. From the beginning of time, the great empires fought one another not so one emperor could sit on a taller throne than the other, but to take from the other empire, whether it be territory, gold, or the ability to enslave the conquered citizenry to do his bidding.

That was Holloway's philosophy, so the tactics, strategies, and operations he employed were focused on this singular goal.

CHAPTER 44

January 11
The Calvert Estate
6200 Georgetown Pike
McLean, Virginia

Within the secured grounds of the Central Intelligence Agency's headquarters located in the Langley neighborhood of McLean, Virginia, sits a four-story Georgian Revival home. The house, built in 1926, was the oldest structure within the CIA's complex and part of an estate that had coexisted with the CIA for seventy-five years. After the deaths of Margaret Scattergood and Florence Thomas, the two original owners of the Calvert Estate named after George Calvert, a Brit and the first Lord Baltimore of Maryland, the CIA converted the home into housing for their K-9 units. The property literally went to the dogs.

The beautiful home had fallen into disrepair and ruin due to the agency's neglect. Finally, during the Bush administration, a new head of facilities arrived at the CIA and saw the potential of the Calvert Estate. The manor home underwent a complete renovation to become a state-of-the-art conference center together with museum and reception rooms.

In addition, any CIA employee would be remiss not to include some clandestine feature to one of its facilities, and the manor home was no different. In the dark basement where the casual observer might see furnaces and dusty wooden shelves, there existed a secured room, impenetrable to curious listeners.

When Billy Yancey began any operation so dark that it was beyond the purview of the president, like the assassination of Kim

Jong-un, for example, he utilized this part of the Calvert Estate. Today, he didn't assign the task to an underling. There was no middleman to pass orders on to the operatives. Yancey wanted no witnesses.

Yancey had never met this operative although he'd been used on multiple assignments. The shooter had never failed. Yancey also wanted to meet the shooter and observe his reaction to the target. Everyone knew of each other in this industry. Some assignments might seem objectionable despite a shooter's loyalty to his country and the men who ran his operations. Yancy needed a read on this before he gave the order.

Yancey entered the room, which was dour in its furnishings compared to the opulence on display in the rooms above them. There were white walls on three sides, with the fourth wall a stone and mortar combination that was part of the home's foundation. A simple gray folding table sat in the middle of the room, with a few stackable chairs scattered around the cramped space.

This room was not intended to be comfortable. If someone managed to stumble across it, they might think it was used for storage. It suited Yancey's purposes, however.

He and the shooter were the sole occupants of the room. The shooter sat quietly across the table with his hands clasped in front of his chest and his legs crossed. His black hair, two-day-old beard and chiseled jaw gave him the look of a Guess model.

According to his personnel records, he was thirty years old, five feet eleven, and only one hundred eighty pounds. His lean frame concealed its potential for strength and quickness, and its capacity to inflict death. The shooter's steely blue eyes stared at Yancey, emotionless and difficult to read. Yancey would have to connect a polygraph to the shooter in order to determine his veracity under questioning, and even then, he'd have his doubts.

Yancey returned the man's stare and chose not to say a word. He slid a file across the table and waited for the shooter to pick it up. He'd dealt with hard-core operatives in the past, but they did show some form of emotion. An imperceptible smile. A nod. Even a deep breath with a corresponding exhale.

Not this shooter. He barely moved his body as he pulled the file toward him and rested it on his leg. When he opened the folder, it was the first time he'd broken eye contact with Yancey.

He thumbed through the packet of materials, beginning with information on his target. He provided the rest of the folder a cursory glance.

Without looking up, he asked, "When?"

"Your flight will leave Atlantic Aviation at oh five hundred day after tomorrow," replied Yancey. Hyde Field was an executive airport just outside Newport News, Virginia, where the shooter lived on his sailing yacht.

"Deadline?" he asked, making eye contact with Yancey again.

"No. First opportunity would be best, however," replied Yancey. "Do you have any questions or concerns?"

"Nope. This is all I need."

Yancey reached into his jacket pockets and slid two envelopes of newly minted Texas one-hundred-dollar bills totaling twenty thousand Texas dollars across the table.

"Spending money," said Yancey.

The shooter removed a handful of the bills and studied them. The Star of Texas was imprinted on the back and a picture of Sam Houston on the front. He thumbed through the new currency and then shoved it back into the envelope.

"What else?" the shooter asked.

"That's all," said Yancey before adding, "Shoot straight."

The operative stood, tucked the folder and the money against his chest, and never responded.

CHAPTER 45

January 11
Eunice, New Mexico

Each day, Lee sent scouts to the New Mexico border with Texas to surveil troop movements and border patrol strength to establish a pattern to the military's protective measures. Not surprisingly, activity was at its lowest in the early morning hours between three a.m. and dawn, which was around six thirty a.m. A shift change occurred at eight in the morning when the manpower at the checkpoints was doubled. However, during the handoff, the patrols on the perimeters were called into the checkpoints, leaving the fences unmanned and vulnerable.

Lee traveled fifty miles to Eunice, New Mexico, where a checkpoint with very little activity was located. Using his field glasses, he studied the security as the change was made. The number of refugees huddled near this checkpoint were minimal compared to the fenced borders to the south.

On the New Mexico side of the border stood the URENCO nuclear enrichment facility. The plant had begun operations in 2010 after the first centrifuge was installed and made operational. One of the largest enrichment services of its kind in the U.S., the facility spun uranium in its natural form until it was made into the highly concentrated U-235, the main element in nuclear weapons.

Lee's commandos captured a scientist leaving the facility one evening and interrogated him. They learned the facility had been taken off-line due to the power outage and to protect its uranium supply. When power was restored to the region, the two-hundred-thousand-square-foot facility could be up and running within days.

Lee considered URENCO to be a prized acquisition for Dear Leader in the event North Korea looked to expand into the United States. Otherwise, Lee would find a way to destroy the facility, rendering it useless and an environmental disaster for years.

After spending an hour surveilling the checkpoint, Lee moved southward along gravel and dirt roads, periodically studying the refugees at the border. He was sickened at the smell of dead bodies smoldering on the funeral pyres, which could be seen every half mile or so. Lee gave credit to those pressing against the fences, begging to gain entry. Their perseverance might be rewarded at some point soon.

Lee studied the map of Texas his men had taken from the URENCO scientist's vehicle after killing the man. There were very few roads to travel, but the military transport trucks they'd obtained were capable of travel on all types of terrain. If he could get his men through the border fencing, then the transports could take the commandos deeper into Texas, where they could meet at a predetermined rally point.

He instructed his driver to return to Carlsbad Caverns, where he would put the final touches on their invasion plans. He would assign unit commanders the task of picking their men, arming them, and establishing a transportation plan. He had three days to get ready before his next scheduled conversation with Holloway, during which he planned on setting a day and time to commence their mission.

CHAPTER 46

January 12
Austin, Texas

The hastily called Texas State of the Union address drew immediate criticism from the president's political opposition. They argued there was insufficient time to coordinate their response, which they assumed would be broadcast over the Texas AM band airwaves immediately following the president's speech. When they were told a political response wasn't going to be aired, that really sent them into a tizzy.

As President Burnett entered the capitol building in Austin to address the joint session of the newly installed Congress of the Republic of Texas, she didn't know if this was going to be a fairly respectful affair, like those exhibited in Washington in years past, or a raucous shouting match, which often occurred in the United Kingdom and other politically charged nations.

Either way, she was going to stick to the script and her goal of providing a unifying, uplifting address to carry Texans until relief arrived. Her speech would focus on the accomplishments of becoming a new nation, installing a government, and protecting their borders. She would also focus on the malaise that had begun to come over Texans due to the lack of food and the uncertainty of their future. The next topic would address the issue of the refugees. It was time for her to state in no uncertain terms the reasons she'd refused their admittance. Texans would understand.

There were no television cameras allowed into the chamber on this evening. TV broadcasts were nonexistent in Texas, and the cameras would only serve to provide news footage to international networks, which had treated the Burnett administration and Texas very poorly.

After shaking hands and speaking with members of the Texas Congress seated in the gallery, President Burnett made her way to the podium.

She made her introductory remarks and spoke about the history of Texas and the great leaders who'd fought to make it strong and free. She patted herself on the back for her foresight in preparing the former state for this moment, both politically and with respect to the power grid.

With the preliminaries out of the way, President Burnett got into the meat and potatoes of her address.

"This is the first State of the Union address to be delivered to our new nation, and I don't take the fulfillment of my duty lightly. In order to discuss the details, I must first affirmatively state that the Texas spirit has never been higher than it is today, despite strains placed upon us. I am pleased to say that Texas is in fact free, and Texas is stronger than ever!"

The president knew this line in her speech would generate the most animus from her political opponents. Despite the overwhelming cheers and applause from her political allies, she could hear the catcalls and boos from the other side of the aisle. This was planned, as she intended to paint them as obstructionist and anti-secession. If they disagreed with the majority of Texans, she'd be glad to show them the door back to the United States.

"The vast majority of Texans have never been more deeply determined to face the solemn tasks before them. The response of my fellow Texans to this catastrophe has been instantaneous, and it will be sustained as long as we assure our families and neighbors of security, survival, and a better future.

"I've traveled across the country and seen the efforts you've made to overcome these trying times. I have watched you face reality, help one another, and be a good steward of our limited assets until we can establish trading partners to restock our food supplies. Together, my fellow Texans, we will withstand this crisis, band together in a spirit of unity as winter settles in, and with the coming spring, a sense of renewal will overcome our collective spirit in a manner our detractors could never imagine."

President Burnett paused once again as part of the chamber roared its approval while the other side sat with sour faces, hating every word of her speech. She suddenly wished the cameras were rolling to broadcast their discontent to the world.

"Texans may be judged by outsiders, but we understand what it takes to survive. The first step is for all Texans to come together, not just those who agree with me politically. Texans expect us to carry out our duties to preserve and protect our fledgling nation without partisanship, but rather, with a cooperation necessary to restore our well-being and to ensure the safety of our borders.

"My fellow Texans, I never expected to be a wartime president, and many of you might ask, *who are we at war with?* Let me answer that for you. We are still at war with Washington, who fights us at every turn as we attempt to feed and protect our people. We are at war with an international media, which portrays us as cold and heartless because we won't open our borders to all comers. We are at war with those who wish to enter our country and take food out of the mouths of you and your children. People who didn't plan ahead like Texans did, and now expect us to open our homes and food pantries to keep them alive.

"If history judges me to be cruel and callous for not allowing hundreds of thousands of people to flood into Texas and decimate our dwindling food supplies, I'll take the heat for that. I do believe that you, my fellow Texans, will judge me on what I did for you and your fellow citizens.

"Toward that end, I come to you tonight with a warning. We are going to enter a short period of time that will test your will and morale. Food will run short, services will be spread too thin, and based upon the masses of refugees amassed at our borders, the possibility of a breach looms large.

"When times are tougher, I will call upon you to step up for your country. Texas isn't just a place on the map, it's a spirit that resides in the hearts of our people. With everything you do and every decision you make, I call on you to remember these words—Texas strong! Texas free!"

The majority of the attendees jumped to their feet and began to chant the phrase, which had permeated President Burnett's political rallies for decades.

Texas strong! Texas free!

CHAPTER 47

January 12
The Armstrong Ranch
Borden County, Texas

"Well, that surely got the emotions stirred up," said Major before adding, "On both sides of the political equation. If her opponents voice too much in the way of political opposition, they'll appear anti-Texan."

"Daddy, you really know this politics stuff," said Riley. "Did you ever consider running for somethin'?"

"Nah, son. The politics within the Texas Rangers was enough for me. You know, it wasn't enough to be a good lawman, working hard, solving crimes, and paying your dues as you rose through the ranks. If you wanted to get to the top, there had to be a certain amount of ring kissin' of politicians."

"Did you have to kiss Marion's ring, dear?" said Lucy sarcastically as she tilted her head to the side. Major studied her body language and immediately recalled what he knew about marital politics. *Proceed with caution!*

"Well, um, naturally, anytime a statewide officeholder appeared in Lubbock, they expected to see their number one lawman and other local muckety-mucks. Plus, the Burnett family and the Armstrongs have kept close friendship ties for generations. I didn't, however, kiss the proverbial ring. Marion knew better and wouldn't expect it. Frankly, any help she gave me to rise to the top of Company C was based on respect for my accomplishments."

Lucy stuck her chin out a little bit and nodded her head. "Why do you think Marion never got married?"

Riley interrupted. "Wait, what? Our president is single?"

"That's right, son," replied Major. "Marion has always been focused on her political career, often to the detriment of the Four Sixes Ranch's operations. After I retired, that was the first time she approached me about something remotely related to ring kissing, but it was the other way around. She wanted me to oversee the Four Sixes Ranch."

"Hey, you never told me that," said Lucy, who immediately appeared to be hurt by the slight.

"Honey, I never gave it a second thought," said Major quickly as he scooted a little closer to her on the sofa. "This was years ago when Palmer and Riley were still in high school. Cooper was still too young for additional responsibilities, and Duncan was off at war and never showed an inclination for ranching."

"Speaking of which," started Duncan, who changed the subject to protect his father from an awkward conversation that he imagined wasn't quite over. "They're expecting an answer from me day after tomorrow."

"Have you heard from them?" asked Cooper.

"Yes, Captain Harris called earlier today," replied Duncan. "It was not a high-pressure call. He wanted to remind me that the colonel expected an answer and that he was available to answer any questions. I confirmed with him that he'd be my immediate superior and that my unit would operate separately from the military operations ordered by the adjutant general or the president."

"Why's that important?" asked Palmer.

"Purely selfish reasons that can never leave this room, understood?"

Everyone either nodded their head or replied yes, so Duncan continued. "I took the opportunity to speak with the guards assigned to Arnold Oil while we were in Odessa getting fuel. Granted, they were brief conversations, but their opinions were near unanimous. The fence won't hold the refugees out much longer."

"Are they going to bust through?" asked Riley.

"At some point, yes. People are dying on the other side, and they're realizing there's nothing to lose. Because I was still a civilian when I asked about this, the soldiers were hesitant to give me a straight answer."

"About what, son?" Major interrupted with a question.

"I believe they have shoot-to-kill orders, especially after the situation north of Wichita Falls. The hostage situation at Midwestern didn't help the refugees' cause either. It just provided the administration an example to instill fear into any Texans living near the borders."

"Duncan, are you saying you'd disobey the shoot-to-kill order?" asked Cooper.

"I don't know, Coop. Here's my problem. These folks are Americans, just like we were a month or so ago. Okay, so they break in, and out of desperation, they choose to loot and steal. Should our soldiers shoot them just because we *believe* they're going to loot or steal?"

"Well, they've proven they're capable," replied Cooper dryly. "The bodies are piling up around our ranch too."

"And they're Texans," interjected Riley. "These refugees will stop at nothing. What would we do if a pack of them came after our ranch?"

"We'd defend it as we have been and shoot them if they tried," replied Duncan.

Cooper stood and sat next to the fire. "Then if we believe that's the right thing to do—to protect our ten-thousand-acre ranch, wouldn't it be the right thing to do for the president to protect Texas?"

The room grew silent for a moment as they contemplated Cooper's statement. The duty to protect was all relative, whether it was your home, ranch, town, or country.

"Wow, Coop sounded just like Daddy," said Palmer. "Maybe you oughta be a politician."

"Forget it!" said Cooper as the family laughed at the suggestion.

Major turned the attention back to Duncan's reasoning for joining the TX-QRF. "Son, if the quick reaction force doesn't focus on border protection, where do you see them helping Texas the most?"

"Two places, Dad. One is to deal with the threat that Sook and I believe is coming. There are Koreans gathering out there somewhere—either in New Mexico or, heck, they could already be in Texas. I wanna focus my unit's efforts on dealing with them."

Major nodded in agreement, and then he asked, "What's the other place?"

"Right here," Duncan replied. "I plan on making my men loyal to me and what I need done. If Texas is going to battle an onslaught of refugees or North Korean operatives, I want my guys ready to step in and help defend the ranch if need be. I'll have tremendous resources at my disposal, which I will not have if I refuse the job. It's the only way I could agree to leave the ranch without the benefit of my gun and experience."

"Are you ready to give them an answer?" asked Lucy with trepidation.

"Not yet, Momma," replied Duncan. "Antonio is scheduled to make another cattle run in a couple of days. I think I'll drive into the city at the same time and meet with Captain Harris and, you know, take a look around. I'm sure he'll be trying to impress me, so it'll be the perfect time to ask for additional perks."

"I'll ride with you, son," added Major. "While you talk with Harris, I'll see what I can learn too."

"Deal."

CHAPTER 48

January 13
Perryton-Ochiltree County Airport
Perryton, Texas

The shooter looked out the porthole windows as the pilot made his final approach into Perryton, Texas, a small town located in the northernmost reaches of the Panhandle at the border with Oklahoma. He made the trip from Newport News to Texas in a Maltese-registered Dassault Falcon 50, which had been flown into the States from the air branch of the special activities division of the CIA.

The rendition aircraft, often used for the transfer of high-value prisoners from the Middle East to CIA locations around the world, had become a useful tool in the practice of sending terrorist suspects to locations that were less vigorous regarding the humane treatment of prisoners. Away from American media scrutiny, the terrorists could be influenced to give up information on others within their cell.

Perryton was chosen as his destination because of its close proximity to the Texas border. If he had been inserted deeper into the country, his flight might draw the attention of the various military installations spread around Texas. This would require a considerable drive south toward West Texas, but it would give him time to consider his mission.

As the plane taxied to a stop, he scribbled his destination on a piece of copy paper ripped from a page in the folder given to him by Yancey. He was assigned one CIA operative, who'd remained in Texas and would act as his driver, spotter, and security. The shooter was not used to working with an unknown quantity as his spotter, especially a spook. After he took the shot, he'd have to remember to watch his back.

The shooter vowed he'd treat this kill like any other, regardless of the target's history of serving his country. The man was just a target, nothing else. He would, however, become intimate with the target's routine, surroundings, and security he employed.

He would be patient and bide his time in order to achieve success. His orders did not provide a deadline, which was rare in his business. Usually, higher-ups were anxious to move along with phase two of an operation, with phase one being the kill.

He was not made privy to the big picture, nor did he care. When the opportunity presented itself, he'd squeeze the trigger. Boom, done.

Then he'd go back to his new sailboat, the *Miss Behavin'*, located in Newport News, and chill. Heck, he might even take her back up the coast to Marblehead off the Massachusetts coastline for old times' sake.

Part Four

CHAPTER 49

January 14
TX-QRF
Texas National Guard Base
Lubbock, Texas

It had been ten days since Major, Preacher, and Duncan had traveled into Lubbock to assess their slaughterhouse options. Signs of the city's collapse had begun to manifest themselves in the form of out-of-control fires, shuttered businesses, and angry mobs gathered around governmental buildings. The departure of the Texas military from assisting the local law enforcement had taken a toll on a vibrant midsize metropolitan area, which had once earned the nickname the Hub City. Lubbock was looked upon as the economic, educational, and health care hub of the South Plains, the nickname this region of the Texas Panhandle had earned.

The interstate, which ran north and south through the heart of the city, was once again closed to civilian traffic, both vehicular and those on foot. Until Duncan formally accepted the position commanding the regional quick reaction force, he would have to approach the National Guard facility like other civilians.

Early that morning, Duncan had contacted Captain Harris via the satphone to set a time to meet. Duncan had several questions and was anxious to see the facility. On the ride into town, he and Major confirmed their game plan while touring the base. Duncan wanted to feel comfortable that he'd have both the authority and resources to help Armstrong Ranch if it came under attack.

Very few vehicles traveled the streets of Lubbock that morning. Offices and businesses were closed, looted, or burned to the ground.

Evidence of the economic collapse associated with this catastrophe was everywhere.

Like the rest of North America, whose economy was driven by consumer spending, when the U.S. was beset by an event of this magnitude, the engines of trade, manufacturing, and services came to a screeching halt. The nature of the world economy was based upon spending. When the ability to earn was squashed, then spending stopped, and the vicious cycle brought the society downward to its most rudimentary levels—survival of the fittest.

The retail businesses of Lubbock went weeks without an acceptable currency in place, so they attempted to close their doors and wait for the anticipated recovery. The people of Lubbock refused to wait. They began to demand access to those goods, and when they had nothing of acceptable value to trade for them, people took more extreme measures, which necessarily included violence.

The downward spiral of society into collapse was an inevitable result as people competed with one another to obtain food. It could take months if not years for a new nation to become self-reliant. Crops didn't grow overnight. Sources of meat didn't reproduce in a short period of time. Manufacturing plants needed to be built to create the prepackaged canned goods that the citizens were accustomed to purchasing in grocery stores.

It all took time, and as a result, people died from starvation or at the hands of their fellow man—whether the lights were on or not.

"Identification, please, and state your purpose," said a guard at the entry gate to the base. Security was heavy, reflecting the increased violence in the Lubbock area. Several groups walked the sidewalks around the camp, attempting to get the attention of the roving patrols. Most asked for food while others sought information.

Major and Duncan responded and provided their identification. They were instructed to exit the truck while it was searched, and then they were patted down as well. As the process was completed, Captain Harris arrived in a Humvee. After speaking with the sentries, the Armstrongs were waved through and followed Captain Harris to the administration buildings. After they parked the vehicles, Captain

Harris was apologetic.

"Sorry about that, gentlemen," he began as the men shook hands. "Putting you on the visitors' list totally slipped my mind although you would've been scrutinized to an extent anyway. Welcome to Camp Lubbock."

"Not a problem, Captain," said Duncan. "The amount of activity here warrants the additional security, and that applies to both sides of the fences. We were in Lubbock ten days ago, and the city seems to have taken a turn for the worse."

"Sadly, that's true," said Captain Harris. "Even with Texas taking control of Fort Bliss and Fort Hood, where I'm stationed, the number of active-duty personnel and reservists is less than one hundred thousand. Texas has a lot of area to protect, especially when you consider we have to guard a border of this size. Using the regular military to control the streets of our cities wasn't feasible. Frankly, that's part of the reason for expanding the TX-QRF into our regional bases. We hope the quick reaction teams can supplement law enforcement in dealing with local issues while the Texas Army and National Guard focus on border protection."

"Makes sense," said Major as Captain Harris motioned for them to follow him inside. "Have you divided the country into regions? For example, what areas will Camp Lubbock assist?"

"That's a great place to start. This is my temporary office, until I hire a successor, of course." Captain Harris chuckled as he led them into a spacious room, which included maps, whiteboards, and television monitors.

"I assume you're referring to me," said Duncan.

"Well, I do need an answer by tomorrow, but today will suit me just fine too," said Captain Harris as he walked up to a map.

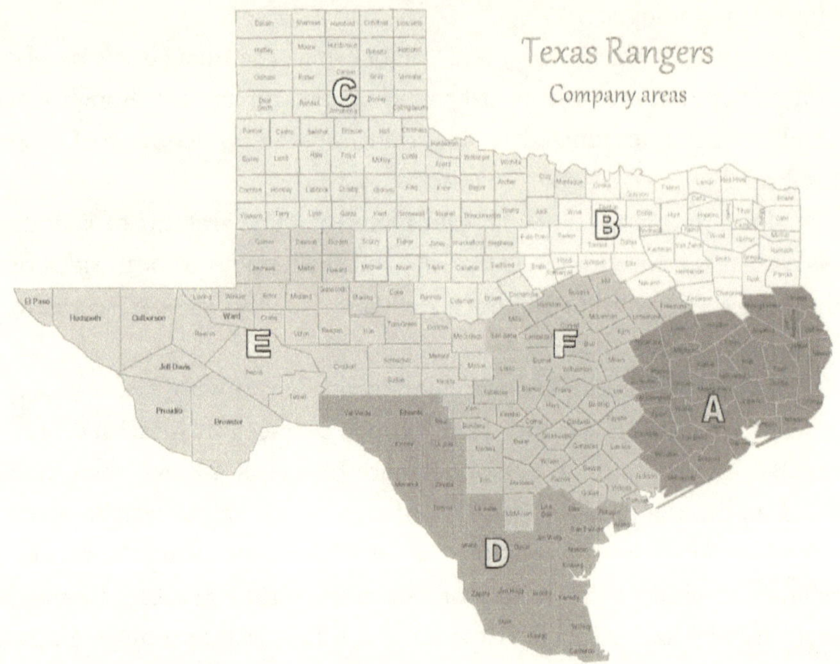

"Well, this certainly looks familiar," quipped Major as he ran his hands across the map. "If I didn't know better, this came right out of my old office."

"Good memory, Major, because you are correct," said the captain. "The investigative functions of the Texas Rangers have been consolidated into Austin for the time being as the newly formed Department of Justice prepares for a future following the collapse. In my opinion, the president has changed her focus from crime investigation to crime prevention as she tries to stabilize our cities. It would be impossible to investigate the number of murders that occur on a daily basis."

Duncan studied the map closely as his father's old region stood out in pale yellow. It encompassed the entire Texas Panhandle and areas to the east along the Red River. But, as he recalled from his days at home when his father still presided as major of Company C, Borden County was not included. At the time, it had turned out to be a good thing, as his father could never be accused of a conflict of interest when the Rangers were investigating any matters in Borden

County. However, for Duncan's purposes, he wanted the ability to dispatch his teams to the ranch if necessary.

"Captain," Duncan interrupted, "Borden County, where our ranch is located, falls outside the Lubbock region. Granted, I don't expect any civilian uprisings in a county that once had six hundred residents and probably half that now, but if necessary, I'd want permission to assist in protecting my home county."

"Consider it done," Captain Harris quickly replied as if he expected the issue to be raised. "Now that you've seen where you'll be hanging your hat, let me show you around the base."

The men walked through the facility and inspected the armory. Duncan was pleased that every infantry weapon available to the U.S. military was included together with body armor and other tools like night vision.

They toured the outside of the permanent buildings, which included temporary tent housing, portable buildings obtained from FEMA for housing of personnel, and rows of military vehicles to be used in combat and patrols.

"Very impressive," said Duncan. "Now, you mentioned that I could handpick my team. How many men will I be assigned?"

Captain Harris led them out to the parking area near the perimeter fencing on the south side of the base. He nodded and replied, "Company level of roughly a hundred soldiers, which, based upon my analysis of the region, could be divided in three to five platoons, which may vary by unit type, structure, and assigned region within your area of responsibility."

"Where will they be housed?" asked Duncan.

"You can use the base, although the accommodations are not the best for a long-term scenario. My plan was to divide them between Lubbock, Amarillo, and Wichita Falls, each with their own regional command and area of responsibility. Then maintain a permanent force here that would act as a roving unit capable of putting out fires across the entire region."

Duncan didn't respond but opted to soak in the information he'd received. A flash of light or the sun's reflection on a shiny piece of metal across the street momentarily caught his attention. Subconsciously, his hand slid down his side to grip the butt of his weapon. After a moment, he shrugged it off.

Major and Duncan thanked Captain Harris for the informational tour. Duncan advised the captain that he wanted to discuss the matter with the entire family this evening but promised him a timely response. As they reached the truck, Duncan gave the house across Regis Street one more look before they left.

*****

"I'll be damned," Holloway said to himself as he crammed the monocular against his eye. "I can't be wrong about this."

His two lieutenants had learned not to interject themselves into the conversations Holloway tended to have with himself. If he sought their input, he'd ask them directly.

"Was it back in Arizona? Peach Springs? Yeah. He was with that young Korean girl. They kicked the crap out of those guys and then were escorted into the sheriff's office. He had a beard, but I'll never forget the guy's eyes. They were intense. I know an operator when I see one."

Holloway began to think to himself as he recalled the events in Arizona. The proximity of his observations in Peach Springs and the failed ambush near Winslow were no coincidence. He became firmly convinced that this operator was the one who had killed his guys and, by some stroke of fate, was now shaking hands with the top brass at the Lubbock armory.

He set the monocular in the cup holder of the truck and started the engine. "Boys, I've seen enough to know that the armory is out of reach, but revenge for some of our brothers may not be. Let's go."

CHAPTER 50

January 14
The Armstrong Ranch
Borden County, Texas

Major and Duncan returned to a hot dinner of barbecue, courtesy of the hunting expedition resumed the day after the attack on the Slaughters at the Reinecke property. Lucy prepared cornbread, which was oozing with butter made from the dairy cows and complemented with ranch-style beans. The aroma filled the house as the two travelers hung their jackets and stowed their firearms.

Preacher, who'd made the final run to the slaughterhouse with Antonio, which freed up Major and Duncan to spend as much time as needed at the National Guard base, was adding logs onto the fire. The entire family had gathered in the living room, awaiting the guys' return.

Lucy encouraged everyone to make themselves a plate and find a place to take a seat around the fire. It was time for a family discussion.

"How'd it go, Duncan?" asked Riley as Duncan and Sook finished an embrace coupled with a brief kiss. She gently touched his face, which was in need of a shave again.

"Dad, I believe you'll agree," started Duncan in reply, looking to his father for confirmation, "they're very serious about establishing a military presence in Lubbock, in Camp Lubbock, as they now call it. What they have in mind for me is impressive, too."

"I agree, y'all," said Major. "They've divided the state into the same regions as when I operated with the Texas Rangers. Duncan would be in charge of my old stomping grounds. I might be able to give him insight as situations arise."

"What kind of situations?" asked Lucy. She was carefully studying her husband and her oldest child to gauge their truthfulness.

"I have to say that my role with the TX-QRF leans more to law enforcement than it does military," replied Duncan. "It's almost like a militarized SWAT team."

Major nodded and wiped some barbecue sauce off his mouth with his sleeve, drawing a grimace from his missus. "I have to agree. That's an accurate description. Camp Lubbock will be the primary base of operations for border protection, but the TX-QRF is designed to respond quickly to coordinated attacks by gangs or groups of people that can't be handled by law enforcement alone."

"There is an added benefit," said Duncan. "As the head of the Region C arm of the TX-QRF, I will have complete autonomy over the men I choose, the use of weaponry out of the armory, and a variety of vehicles. I can also deploy the teams as I see fit based upon conditions on the ground."

"You could use them anywhere?" asked Palmer.

Duncan took his first bite of barbecue, smiled and gave his mother a wink of appreciation. "Pretty much. I even got authorization to cover Borden County, which is actually part of another region."

Lucy directed a question to Major. "Honey, how does Region C correspond to your old area?"

"Exactly the same," he replied. "Duncan noticed the exclusion of Borden County on the map, which, by the way, came out of my old office. He asked for and received the ability to respond to threats here."

Everyone absorbed the information and continued eating until Cooper spoke up. "So, you gotta decide, or did you tell 'em already?"

The room held their breath as they feared a reigniting of the animosity between the two brothers that had finally been put to rest. If there were going to be any dissenters within the family, it would most likely be Cooper or Lucy, who, of course, held a power of veto that surpassed all of their votes.

"No, I wanted to talk with all of you first," replied Duncan. "This is a tough decision for me. I don't need to do it, but it is an opportunity for us to add some significant assets to our ranch."

"Like what?" asked Riley.

"Well, some of the things we could use include better communications equipment, longer range optics, and night vision, which is the single biggest asset the military holds over civilians. Our perimeter security would benefit greatly from those things."

"What about guns?" asked Preacher. "Will you have the ability to get us more rifles, especially ARs?"

"That's my goal, but I have to move slowly at first as I get the lay of the land. Listen, one thing that has never come up in my conversations with Captain Harris or the colonel is compensation. I don't want their money. Pay me in defensive tools and weapons."

"I don't want you to pay with your life," said Lucy bluntly. "I assume you'll be placed in dangerous situations."

"Yes, ma'am, I'm sure I will be. But know this, while I will never place my people into a situation that I wouldn't be willing to go into myself, I'm not going to risk my life for others. I've been there and done that."

"This is true," said Sook, who spoke up for the first time. Duncan gave her a smile and held her hand.

"Well, this is what I think," said Cooper. "It seems like the ranch is coming under attack every few days. Now they are coordinated and using deadly force. If Duncan can do his new job safely and in the process help us defend the ranch with whatever is at his disposal, then I'm all for it."

"I agree," said Riley.

The other members of the room looked around and nodded their agreement. Finally, all eyes were on Lucy.

She fought back tears as she spoke. "Duncan, no hero stuff, do you promise? I mean it. Do your job but do not risk your life for those who don't appreciate the sacrifice you're making."

Duncan stood and approached his mother. He crouched down onto one knee and took her hands in his.

"I promise."

CHAPTER 51

January 14
Patricia, Texas

The trip into Lubbock was a successful one for Holloway and his men. More vehicles were stolen, and a food cache was uncovered at a warehouse adjacent to the Lubbock terminal of Pro Petroleum, a division of Rip Griffin Fuel & Transportation. The company had once provided fuel and sundries to convenience stores across the Southwest, but now its operations were restricted to Texas locations. Holloway had been in search of a small fuel tanker and came across this facility just east of the airport when they left their surveillance of Camp Lubbock.

He spotted a small five-hundred-gallon fuel truck parked by the warehouse bearing the Griffin logo. His men approached the storage facility, found a single employee occupying the trailer at the entrance, and then had a field day.

After convincing the man to turn over the keys to the storage lockers and the keys to his full tanker truck, they killed him before dropping his body into a dumpster. The packaged snacks and bottled drinks were too much to take in Holloway's pickup, but he believed they could stop by here in the future to pick up more. With the employee missing and his fuel truck gone, hopefully the good people of Pro Petroleum would assume the man had quit his job, taking the fuel with him.

The best part of the Pro Petroleum heist was the fact it was right under the noses of the National Guard base. Holloway was growing more confident with each raid into Lubbock. Today's score was significant in many ways, not the least of which was the identification of the man likely responsible for the death of his people in Arizona.

But first things first. He was preparing for a strategic planning session on the satphone with Lee. The commander was ready to make his move, and Holloway had a plan that would work. It would also gain more respect from his Korean friends.

Holloway made the call. Lee, who'd learned to speak English while he spent ten years smuggling operatives into the United States via Canada, understood Holloway's plan and wholeheartedly endorsed it. The vehicles commandeered by Holloway were greatly appreciated, and as a result, Lee granted Holloway's request to carve out a piece of the pie stretching from Lubbock northward to Amarillo and then to the east and Wichita Falls.

Since Holloway's departure, more commandos had arrived from Mexico, and they'd brought weapons, including more rocket-propelled grenades and launchers. Holloway cautioned Lee to preserve this important firepower as they set about to take down the Texas power grid. He felt like he had identified the critical substations to attack, and the RPGs would make the job much easier.

Finally, the two leaders agreed upon a date. Lee would position his men up and down the West Texas border as soon as darkness set in the next evening. The vehicles utilized by Lee's people would hold back to avoid detection by the Texas forces and wait for the moment to advance.

Once the border fences were breached, they would push into West Texas mingled in with the hordes of refugees. Holloway and Lee discussed whether to arm some of the refugees so that they could occupy any reinforcements that arrived at the border. Unlike Lee's men, who had a specific destination to locate once inside the country, the refugees were likely to scatter in all directions, creating a nightmare for the Texas military as they tried to round them up. Gun battles between the refugees and the military would only bog down the Texas troops, giving the DPRK commandos more time to escape.

Lee ultimately agreed and began to round up the substandard semiautomatic rifles built by the Mexican drug cartels. These weapons, commissioned and purchased with bitcoin by the North Korean treasury, were not considered reliable by Lee. He would instruct his men to give away the weapons to the refugees together with a ten-round magazine.

Finally, Holloway provided specific rally points for Lee's men. They agreed only six hundred commandos were required initially to conduct the raids upon the power plants and governmental facilities. After the grid was taken down, a second wave could enter Texas.

Lee was required to divert many of the new troops across the U.S. to destroy bridges and other infrastructure while disrupting any relief efforts they came across. The idea was to keep Americans beaten down until Lee received further instructions from his commanders in Pyongyang.

Holloway, of course, never admitted that he didn't care about what Lee did to America. In fact, he wasn't really that concerned with the rest of Texas. He planned to pillage his part, find a nice ranch to settle on with a harem of some kind, and live out his days in luxury, surrounded by armed guards.

CHAPTER 52

January 15
West Texas

"This has to be the flattest place on the planet," said the shooter, making no effort to lower his voice or hide his location. He and the spotter had spent the day observing their prey from a safe distance, which was over a mile away. Sitting atop a hill no more than six hundred feet above the ground where the target was frequently observed, the shooter lamented the lack of elevation, which would give him an advantage.

The shooter didn't make small talk with his assigned companion. He focused on his weapon, cover, and timing. Despite the long distance between his hide and the target, which prevented detection, the shooter continued to maintain his routine. For now, he sat against a bur oak with his rifle across his knees. This was the shooter's gift—tranquility. It was a trait he'd acquired over time without instruction or practice. It came to him naturally, an overall peace where stress was nonexistent.

A burst of cold air blew down the hill, carrying with it fine dirt and pine needles. It was colder than he expected, but he didn't wear bulky clothing regardless of the shoot's locale. He gritted his teeth and shook off the chill.

The shooter took the Swarovski BTX spotting scope from his companion and studied the ranch below them. The 35 x 95 zoom capability allowed him to see the details on his target's face. Rugged, with a chiseled jaw, the man was a warrior, respected by many. He was one of their own, yet someone had signed his death warrant.

Was it the CIA guy who ordered the hit, perhaps acting on a

vendetta? Or a higher-up, as in the White House? Maybe he was a traitor and chose Texas as his hideout? With all the trouble America was in thanks to Kim Jong-un, was it really necessary to kill this vet at this time?

The shooter considered all of these questions and weighed hypothetical answers. He could walk any time he chose although he imagined his handler, also holding the position of helpful spotter and wheelman, probably had orders of his own in such an event.

The shooter considered taking out his companion and leaving him under this scraggly oak tree as food for whatever four-legged critters resided on this hill. He'd pack up his rifle, make his way back to Newport News, and sail away. They couldn't find him on a good day, much less after the apocalypse.

Putting the *why* out of his head, the shooter began to focus on the *how*. The target was always near buildings and people and horses. Distractions that prevented him from standing still. At the mile-and-a-quarter distance between them, a miss was entirely possible. He chose to wait for a better opportunity, one in which the unsuspecting target left his protective cover. Perhaps the target would leave his comfortable surroundings and expose himself. The shooter's setup and planning would have to be on the fly, but a skilled marksman could overcome those obstacles when the distance was reduced to a thousand feet instead of seven thousand.

For once, the shooter had the luxury of time.

CHAPTER 53

January 15
West Texas

There were three checkpoints located to the south of Lubbock along the West Texas border with New Mexico. Just after six o'clock that evening, activity began to take place on both sides of the border. Lee transported his men as far north as the Highway 82 checkpoint, located an hour to the southwest of Lubbock, and also toward the southernmost border checkpoint at Texas Route 176 leading into Andrews, which was due east of Carlsbad.

This stretch of the border spanned eighty miles. With the estimated number of refugees per the radio broadcasts monitored by Holloway being a thousand per mile, with more congregated in the New Mexico border towns of Knowles, Hobbs, and Nadine, he expected a big crowd would burst their way through when the action began.

Holloway's unit spent the late afternoon systematically transporting their fleet of stolen pickup trucks to within two miles of the border. As early evening approached, they moved vehicles into position, spaced a mile and a half apart.

The operation had several facets, all of which relied upon surprise, speed, and a bit of luck.

Holloway's job was to attack the checkpoints, take out the sentries, and open gaping holes in the border fence. Holloway's men would hook chains to the fencing and around their truck's trailer hitches. When the border guards had been disposed of, the pickups would pull the fences down, most likely aided by the refugees desperate to enter.

At the stretches of the border where checkpoints didn't exist, Lee would use the M35 transport trucks they'd commandeered and crash through the fences. These trucks full of commandos would head directly for Patricia to seek cover under the large buildings at the cotton gin.

Lee's men on foot would work in groups of ten using the buddy system. Once they broke through the border and moved into Texas, they were instructed to locate a vehicle, which included instructions on how to locate the Klondike High School.

Holloway's prior surveillance of Camp Lubbock had served another purpose. He'd wanted to confirm there was no air support for the border checkpoints. That would complicate the operation, but he was in luck, as the equipping of the new base wasn't that far advanced as of yet. Any air support, most likely in the form of attack helicopters, would have to come from Fort Bliss.

By the time Texas Homeland Security would be notified of the incursion, it would take time for Fort Bliss to respond and send the choppers toward the Lubbock region. His parked vehicles and the incoming M35s would be long gone an hour after the breach.

The most difficult checkpoint was located at Hobbs, New Mexico. Because of the large number of refugees situated in the town of thirty-five thousand full-time residents, those who had no intention of entering Texas because of the security hassle might change their minds when the welcome mat was rolled out, courtesy of Holloway and Lee.

Security established by the Texas military was greatest at the four-lane divided highway stretching from Hobbs eastward toward Seminole, Texas. The firefight here would be more intense, prompting both Holloway and Lee to want to be a part of it. Accordingly, the two men agreed to attack the Hobbs checkpoint from both sides, kicking off the operation.

CHAPTER 54

January 15
Camp Lubbock
Lubbock, Texas

"Whadya think, boys?" Duncan asked Riley and Cooper as he completed his enlistment paperwork and handed it back to Captain Harris. Duncan's status within the United States government and his former military rank were irrelevant in Texas, although a system of assigning rank based upon prior U.S. experience was left to the discretion of the commanding officer of each unit. The new nation was going through enough growing pains without dealing with the bureaucratic minutia of converting the former U.S. military to the new Texas armed forces.

"Pretty impressive," replied Riley. "Is it official now?"

"Yeah," said Duncan. "After a swearing-in ceremony, which will take place tomorrow, I will officially be the commander of the Republic of Texas Quick Reaction Force of Camp Lubbock, Region C."

"What happens next?" asked Cooper.

Captain Harris returned to the conference room and answered Cooper's question. "Today, we'll assign you a driver and a vehicle. Also, we'll get you fitted for uniforms, and lastly, we'll assign weapons. Tomorrow, after a brief ceremony attended by probably three or four people, you'll sit in this room and start going through personnel files to pick your teams. I've been working on that project for a couple of weeks and have some suggestions, but the final say will be up to you."

"I really don't need a driver," said Duncan. "I can drive myself."

"Well, he's more than a driver," said Captain Harris with a chuckle. "I've been using Corporal Gregorio Esparza as my aide-de-camp, as well as my driver. Esparza is a fifth-generation Texan whose great-grandfather fought at the Alamo. His great-grandfather was the last Texan to enter the Alamo as the siege commenced in March 1836. He's bilingual and has an impressive combat record with the 101st Airborne. Espy had just transferred to Fort Hood to work under me when the EMP struck."

"Espy?" asked Duncan.

"Yeah, like the ESPN awards," replied Captain Harris. "That's his nickname."

Harris reached into his shirt pocket and removed a temporary security badge with Duncan's name imprinted on it. He continued. "This is not your official facilities badge yet. That'll come tomorrow after your swearing in, etcetera. It does allow the ability to take your brothers around to give them a look at our operation, plus you can report to logistics to get your gear squared away. In the meantime, I'll have Corporal Esparza ready a Humvee, and I'll turn him over to you, assuming, of course, you agree to using him."

"I'm sure he'll be fine," said Duncan.

Captain Harris left them alone, and Riley immediately put in his request for the first stop. "Hey, can we go see the guns now?"

Cooper started laughing. "No surprise there. But we've gotta start somewhere, right?"

Duncan laughed and swatted at both of his siblings. He was enjoying the comradery with his younger brothers after being absent from their lives for nearly ten years. Duncan wanted to fill the void Dallas had left when he departed the ranch for the Middle East and never returned.

"Okay, let's go see the toys."

As they made their way from building to building, the military personnel gave them the occasional odd look because they were civilians. On a couple of occasions, military policeman asked to see Duncan's credentials, which allowed him to pass without further questioning. He wasn't sure what the various designations on the badge meant, but he supposed the title commander must mean something around the base.

"Here we go, guys," started Duncan. "Now, Riley, don't get too excited when you see what's in here."

Duncan swiped his badge, and the locks popped open, providing them access to the armory. "I haven't picked out my weapons yet. The Barrett that I brought back from North Korea isn't the ideal battle rifle. It's really a sniper rifle that will make do in battle if necessary."

"Are you gonna choose common calibers with our rifles at home?" asked Cooper.

"That's a great idea, Coop," said Duncan, who wanted to provide his brother some kudos although he'd already considered the idea. "Here's the one I have in mind."

Riley and Cooper followed Duncan down a long row of M4s and M16s to a separate rack labeled *NATO 7.62.*

"These are the AR-10s like Dad's new gun. This Mk 14 EBR was used by the units under the U.S. special ops commands, like SEAL teams, Delta Force, and certain task-specific Green Beret units. Here, check it out." Duncan handed Riley the weapon.

"I like it. In fact, I'll take this one."

"Very funny," said Duncan as he looked around to see if they were alone. "All in due time, Riley."

Cooper walked to the rack and studied the green metal ammo cans stacked underneath the gun rack. They were all labeled 7.62. "Just like our .308 hunting rifles," Cooper mumbled to himself.

"That's right, Coop, which fits with what you said earlier. I like this rifle because it gives me the ability to engage enemy targets beyond the range of M4 carbines and M16 rifles, but also the caliber matches many of our weapons."

"Duncan, what about handguns?" asked Riley.

"Follow me," said Duncan. He led them to the center of the large open auditorium-style building to several rows of glass cases, which displayed the military's sidearm selections. He stopped in front of a sign labeled *M17.*

"This is one of the finest pistols ever made. It's the military version of the Sig Sauer P320, which is designated as the M17." Duncan slid open the case and pulled out a black matte version of the M18. "This is the compact version of the larger M17. Same firepower, just smaller. I'll probably carry one of each when in the field."

"Nine millimeter?" asked Cooper.

Duncan leaned in to whisper, "Yes. Matches everything else, understand?"

Cooper nodded as he took the gun from Duncan and weighed it in his hands. He nodded his approval. The guys were examining the various handgun models when they were interrupted by Captain Harris.

"I suspected I'd find you in here," he said with a smile. He pointed to the M17 chambered in .45 caliber. "That's what I carry daily. Actually, this one, with the fiber-optic front sight. It's never failed me."

Duncan returned the weapons to the case before Captain Harris interrupted him. "Commander, have you made your selections? If so, we can assign them to you today while you get the rest of your gear in logistics."

Duncan quickly retrieved both an M17 and an M18 in their hard plastic cases. "Ammo too?"

Captain Harris nodded and pointed below the shelves. Duncan instructed Cooper to take a thousand rounds of .45 caliber together with three extra magazines for each weapon. Afterwards, they did the same thing for his new battle rifle.

When the day was done, Duncan looked the part of a soldier. He no longer worked in the shadows in the dark world of special operators. Tomorrow, he'd be in uniform, in command of a hundred men, and capable of responding to all contingencies, including those that threatened his family.

Chapter 55

January 15
The Armstrong Ranch
Borden County, Texas

It could've easily been a somber dinner as Duncan came back to the ranch for one last night before he officially took over the reins of the TX-QRF in Lubbock. It turned out to be anything but solemn. Cooper and Riley became the life of the party as they teased their mother with jokes about becoming soldiers. Palmer laughed that they'd seen more action at the ranch than those guys walking the fence.

Corporal Esparza, Espy, was an instant hit. His Latin good looks and charm were irresistible to Palmer, who immediately took a liking to the single young man. At first, Espy was overwhelmed by the Armstrong family and how they interacted with one another. Quietly taking it all in, he sat politely at the dining table next to his boss on one side and Palmer on the other. However, as the evening went on, he came out of his shell and spent some time razzing Riley.

Riley insisted wrestling a steer was far more difficult than Espy's favorite hobby, soccer. After being transferred from the 101st to Fort Hood, he'd commuted to Austin to play on the semipro Austin Real CHC football club, a men's outdoor soccer team that competed with others like it throughout Texas.

Espy insisted that soccer was a contact sport and he had the broken ankles and concussions to prove it. He explained how humorous it was for parents to insist their children play soccer rather than football in order to avoid injuries. At least in football, he laughed, you get pads to prevent getting kicked in the head.

The conversation then turned toward Cooper's exploits, especially aboard One Night Stand. This was a story they'd never told Sook, who listened in horror as Cooper described what had happened on that night last October.

By the end of the evening, bellies were full and the Armstrong family was welcoming Espy in with open arms. As the evening had progressed, Duncan came up with a plan that would not only garner the loyalty of his new aide-de-camp, but also provide him the ability to work from the ranch rather than be away in Lubbock for days on end.

Duncan pulled his father aside and asked if Espy could live in one of the ranch houses outside the perimeter. That way, the two could become inseparable allies, and Duncan could use Espy's talents to help defend the ranch.

Major had a better idea, one that might suit Espy if he didn't mind the spartan furnishings. He could live in the bunker. Preacher had modified the tri-fuel generator to harness the sun with solar panels they'd discovered at the Reinecke complex. After further discussion, Major and Duncan took Espy outside and made their pitch.

Twenty minutes later, Espy was accepting the offer and thrilled at the prospect of moving out of the temporary tents surrounding Camp Lubbock to sleep in the *submarine*, as he called it. He asked Miss Lucy twice if she didn't mind another mouth to feed. He promised to eat leftovers, volunteer for KP duty, and help teach the kids on the ranch how to play soccer.

While the group sat around the fire and traded stories and jokes over hot chocolate, Duncan caught his father's eye and nodded toward the kitchen as a signal for Major to join him. First Duncan and then Major slipped away to talk privately.

"Son, I have to be honest with you," began Major when he entered the kitchen. "I had my reservations about your involvement in the TX-QRF. After our trip to Austin, it was in the back of my mind that Gregg could be behind this. You know, purposefully putting you in danger to silence the only remaining witness to his failed attempt on Kim's life."

"We haven't really talked about that, Dad, but I believe I'll have access to information that may give me answers. If this was a setup by Gregg and the men who are loyal to him, then I need someone to watch my back. I think Espy is our guy."

"No doubt, son. He fit right in with the family. He seems like an appreciative young man who'd work with you and not against you. Offering him a place here was a good move."

Duncan laughed. "Plus, I think he's sweet on Palmer."

Major pulled up a chair and gestured for Duncan to do the same. "Oh, I noticed that, and I'm sure your eagle-eyed mother did as well. Well, he'd better be careful about what he wishes for because she was very flirty with him tonight, a side I haven't seen of her in a while."

"Dad, if you need me to create some boundaries, I'll do it," said Duncan. "I need him focused and not concerned with my little sister."

"They're fine, son. Let it play out. Your young corporal seems like a good man, and he's practically under our roof, where we can get to know him."

Duncan hesitated and leaned back in his chair to glance toward the family room. He didn't want to be interrupted but thought it would be too obvious to drag his father outside, which would pique everyone's curiosity.

"Son," whispered Major, "is something on your mind?"

"Dad, I need to talk to you about me and Sook. I, um, well, I love her, Dad. I think I'd like to marry her, but I want to make sure it's, um, okay."

Major leaned forward and patted his oldest son on the arm. "Son, of course it's okay. It's more than okay, actually. Your mother and I love this young woman like she was one of our own. And not just because of how she saved your life. There is a beauty about her inside. She's giving, unselfish, and completely honest. I've never seen anything like it since I fell in love with Miss Lucy."

Duncan fidgeted and then continued. "I can't believe I'm about to say this out loud, but it has to be said. Daddy, she's Korean, and life may be tough for her here. Am I doing her a disservice by being selfish and not giving her the opportunity to return to South Korea, where she might still have family?"

Major furrowed his brow and nodded. "As for the last part, that's something that you'll need to discuss with her when you two assess your future. But as to her race and heritage, I can assure you no one in this family cares about that, and we're all that matters. Listen, I've said before that this world would be a better place if all of us would stop viewing each other through the prism of race, color, and religion. Only a color-blind society can be truly racist free, and that goes for those who ordinarily scream racism the loudest."

Duncan smiled. "Do you think it's too soon? We've only known each other for a couple of months."

"True, but in those two months you've been through more than most courting couples do in a year, or a lifetime, frankly. Love can come from out of nowhere. It's an extraordinary feeling when you know the woman you love also loves you back. There is no doubt in my mind that Sook loves you as much as you love her."

"I'm gonna go for it, Dad," said Duncan with conviction. "Not tonight, though. I feel like we're having a family reunion. I mean, listen to them out there. They didn't even notice us missing."

Major laughed and stood. "You're wrong, son. Two people did—Lucy and Sook. The ones that love you always miss you when you leave the room."

Chapter 56

January 16
West Texas near Hobbs, New Mexico

In the year 27 BC, two thousand and fifty years ago to the day, a thirty-six-year-old military hero named Julius Caesar was bestowed the title of Augustus by the Roman Senate, marking the beginning of the Roman Empire. His reign was one of the most effective in human history, fostering in the era known as Pax Romana, a period of two centuries in which the Roman world was free of large-scale war. But, as always has been the case, all empires collapse eventually. They're either defeated by a greater, more powerful enemy, or their financing runs out.

On this 16th day of January in 2023, the newly formed empire known as Texas would begin a period that would test the mettle of its leaders and the will of its citizens. History would judge the actions of all sides who participated in the events to come.

There was one seminal event that would be universally accepted as the trigger—the moment Texas would find its way into the world's history books, not as a footnote to the devastation associated with the attack on America, but a chapter in its own right.

Joseph Manuel Holloway, age thirty-six, led his twenty men into position. His plan made several assumptions, the most important of which was predicting the reaction of the border security. Based upon their surveillance, the checkpoints demanded the most attention of the Texas military.

While there were an increasing number of roving patrols that drove the fences twenty-four hours a day, the checkpoint entries had the largest number of refugees congregated around them, therefore garnering the most firepower by the Texans. He assumed the roving patrols would descend upon the checkpoints once the assault began, but by then, it would be too late, as refugees would be pouring through the fence.

Using the element of surprise, he'd attack two of the three checkpoints with four-man teams while he would lead his best four guys against the Hobbs entry point. His remaining men were situated equidistant along the border fence. Once the roving patrols left the more remote areas of the Texas border to assist at the checkpoint, his men would pull down the fences, allowing commandos and refugees to enter. The mass confusion would enable Lee's men the cover necessary to make it to their transportation.

Holloway looked to the eastern sky and saw the sun beginning to peek over the horizon. It was 6:15, and the sentry guards would be preparing themselves for a shift change soon. Minutes earlier, he'd contacted Lee and confirmed they were in place.

In the last hour, they'd cautiously approached the checkpoint from the east, with each man driving his own vehicle. A neighborhood on the Texas side of the checkpoint and a local RV park provided a plausible explanation for the presence of an approaching vehicle, although the sentries at the checkpoint rarely had a traveler from Texas attempting to leave.

His men gathered outside a mobile home situated a hundred yards from the checkpoint. The ten-foot fencing marking the border met under the Welcome to New Mexico sign stretched across Seminole Highway. Atop the sign, annoying flashing yellow caution lights had been attached, creating a constant warning to anyone approaching the checkpoint that they were, in fact, not welcome in Texas.

"All right, gentlemen, it's go-time," said Holloway as he gave the checkpoint one final glance. "Remember, we've got about ten minutes to take care of business before reinforcements arrive. This will be over and done in far less time, if we execute according to plan."

He patted his guys on the shoulders and pointed them toward their positions. His four men approached from different angles, with

Holloway walking straight up the divided highway toward the guards. Once he was in position, he'd open fire and his men would converge upon the gates, killing anything that moved.

Holloway would then peel off and cover a block barn building, which had been converted into a barracks. Based upon their surveillance, no more than eight men slept there before the morning shift took over.

It was 6:30, almost sunrise on a glorious new day, for some.

Holloway casually approached the command trailer and glanced inside the windows to locate the unit commander, who was having coffee with one of his soldiers.

"I'll see you two in a minute," Holloway calmly muttered as he walked past the wooden stairs that entered the trailer. He raised his automatic weapon, flicked off the safety switch, and quickly counted his targets.

Eight men stood before him, facing the fence and the refugees, who were beginning to stir as the morning sunlight struck their faces. All of the soldiers had their backs to Holloway as his shadow began to grow on the asphalt highway behind them.

It's been said to shoot a man in the back is a cowardly act. A man of honor, a gentleman, would allow his adversary the opportunity to face his attacker. Holloway sneered at the thought. Killing was neither honorable or gentlemanly. For some, it was self-preservation. For others, it was simply their job.

For Holloway, it was fun.

He dropped to a knee and opened fire on the men at the center of the sliding chain-link fence. No head shots, yet, he reminded himself. Center mass, take them down, finish the job seconds later.

As his automatic weapon emptied its first magazine, shrieks of fear filled the air from the refugees. Gunfire erupted like blasts from stereo speakers in a movie theater as his men converged from both sides to kill the guards to Holloway's left and right.

Trusting in his men's capabilities, he rose, quickly pivoted, and jammed another magazine into his weapon as he walked calmly toward the entrance to the trailer, with his rifle's sights trained on the door. First a female soldier, then the unit commander burst through the door with pistols raised. They were dead within seconds.

"The barracks," shouted one of Holloway's men.

He swung around and saw that several soldiers had bolted out of their sleeping quarters, ready for battle. They fired upon Holloway first, but missed as he quickly ran for cover at the side of the command trailer.

His men returned fire, killing one soldier, but the others took cover behind a Humvee towing a trailer.

They began to fire at Holloway's men, missing them but finding plenty of victims on the refugee side of the fence. This resulted in a mass exodus by those who'd waited weeks to enter Texas as they pushed and shoved to flee the gunfire. The moans of the injured and the screams of the frightened filled the air.

"You two, open the gates!" Holloway began shouting instructions. "The rest of you provide cover and converge."

Bullets began flying in both directions. Another soldier attempted to join the fray as he burst out of the barracks, raining automatic gunfire towards Holloway's position. He was cut down in seconds by one of the commandos. Now they had the numbers.

The gate began to open, creaking on its dirt-filled, rusty gear mechanism. Refugees began to spill through the opening as soon as they were wide enough to fit through. The mad rush in the opposite direction turned on a dime, and the scramble for the Texas soil became more important than their fear.

With the rush of refugees came the DPRK commandos. Dressed in civilian attire, only their Korean faces gave them a different look from the Americans seeking refuge. They charged forward screaming in Korean.

"*Manse! Manse!*"

The term had often been used as a tribute to wish Kim Jong-Il a long life, and it was also used for Kim Jong-un. Similar to the term *banzai* used by the Japanese during World War II, *manse* was often used by the Korean People's Army as the Korean equivalent of *victory*.

The commandos were fearless as they raced past Holloway and

charged the soldiers pinned down behind the Humvee. When a rifle was raised to shoot over the hood, the fearless commandos shot it out of the gunner's hands. If a body part broke cover, it was torn to shreds by a salvo of bullets.

Their approach was relentless, and the three soldiers were quickly dispatched. By Holloway's count, there was one last man hiding in the barracks. He ordered the building surrounded as refugees ran past him down the center of Seminole Highway. Approaching vehicles grabbed his attention, and he swung around to find the source of the rumble.

A caravan of U.S. military trucks approached, passed through the gates, and slowed to a stop next to him.

"Excellent, Holloway!" shouted Lee.

"We have one more to—" began Holloway as automatic gunfire exploded behind him. The last of the military guarding the Hobbs checkpoint was killed as he exited the barracks.

Holloway stood on the running board of the M35 and held onto the side mirror bracket. "Get to your rally points! Watch for the roving patrols!"

"What about their weapons?" shouted one of his men.

"Leave them for the refugees," he yelled in response. "Go!"

Lee's driver paused while some of the commandos returned to their truck. As the men loaded up, Holloway asked Lee to drive him to his pickup and accompany him to Patricia. There was a lot to discuss.

CHAPTER 57

January 16
West Texas near Hobbs, New Mexico

"Welcome to Texas, General," said Holloway with a chuckle as the men settled in for the ride back. The first twenty minutes in the truck were spent checking in with their teams. The surprise attacks on the three border checkpoints were a success. No casualties or injuries were reported. As expected, the border patrols raced to assist their comrades at the checkpoints only to be greeted by thousands of refugees blocking their path. One of Holloway's men reported that the refugees fired upon the military vehicle using the guns his men had left behind after their successful assault. This resulted in a massacre of refugees as the military returned fire indiscriminately out of anger.

Holloway checked his watch. It was seven a.m. He looked out of the passenger's side window, where he was seated, and scanned the sky for chopper support. Only clear blue skies returned his gaze. *Just as planned*, he thought to himself with a smile.

"Texas is flat here, and we're in open view of their forces," said Lee.

"General, not to worry. The Texans have much bigger refugee problems in other parts of their territory. They have only recently established a military base in Lubbock to our northeast."

"Will they not hunt for us?"

"Eventually, but you and your men are going to move on before then," replied Holloway. "Today, we focus on getting the Lightning Death Squads to safety at a location I have picked out. I have identified the power substations around Texas to attack. We will establish a plan of attack for those."

Lee looked at a map provided by Holloway. "The biggest cities are many miles away. We will need days to reach them and prepare our attacks."

"That is true, but the Texans will be preoccupied with the West Texas border. We should be prepared for one new wrinkle."

"Wrinkle?" said Lee inquisitively.

Holloway remembered he should avoid American idioms. "Wrinkle. You know, a minor problem."

"Yes, what problem?"

"The refugees may be captured and tell the Texas military about the Koreans who entered the country with guns and military trucks. Your men will have to disguise themselves to avoid detection as they travel. It's likely that roadblocks will be established on the major highways."

"What do you suggest?" asked Lee, who had spent a decade smuggling North Koreans into America but who never had to caution them about hiding their race from others.

"As they travel to their destinations, tell them to avoid traveling in large groups, which might draw attention. Find clothing, which includes hats and sunglasses. Avoid the locals, and make every effort to avoid any more gun battles."

Lee looked out the back window of the Ford pickup and watched the convoy of vehicles rumbling along behind them. "Good advice, of course. The timing of our attacks is just as important as the assaults on the soldiers today. Once the first power plant is taken down, then the military will move quickly to defend the others."

"Correct, but if the ERCOT employee who educated me was telling the truth, not all of the substations will need to be destroyed. He called it a cascading effect. The power stations will go off-line, as he called it, but the other substations will continue to make power until they are overloaded. The failure in the system of a few parts will trigger the failure of the other parts."

Lee nodded his understanding. "Maybe the failure of the Texas power grid will destroy the Texans' will to fight."

CHAPTER 58

January 16
West Texas

The shooter had endured three nights sleeping in a car and spending his days studying the target's surroundings. Before dawn, he took up his customary position leaning up against the oak tree with his spotter seated to his right. He looked at his watch. It was 6:30. He rolled his neck on his shoulders to work out the kinks. He didn't need long-range optics to describe the scene unfolding below him.

"He'll be walking out any minute with a mug of coffee in his hand. He'll make small talk with someone, anyone who might wander into his path. Maybe he'll stretch to loosen his body, but eventually he'll make his way to the barn and locate his horse."

The spotter studied the area near the barn with the high-powered optics. Periodically, as the shooter spoke, the spotter would look over in his direction to see if he was somehow cheating and using his rifle scope to observe the target for himself. He nodded and shrugged, amazed at the shooter's uncanny ability to predict the target's routine and movements without observing him.

The shooter continued, clearly enjoying his musings. "What is it with these Texans and their horses. The stereotypes that define these people are spot-on. Tumbleweeds blowing down a deserted highway until they lodge on a front porch of a ramshackle house abandoned on the side of the road years before."

The spotter continued to watch the target as the shooter spoke more words than he had since their arrival. A woman joined the target for some conversation. This was out of the norm compared to the last couple of days and created some interest for the spotter.

"They're boot-loving, gun-toting cowboys who ride horses to oil-drilling jobs, or to rustle cattle, or out of sheer boredom. Anyone who doesn't work in an oil field is either a farmer tilling this rocky dirt, or he's fighting banditos who managed to wander onto his ranch looking for a better life."

The spotter, who was a Texan, rolled his eyes but maintained his composure. He was warned about the ego of the shooter, but he never thought he'd have to listen to his incessant ramblings. This was an unwelcome change in their joint assignment.

"And look at this wasteland. The only trees are scrub oaks like this one or tall cacti. Really. I don't get it."

The shooter suddenly became quiet. He sat a little taller against the tree and pulled his McMillan TAC-50 rifle into his lap. This was his weapon of choice for long-range operations like this one. A manually operated, bolt-action rifle, the TAC-50 was a sniper's favorite because of the rifle's relative light weight to comparable rifles and the ability to use five-round magazines.

The optics were state of the art. The Nightforce NXS 8-32x56 telescopic sight could bring the target into the shooter's eyes, making the kill up close and personal.

Like its counterparts, the fifty-caliber round packed a heckuva punch on impact, traveling faster than the speed of sound, as it was capable of flying a mile in just two seconds. At the shooter's present range from the target, he was near the one hundred percentile in success probability for his skillset provided there were no unexpected obstacles.

He slowly moved the rifle so that the barrel rested on the top of his foot in the direction of the target. With his left hand, he pulled a few blades of grass and slowly dropped them from his fingers. They fell straight to the ground. He reached for a few dead oak leaves and crumbled them in his palms and repeated the process. The dried remnants fell directly below as he unfurled his fist. This drew a smile from the shooter.

Finally, he looked toward the sky, not seeking guidance from above, but to study the movements of the clouds. His smile widened as the perfectly clear baby blue skies reached into the heavens.

"Hey, something's happening," said the spotter. The urgency in the man's voice would startle most anyone else in this situation, but not the shooter. It was as if he expected the proclamation.

CHAPTER 59

January 16
The Gregg Ranch
West of San Angelo, Texas

In the several days Vice President Gregg spent at his ranch located twenty miles to the west of San Angelo, he'd tried to reconnect with his wife. The once vibrant woman who had grown accustomed to their Georgetown surroundings and the Washington social scene was now withdrawn and distant. Their home was decorated in antiques and bore little resemblance to the traditional-style Texas homes surrounding San Angelo. Over time, his wife had abandoned her Texas roots for Washington, using only the occasion of the EMP to force her out of Raven Rock and back to San Angelo.

For the first couple of days of his vacation away from Austin, he and his wife had ridden around their spacious four-hundred-acre ranch. No longer an operating ranch, it had become a large parcel of property with a handful of horses and their home.

The rides were enjoyable although the conversation was not. On the third day, he awoke in his separate bedroom and readied for their ride, but stood standing near the horse barn alone, as she never emerged from the house. Gregg decided he would ride nonetheless, finding the time alone as he traveled around the perimeter of his property to be very therapeutic.

It provided him an opportunity to change his perspective on the current state of his career and the relationships he'd lost as a result of his move to Texas. In hindsight, he felt like he'd betrayed the country he once loved and protected with his life. He was a highly decorated leader, respected by all whom he commanded, and revered by those who worked closest with him.

He recalled when he was first drawn into the dark side of the Washington political apparatus, the so-called deep state, which existed like the Mafioso of the mid-twentieth century. Working in the shadows, career employees of the government made decisions that changed the course of a nation. With the decision to assassinate Kim Jong-un, Gregg had made a dangerous play, one that had backfired and ultimately led to the collapse of the greatest empire in human history—the United States.

Gregg stared at the house, wondering if his wife would stand him up two days in a row. As he waited a few more minutes for her to emerge for their morning ride, he began to nervously kick at some rocks in the dirt. He popped open the lid of his travel mug and gulped some of his lukewarm coffee.

His mind wandered back to his regrets as he continued to self-analyze his actions and punish himself for his transgressions. The failed attempt on Kim's life was a defeat every bit as harsh as a loss of men on the battlefield. It was a failure he'd regretted every moment since, but not just because Kim survived the attack or the resulting decimation of America.

When former General Montgomery Gregg sent his men into battle, he watched over them by staying in constant contact with the commanders in the field who were responsible for monitoring the troop movements. When his men died, he took it hard and personal, often taking the time to greet the remains when they flew in through Andrews Air Force Base. And if he couldn't be there in person, he'd certainly find a way to speak with the families by phone.

Gregg looked toward the house and then at his watch. He realized his wife had stood him up for a second day in a row. He called for his ranch hand, who retrieved his wife's horse to return the mare to the stable. Gregg took a moment to rub the muzzle and forehead of his prized Lipizzaner stallion, one that was nearly identical to General George Patton's white steed.

"Old buddy, I sent two men into battle and left them behind. On my orders! One died and the other came back, and now I've ordered his death. What's wrong with me? How could I have committed such an act of betrayal? I've got to call it off. I need to tell Yancey to stop the hit on Armstrong."

Gregg was becoming emotional and considered forgoing his ride. He hung his head in shame for a moment until his thoughts were interrupted by his wife screaming his name.

"Monty! Monty!" she yelled as she raced off the front porch, holding her housecoat together with one hand and the satphone high in the air with the other. He walked toward her, leaving his horse behind.

"What is it, dear?" he asked in his normally calm demeanor.

"It's Austin. Something has happened. They need you!"

Gregg took the phone and began to raise it to his ear. His wife turned to walk toward the house, but he reached for her arm. "Dear," he began as Gregg suddenly felt the need to receive absolution. He had to seek the counsel of his wife. "Will you wait with me? I need to tell you something."

She nodded, pulled her housecoat together, and quickly returned to his side. After giving her a smile and a nod of thanks, he addressed the caller.

"This is Vice President Gregg."

CHAPTER 60

January 16
The Armstrong Ranch
Borden County, Texas

Duncan walked out of the house after filling his belly with Miss Lucy's biscuits, grits, country ham, and red-eye gravy. His mom had a way of making gravy that was very different from what you might find in restaurants. After she cooked the ham, which came from the wild pig his brothers had hunted, it was removed from the pan. She then added a mixture of coffee and water, stirring it with a wooden spoon until there was a good consistency. Finally, she worked in butter and a beef bouillon cube for more flavor. It was a delicious breakfast that had always been his favorite, so Lucy thought it was appropriate to fix before he left for his first official day as commander of the TX-QRF.

Espy wanted to spend some time in the barn with the ranch hands to watch how they readied the horses for the day. Duncan told him that he wanted to take a ride with Sook before they headed for Camp Lubbock, and his new aide-de-camp seemed to have no problem being tardy for their first day of work together.

Duncan really liked Espy on a personal level and felt like he could trust the younger man as they put together a unit capable of protecting their fellow Texans.

He reached his hand inside his fleece-lined jacket to a pocket next to his heart. A small box was there, which contained the engagement ring Pops had given Duncan's grandmother after World War II. Major and Lucy had kept the ring for use by the boys in the event they found a bride. After Duncan's conversation with his dad the night before, he wasn't surprised that his mother had embraced him this morning, teary-eyed but full of joy.

She'd retrieved the engagement ring from the safe and reintroduced it to Duncan. It was simple in its design, but its significance to the Armstrong family was priceless. He patted the ring against his heart one more time as a symbolic gesture to combine Pops's love of his bride with the love Duncan held in his heart for Sook.

He finished off his coffee and snapped the lid shut on the travel tumbler. After shoving it in his jacket, he turned toward the house as he heard Sook emerge through the front door.

She was adorable as always, bundled up in her blue jeans jacket and scarf, which had been given to her by Palmer. Sook never once complained about the slightly ill-fitting clothes. She'd gained some weight, *filled out*, as his mother lovingly observed, which made the hand-me-down clothing fit better.

Duncan rubbed his palms, which were sweaty despite the chilly morning temperature. He never experienced this type of nervousness when he was on a mission. That was work, this was life.

"I'm ready," Sook announced as she playfully skipped toward him before wrapping her arms around his neck. She squeezed him so tight he was afraid she'd notice the ring box under his jacket.

He enjoyed the embrace for another moment until he called for their horses. Instead of the horses, Espy came running out of the barn.

"Commander! We're needed back at the base!" he shouted to Duncan.

Espy ran to Duncan and handed him the phone. "There's been an attack on the westernmost perimeter checkpoints to the north and south of Hobbs. It's all hands on deck, sir."

Duncan took the phone and immediately noticed Espy had reverted to Corporal Esparza.

"Get the truck ready!" instructed Duncan as he took the phone. He looked at Sook, who appeared dejected. In that moment, Duncan wondered whether he'd made a mistake taking the position. He hadn't even left for his first day and the love of his life was disappointed, not to mention his plans to propose to her were derailed.

He looked down into her eyes, which had begun to well up in tears. "Sook, I am so sorry. I have to deal with this."

She sniffled and pouted a little, but Duncan knew it wasn't to make him feel guilty for leaving. She genuinely looked forward to their time together, and out of love, she wished they never had to be apart.

"I understand, Duncan. You are a soldier again and must protect your country."

"I will miss you, but I promise that I'll come home to you safely. Okay?"

Sook smiled and wiped away her tears. She gave Duncan a kiss with another hug as Espy was pulling up in the Humvee.

They broke their embrace, and Duncan walked toward the truck. "I love you, Sook. Tell Daddy I will call him on the phone."

"I will, I love you," she shouted back.

Duncan stood for another moment, not wanting to leave. Then a smile came over his face. Sook came racing back to him.

"One more kiss for good luck!"

CHAPTER 61

January 16
West Texas

The shooter calmly slid his rifle up in a smooth, efficient motion, one honed by many years of repetitive practice. Despite the chilly conditions and the inhospitable ground underneath him, he masterfully slid into a prone position, the most stable for long-range shooting. His tripod was extended, and it lay perfectly in place, as he'd practiced since he'd chosen this sniper hide.

The shooter slid under his rifle and gripped it using all of the skill learned from many kills. His spotter's eye slid behind the Schmidt & Bender scope. The exceptional optics snatched every bit of light from the rising sun and provided him an intimate view of the target. The target turned toward him, having no idea he was making the job much easier.

With his thumb, the shooter flicked off his safety and settled in.

"Ready," he whispered to his spotter, who continuously looked through the spotting scope. He began to call out the numbers needed by the shooter to be precise and deadly.

"Distance, one thousand nine hundred six yards. Altitude, two thousand three hundred twelve feet. Temperature, thirty-nine degrees. Windage is one-point-five mils left. Elevation is sixty-point-two mil. Twenty-four-point-seven in rail, twenty-three-point six in turret, and ten-point-seven in hold over."

Okay, the shooter thought to himself as he made the last second corrections to his scope and settled the crosshairs on his target. *My apologies, brother.*

He gently squeezed the trigger. The shooter knew as the gun

slammed into his shoulder and his line of sight to the target disappeared as a result of the recoil. He'd made the perfect shot, one that could only come from years of experience and mental preparedness during all of these hours sitting on a hillside in West Texas.

At the split second when the firing mechanism of the TAC-50 sent the heavy-caliber bullet toward the target, his trained brain was able to analyze the shot in mere milliseconds. It was an incredibly brief moment in time that was impossible to comprehend. His rifle had held true. The scope, zeroed in to the precise distance and under exact conditions, placed the crosshairs exactly where he wanted them. The trigger pull was smooth, unhurried. His shooting position was solid. There was no last second twitch or flicker of doubt.

He whispered the universal sniper's motto.

"One shot, one kill."

THANK YOU FOR READING *TEXAS STRONG*

If you enjoyed it, I'd be grateful if you'd take a moment to write a short review (just a few words are needed) and post it on Amazon. Amazon uses complicated algorithms to determine what books are recommended to readers. Sales are, of course, a factor, but so are the quantities of reviews my books get. By taking a few seconds to leave a review, you help me out, and also help new readers learn about my work.

And before you go…

SIGN UP to Bobby Akart's mailing list to receive special offers, bonus content, and you'll be the first to receive news about new releases in The Lone Star Series, The Pandemic series, The Blackout series, The Boston Brahmin series and The Prepping for Tomorrow series—which includes sixteen Amazon #1 Bestsellers in thirty-nine fiction and non-fiction genres. Visit Bobby Akart's website for informative blog entries on preparedness, writing, and his latest contribution to the American Preppers Network.

www.BobbyAkart.com

www.ingramcontent.com/pod-product-compliance
Lightning Source LLC
Chambersburg PA
CBHW020933310726
48980CB00007B/759/J

* 9 7 8 0 6 9 2 1 0 5 3 4 4 *